"I want the whole damned picket fence."

Cressa didn't know what to say, how to answer Adam's proclamation. The wide-open spaces of the Galveston coast suddenly seemed too big. She felt swallowed up by it all. She was filled with a need for the green hills of home, for the safety of Aroha Bay. For a world where the scale was reasonable and the people predictable. Where the men were manageable. Only Adam, she thought bitterly, could make a proposal sound like a challenge. But before she could begin to frame an answer, Adam stepped close and clutched her arms.

"Don't say it," he whispered. "Don't you dare." His face was very close to hers, his breath warm on her cheeks. "You know what, Cressa? I'm going to save us both from repeating patterns. To save you from being the one who quits yet again and me from being the one abandoned. I've had one wife walk out on me. This time I'm going to walk away."

Dear Reader,

Have you taken any risks lately? The gatekeepers to dreams, risks have to be braved before we can move forward or upward. Yet the task of identifying risks can be a slippery one as they are intensely personal; one person's risk is simply another person's thrill. Also, while many risks are physical or financial, some of the scariest are emotional. In the worst extremes, we risk our lives. In love, we risk our hearts.

We take the risk when the dream is more powerful than the fear.

We know this. We have age-worn sayings to remind us: faint heart never won fair lady; nothing ventured, nothing gained. We know—and yet all too often we hesitate. Fools rush in, we tell ourselves. We fear failure. We are afraid, even more, of people witnessing this failure.

And so what if we are afraid? It doesn't need to stop us! I had a lot of fun writing this book in which the daredevil hero and heroine would infinitely prefer to jump out of airplanes than risk confronting their deepest, secret desires and pain. It is a book about past demons, conflicting goals, disguised defences and, above all, love in all its glorious, messy confusion.

Here's to you and your pursuit of dreams—despite all their pesky attendant risks and fears.

Zana Bell

P.S. I love hearing from readers. Please contact me c/o Harlequin Books, 225 Duncan Mill Road, Don Mills, ON, M3B 3K9, Canada.

A Risk
Worth Taking
Zana Bell

TORONTO NEW YORK LONDON
AMSTERDAM PARIS SYDNEY HAMBURG
STOCKHOLM ATHENS TOKYO MILAN MADRID
PRAGUE WARSAW BUDAPEST AUCKLAND

Recycling programs
for this product may
not exist in your area.

ISBN-13: 978-0-373-71715-6

A RISK WORTH TAKING

ABOUT THE AUTHOR

Life used to be full of risks for Zana Bell, who grew up in Zimbabwe, went to university in South Africa then lived hand to mouth in Scotland, England and Greece where she took a wide variety of jobs, each of which presented its own challenges. Then she immigrated to New Zealand and she now lives a richly blessed life with her family in a beautiful seaside cottage. Adventures are still to be had in Paradise, however, as on a regular basis New Zealand provides cyclones, floods, earthquakes and even the odd volcanic eruption. But as her deepest fear is public humiliation, signing up for dancing lessons when she lacks any sense of rhythm whatsoever might yet prove to be the scariest venture of all....

Books by Zana Bell

HARLEQUIN SUPERROMANCE
1625—TEMPTING THE NEGOTIATOR

To Sally and Alan,
who constantly blaze new trails.

You are an inspiration.
Special thanks also to my splendid editor,
Victoria Curran.

PROLOGUE

THIS WAS THE HAPPIEST DAY of her life. That's what everyone said. Cressa stared out of the window of the limousine, as the world spun past her. Everywhere in the city people were going to movies and restaurants or to the beach or playing sports, and here she sat, imprisoned in this white, beribboned Jaguar.

It's just nerves, she thought to herself. Again. *All brides have them.*

She glanced at her father, seated beside her. He looked so handsome and proud. He smiled at her and patted her hands, clasped in her lap. "Nearly there."

He thought she was being impatient. Her stomach rumbled, soured by champagne and doubt, and she rubbed it. Only a month ago she'd carried life there. For such a short time, really, yet it had created a nightmare of intense, conflicting emotions that she still did not know how to deal with. But now wasn't the time. Not the place. She resolutely pushed the feelings aside.

"Dad," she said. "I've got to pee."

"Now?"

"Yes."

"But…" He gestured helplessly out the window. They were driving through the outskirts of Auckland. The church where Brian was waiting for her was set on a hill surrounded by fields. Perfect, her mother had said, for photos.

"Please, Dad."

He leaned forward and tapped the chauffeur on the shoulder. "We need to find a restroom."

The driver flicked her a startled glance in his rearview mirror.

"Better text your sisters," said Dad. "They can go on and tell people we're coming."

"Fine."

She'd just texted the car behind, containing her four very excited sisters, when the chauffeur said, "There's a petrol station up ahead."

"Perfect."

The car with her bridesmaids shot past them as they turned into the gas station. All her sisters waved madly and pulled silly faces. Cressa would have laughed if she hadn't been so close to tears. As soon as the Jag stopped, she opened the door, then paused.

"I won't be long." She kissed her father on the cheek. "You're the best, Dad."

"I know all about performance nerves," he assured her. "I always feel nauseous before I go onstage. Take as long as you need, sweetheart. This is your day."

She heard good-natured laughter from the other customers and saw pointing fingers as she dashed through the convenience shop to the loo outback, but she didn't care. Her veil was a nuisance, though, and it snagged on some boxes of biscuits on one of the shelves. She tugged and several boxes fell as her veil came loose. As she bent to pick them up, she realized she was still clutching her cell phone.

"Don't worry," said a teenage girl, rushing forward. "I'll get them." She smiled shyly. "You look beautiful."

Cressa could see envy in the girl's eyes. What would

she have said if Cressa had asked, "Want to swap places?"

Fortunately, the restroom was a wheelchair one, so her voluminous dress wouldn't get crushed. The size of the cubicle also meant she could pace, two steps forward, two back, her skirts sweeping the concrete floor. She couldn't bail. Couldn't do that to Brian, to her parents, to her sisters, to all the guests.

But she couldn't say the vows, either.

She was sure to the pit of her stomach that she would never be able to utter those two words, *I do.*

Why did it have to be today that all her fears, all her misgivings had finally crystallized into one big, fat, undeniable conviction that she was on the brink of making the worst mistake of her life? A week ago wouldn't have been so bad. Yesterday would still have been salvageable. But today? Now? Ten minutes away from the church? To be having these thoughts now was *unforgivable.*

She crossed to the sink, put her cell phone down and turned on the tap. She wished she could splash water in her face but didn't dare spoil the lovely makeup that had taken over an hour to do. Instead, she held her wrists under the cold water.

Above the sink, her white reflection stared back at her in a fly-spotted mirror. The light wasn't good, and the window above the loo had misted glass that probably enhanced her ghostly pallor.

The window.

She turned slowly, gazed at it, then shook her head. She couldn't. Then she thought of standing at the altar, saying her vows and becoming Mrs. Brian McKenzie forever.

Cressa shut off the water, grabbed her phone, flipped

the toilet lid down and scrambled up on it. Luckily, the window was hinged at the top and quite wide. She hoisted herself up and landed half in, half out of it. Her veil fell forward over her head and dragged in the dust below. A couple of hairpins dislodged and she felt some of her heavy hair come free from the elaborate bun. The window frame dug into her stomach. Her feet no longer reached the toilet seat, but scrabbled against the wall, tangling in her skirts as she levered herself slowly forward. It wasn't easy, especially since she still clutched her phone.

Her father would be wondering what had happened to her. At the sound of fabric ripping, she winced. *Sorry, Ma.* The dress had snagged on the window catch. Cressa wriggled to free herself. Then she was hanging, her thighs on the ledge. Only one way to go now. She gave an extra heave and slithered headfirst down the cobwebby wall to crash onto the grass, banging her elbow painfully. She scrambled to her feet, veil hanging over her face, hair in tangles. With a jerk, she wrenched the veil from her head, causing more locks to fall free. Then she picked up her cell phone, which she'd dropped, and looked around.

Two guys were sitting in a pickup, hamburgers halfway to their mouths, gasping in astonishment. Did white knights come with adolescent pimples and scraggly hair?

She ran over to the truck window. "You've got to get me outta here," she said in a low voice.

They nodded mutely.

"Now!"

At her tone, learned over the years from her mother, a high school principal, they jumped in response. As Cressa pulled open the door, they swallowed their burgers like baby pythons, not stopping to bite or chew. She admired their economy of movement.

"Move over," she ordered, and hauled herself and her skirts into the tiny cabin, realizing she'd have to crouch at their feet. She squished down, her wedding dress nestling like a marshmallow around her. The cabin was filthy, but dirtying her dress was probably the least damage her actions of the past five minutes would cause. The guys' boots were eyewateringly malodorous, but she didn't care. A sense of appalled elation was bubbling up inside her.

"Let's go," she urged. "Quick."

The boys exchanged grins and the pickup roared off with a wheelie that was completely gratuitous, but somehow suited the occasion. She fell sideways as the truck rounded the corner of the gas station, then she was slammed again when the youthful rescuer driving the truck pulled another squealing wheelie as he turned onto the road and sped off.

Her heart was still pounding, but for the first time that day, her mind was completely calm as she began to text her sisters once more.

CHAPTER ONE

Two Years Later

THE HARDEST THING to explain, either to herself or others, was that she had no aversion to weddings as such. There was, in fact, lots to enjoy about them. Right now, Cressa was taking malicious glee in watching her cousin Jake, usually the supercool surfie, straighten his vest for the third time in as many minutes as he stood on the deck of the sleep-out, waiting for his bride to emerge from the main house.

As for the setting of this wedding, it was perfect. A house on the beach in Aroha Bay—Bay of Love. What could be more fitting? The harbor provided the backdrop for the groom, best man and celebrant, with winter sunlight reflecting off the tranquil high tide. Behind the guests, tables with white cloths, laden with plates and glasses, had been positioned under trees festooned with streamers. Fairy lights had been threaded through the branches, ready for the night's entertainment. Cressa had never seen the old house look so festive.

Even the weather was behaving unexpectedly well for an outside wedding, and had provided one of those wonderful Northland midwinter days of blue skies and blue sea. All the guests gathered on the lawn below the sleep-out were wearing sunglasses and many had shrugged off their jackets in the unexpected warmth.

Cressa also loved a good party, and all her favorite people in the world were clustered around her at this one. She glanced affectionately at her parents and her four sisters, Juliet, Portia, Desdemona and Katherine.

"Really, Cressa," muttered her mother. "I do wish you hadn't worn black."

Cressa looked down at the leather miniskirt she'd found in a secondhand shop and the satin top with spaghetti straps, and grinned inwardly. What would a family gathering be without Ma finding something about her to criticize?

"You should be glad I'm not wearing my boots," she hissed back.

She'd foregone her ancient Doc Martens in favor of a pair of high-heeled shoes borrowed from Des, the baby of the family and its fashionista. The shoes were a nuisance, though, because the heels kept getting stuck in the lawn.

Her thoughts returned to weddings and she wondered about the nature of love. People, she was sure, married for all sorts of reasons. Perhaps there was the fear of living alone forever. Maybe they simply confused sex or friendship with something more. And let's face it, after a certain age, going to parties and dinners was way easier to do as part of a couple than as a single person.

Yet Cressa had to admit that denying the whatever-it-was that had such a tangible effect on people was hard. She eyed her cousin. Jake could surf deadly ninety-foot walls of water, yet here he was, as jumpy as a kitten, running his fingers through tousled tawny curls for the umpteenth time as he leaned over to say something to his best man, Rob. Rob shot him a big-brother grin, patted his tuxedo pocket and gave a thumbs-up to indicate that yes, he still had the ring.

"What's keeping Sass?" demanded Des in a whisper that carried to the guests, causing some to glance around. "We've been waiting ages."

As if on cue, the opening chords of Mendelssohn's "Wedding March" erupted from the speakers suspended from the branches of the pohutukawa tree. Everyone turned and a collective sigh rose from the crowd. Sass looked lovely in an ivory dress that hugged her trim midriff, then flared from her hips. Her blond hair was loose and she carried a simple bouquet.

Cressa was certainly not immune to the sight of a beautiful bride. Tears pricked her eyes as she watched Sass make her way down the steps, her mother beside her. She appeared composed and confident, and as she gazed across the guests to Jake, a dazzling smile lit her face. Their union did seem, Cressa had to concede, very much like true love.

Given all the advantages she could see in weddings, her misgivings must therefore have their root in the happily-ever-after bit, she concluded thoughtfully. She just didn't buy that. And if one really did live in marital bliss forever, well, where was the fun and adventure? It sounded like Sunday-school heaven: serene, beautiful— and mind-numbingly boring.

With a deep breath and an inward sigh, Cressa straightened, bracing herself to listen to vows that would lock her dashing cousin and his beautiful, strong-minded Texan wife in bland matrimony for the rest of their lives. But just as Sass reached the steps of the deck, the throaty roar of a motorcycle drowned out the music.

Bride forgotten, all heads whipped around to watch as the bike plunged down the steep driveway at a suicidal pace, swerved just in time around a pothole, only to hit a root. The bike launched and flew through the air for the last few yards before landing with a thump and skidding to a halt in front of the stunned gathering. The rider killed the engine and eased back in the saddle, looking blankly at the guests through his visor as though taken aback to suddenly be the center of attention.

"Adam!"

Sass abandoned her husband-to-be and rushed over to hug the man as he swung off the bike.

"Is that the brother?" whispered Juliet.

"Must be," Portia muttered.

"They're completely different," said Katherine, pointing out the obvious when the man removed his helmet and enfolded his sister and then his mother in great bear hugs, his black hair and olive skin contrasting sharply with their fairness.

"Wow! He's gorgeous," Des murmured. "I bet he's an Eastern European spy."

Cressa smiled, remembering the silly game they used to play when sitting in the mall as teenagers. "Or a Mississippi steamboat gambler," she whispered back.

"Oh, yeah!" Des fanned her cheeks with her hands, as Juliet cast them a withering look.

Juliet's demeanor was another strike against marriage. Since her wedding to Mike a year earlier, she had become exceedingly dull company. Cressa had skipped that wedding because Brian had been Mike's best man. Even Ma had agreed that Cressa's absence might be the best option. Mike was away at a conference this weekend, and Cressa supposed Brian was there, too.

"Adam!" Jake vaulted off the deck and strode across the grass to shake his brother-in-law's hand. "We thought you'd never make it after your flight was delayed."

"Well, there was this real helpful ground attendant…"
His voice was warm and deep, with the same slow Texan
drawl as his sister's.

"Around Adam there always is," said Sass resignedly.
"What was her name?"

Her brother just smiled. "She found a spare seat on a
different airline and voilà." He turned to Jake. "Tell me
I'm not too late to give Sass away. I'd hate to miss the
opportunity of a lifetime." He looped an arm around his
sister and squeezed. "No one else would be rash enough
to take her on."

Sass whacked him with her bouquet. "I might have
known that even at my wedding you'd find a way to
upstage me." She tucked a hand into his arm. "Come
on, you've arrived just in time."

Amid laughter and the buzz of comments, someone
got the music going again and the Texan siblings waited
for Jake to return to the deck before they walked arm
in arm through the crowd as it parted for them. The
brother passed so close to Cressa she could have put out
her hand and touched him, but his attention was on his
sister as he beamed down at her. Sass's blond hair and
classical looks made her brother's dark features even
more dramatic. They mounted the steps of the deck and
Cressa noted he was almost as tall as her cousin. Adam
bent his head and kissed Sass's cheek, before placing her
hand in Jake's. Then he stepped aside and the ceremony
began.

Despite thinking she was completely over her own
wedding-that-never-was, and despite her rationaliza-
tion of the whole marriage scene, Cressa began to feel
slightly sick as the ceremony progressed. Marriage-a-
phobia? She couldn't flee and disgrace herself a second
time. *Think about something else.*

She focused on Sass's brother. Adam. Nice name. Very Genesis. His thick black hair fell straight to his collar, and even though she could see only part of his face, his hawkish nose and knife-blade cheekbones were striking.

He'd handled his bike like a pro. She should know, having nearly hurtled off her own bike when going too fast down that treacherous driveway full of ruts and stones. How long was he staying in New Zealand?

She was dimly aware of soft Texan vows entwining with the more staccato Kiwi ones, so she deliberately turned her thoughts to the bike. She guessed it was a 600. She'd always wanted to try something that big. She looked back at Adam. Would he let her take it for a ride? After all, they were family now. She screwed up her face as she tried to determine the relationship. He was the brother of her cousin-in-law, which would perhaps make them cousins-in-law once removed. Twice, if you took in national differences.

"I now pronounce you man and wife."

The words rang out, snapping her back to the proceedings. As Jake gathered the new Mrs. Finlayson in his arms to kiss her, another audible sigh went up from the crowd. Cressa glanced at her parents and saw they were staring goofily into each other's eyes, as if remembering their own wedding day, and she was surprised to find her formidable mother quite tearful. Cressa was less surprised by her sisters.

"That was so beautiful," said Juliet, dabbing at her eyes with a tissue.

"I know," sniffed Des, wiping her tears away with the back of her hand. "Why do weddings always make one cry?"

"Because they mark the end of freedom, that's why," Cressa said darkly.

Portia gave a watery chuckle, but Katherine rolled her eyes. "Oh, Cressa!" She turned to the others. "Come on, let's go congratulate the bride."

Her family abandoned her and started pushing through the crowd surrounding the newly married couple, but Cressa slipped away and drifted over to the bike. It was a KTM 640 Motard, a lovely beast, and she ran a hand tenderly over the seat.

"In Texas we shoot horse rustlers." The deep, slow voice made her spin around. "You got designs on my bike?"

He was even more gorgeous close up, his face all swooping planes and dark hollows. He looked tired—which wasn't surprising, since he'd just stepped off a transPacific flight, then ridden three hours north—but he was still alert.

"I do," she admitted. "I was wondering if you'd let me take it for a spin."

His interest sharpened. "You ride bikes?"

"I've got a GPX250."

"Yeah?" He nodded approvingly. "That's a tidy little bike."

She snorted. "Little? She'd give your monster a run for its money on the roads around here."

They were mostly unfinished, and Cressa had first learned how to ride a motorbike on the twisting, back-country roads.

Adam surveyed her. "Is that a challenge?"

She stuck her fists on hips and eyeballed him. "Damn straight it is," she said. "My bike's back at the motel, but if you're here tomorrow…"

She watched a smile slowly spread across his face.

"Do you always pick on bikes twice your size?" he asked.

"Well, you know what they say." She put on a leer and waggled her brows. "It's not the size that counts…"

He laughed and stuck out his hand. "I'm Adam Walker. Pleased to meet you."

She took his hand. It was large and warm. "Hi, Adam. Actually, we're family now." His eyebrows rose. "I'm Jake's cousin Cressida, but everyone calls me Cressa."

ADAM FOUND IT HARD not to stare into her wide, gray-green eyes. She had the most direct gaze he'd ever seen in a woman, and her thick, dark hair fell to her ass. Her nose, long, strong and slightly hooked, dominated her face, lending her an imperious air. Right now she was blatantly checking him out.

"Cressida? As in *Troilus and Cressida?*"

"That's the one."

He frowned. "Strange play. I can't recall much of it apart from the dragging of the corpse at the end. I enjoyed that bit. Except, that wasn't Troilus, was it?"

She did a double take. "It was Hector, but I'm impressed. You've actually seen the play? It's not one of Shakespeare's better known ones."

"Way back when. I was only about fourteen then. Wasn't she kind of a bad apple?"

"That's me."

There was something almost wolfish in her grin, and he found himself grinning back. Then he became aware he was still holding on to her hand. She hadn't been in a hurry to claim it back, either. With some regret, Adam let it go. He was in New Zealand only to give his sister away and keep an eye on their mom while Sass was honeymooning. There was no room for flirting. All his time and energy during the next month had to be for studying.

He leaned against the bike as she asked, "How come you went to see the play at that age? Were you studying it at school?"

A gust of wind lifted her hair like a dark cloud around her. The impatient way she tucked it behind her ear suggested she had no idea how sexy it looked.

"My mom's an English teacher. She dragged me to every Shakespeare performance within a hundred miles of where we lived."

"Tell me about it! My dad's an actor. My little sister's first words were—" she put on a baby's lisp "—'Ith thith a dagger I thee before me?'"

He laughed and she joined in. Not that her performance had been that funny, but a weird energy fizzed between them and laughter was a way to express it or release it. Or something. Hell, must be jet lag heightening his senses and jumbling his thoughts this way.

"So where did the bike come from?"

"A rental. I picked it up at the airport once I found out no plane or bus would get me here in time."

She was only about five foot four, but she gave the impression of being taller. She had a nice body—compact, curvy and toned.

"Hey, Adam!" Hearing his name shouted, he glanced away to find his brother-in-law gesticulating from the beach. Adam waved, then turned back to her. "Sorry, Cressa, gotta go. Time for photos. It was real nice meeting you."

She raised a hand in farewell. "See you later, cuzzie bro."

He'd begun to leave, but he stopped and looked back over his shoulder. "'Cuzzie bro'?"

She smiled. "It's a term we use in New Zealand for a loose family connection. You're one of us now."

As he walked away, Adam didn't know whether that warmed or alarmed him.

CHAPTER TWO

OVER THE NEXT HOUR, Sass and Jake introduced Adam to all their guests and he became quite giddy, repeating the same conversations again and again. Yeah, a great flight. Yeah, a little jet-lagged. No, finding the place had been easy—the bike had a GPS. Yeah, the New Zealand roads were pretty different from the long straight Texas roads, but he'd had a great ride up. The country sure was pretty. He'd be here a month. No, he didn't see himself getting bored stuck out in Aroha Bay—what a beautiful spot.

The Kiwis were all very friendly, but he couldn't find Cressa, and tiredness was kicking in fast. He hadn't gotten a lot of sleep on the flight, squeezed into economy, with his legs folded up around his ears. The continual glasses of champagne now being pressed into his hand weren't helping, either, as the reality of what he'd committed himself to began to sink in. Galahad instincts had kept him buoyed on the flight over, but here, standing on the beach at the end of a dead-end road, he was beginning to realize it would be just him and Mom for four weeks. For nine years everyone in the Walker family had led their own, very dissimilar lives. What the hell would living under the same roof again be like?

Even worse, what if Mom wanted to "talk"? Such an awful lot had gone unsaid over the years that, in his opinion, would be best left unsaid. The past was a place he didn't like to visit, even as a tourist. Unfortunately, one of the big drawbacks with women was they usually insisted on talking things out. Mom used to cope by using denial and drink, but now that she was sober....

The one quality all the Walkers had perfected over the years, however, was the art of making everything seem fine, so Adam put his doubts aside as he laughed and chatted and took photos and gave his mom and sis hugs, and everyone smiled to meet such a happy family.

At one point, Sass pulled him behind a big tree where no one could see them.

"Oh, Adam, I can't tell you what this means to me."

He was alarmed to notice tears well. "Hey, don't cry about it. I'm happy to hang out here and make sure Mom is okay. How's she doing?"

Sass smiled. "She's been great these past couple of months. Staying with us in New Zealand has helped. All her old routines are broken, and as you can tell—" she motioned toward the waters of the bay, which were turning silver-blue in the late-afternoon sun "—there aren't any stores around to buy alcohol."

"Great. Well, I'll hold fort for the next month. I know you'll be away for five weeks, but I gotta be back by then. Mom'll just have to go it alone for a few days."

Sass hugged him. "She'll be fine. I'm so sorry I twisted your arm into flying over, but when the cottage came up in Australia—"

"Yeah, I know. Right on the most perfect surf beach where the boys can learn to surf bigger waves. You've already explained several times. Although why the hell you're taking Jake's bad boys with you—but hey, it's your honeymoon."

She laughed. "What can I say? Surfers are crazy and I simply couldn't disappoint them all."

"No worries. I'm here now. It'll be fine."

He sounded confident, but Sass, damn it, was on to him in a flash. "What is it?" she asked.

"Nothing. Jeez, Sass, nothing. Well, nothing major. I just sorta wonder what Mom and I will find to talk about, that's all."

Sass gazed at him for a second. Her voice was gentle as she said, "It's different now that she's sober. She's the mom I remember from when I was a little girl. You were probably too young to recall."

"Yeah?" Adam considered this. At least, he tried to. Jet lag and champagne were not conducive to thinking much at all. "Well, good." Sass was eyeing him thoughtfully, which worried him. "Look, we'll be just fine. I wasn't thinking straight for a minute. Don't worry about it."

"Okay," she said in that tone he knew meant she was already sorting out solutions. He'd been on the receiving end of her solutions too often in the past.

"I mean it, Sass. Leave it."

She gave him that smile he recognized all too well. *Talk on. I'm not listening.* But before he could make a stronger protest, Sass squeezed his arm. "I'd better get back to my guests."

As they stepped around the tree and Sass disappeared to socialize, luck shone down on him. There was Cressa, standing in a group of people, her back to him. Even though no one else had yet noticed him, something made Cressa turn slowly around, and their eyes met.

"Hey," he said.

"Hi." She had the most amazing smile. "Come over and meet my family."

She made a space for him beside her and he could smell her perfume. Light, pretty and a bit spicy.

"This is my mum, Deirdre." She gestured to a tall, dignified woman in a cream suit.

"Nice to meet you, Deirdre."

She smiled, but her eyes x-rayed him in a single glance. "Adam. I hadn't realized you two had already met."

"Yeah, over by my bike."

"Ah, of course."

Again that laser stare. Adam fought the urge to check if his fly was undone.

"And this is George, my dad," Cressa said.

Her dad was tall, with strong features, and Adam figured he must have Maori ancestry. That would explain Cressa's sensational hair.

"An actor, I believe," said Adam.

George feigned astonishment. "You've heard of me in Houston?" He placed a hand across his heart and bowed his head. "I'm honored."

"Oh, Dad, stop kidding around. And these are my sisters, Juliet, Katherine, Portia and Desdemona."

Adam blinked. They were as overwhelming in looks as in names. Juliet, Portia and Desdemona were all fair like their mother. He tried to sort them out. Juliet, sleek bob. Desdemona, long curls. Portia, pixie cut. Katherine and Cressa were dark like their father, but Katherine's hair was short and curly. Their eyes and skin tones were also different. The only thing they all shared was the same strong nose. Adam found it rather cute, but he bet they hated it.

He must have appeared stunned, because George

laughed. "The Curtis women en masse are glorious but overwhelming, I know. Stupidly, we forgot to bring a camera today, and I'd love a shot of all my daughters together, especially looking so beautiful." He pointed to the camera in Adam's hand. "Would you take one of us all?"

"Gladly," Adam said, and raised the camera. "Smile."

Cries of "Cheese" and "Whiskey" arose from the sisters as they squeezed together, and Cressa laughed, her face full of affection as she regarded her siblings.

"Hang on," said Adam. "I'll shoot a few more to make sure." He fiddled with the zoom, clicked a couple more times. "Perfect."

"What about you?" Cressa asked Adam. "Do you come from a big family?"

"Nope. Just one sister, one brother, one mother."

Had he just sounded wistful? Man, he *must* be jet-lagged.

"Lucky you," sighed Desdemona. "More time in the bathroom."

"As if you needed it, Des. You always used to hog it," said Juliet.

"And what do you do, Adam?" Deirdre asked.

He felt as if he was just about to fail an exam. "This and that. Mostly I'm involved in construction."

"Oh."

Amazing how much one small word could convey.

"You're like Cressa," Des interjected. "She doesn't stay in any job for long, either. She's a flibbertigibbet."

"I'm not," said Cressa. "I'm versatile."

That set her sisters off.

"Very versatile," Juliet agreed. "Last month you were a youth hostel manager down in Hokitika."

"And before that you were working in a ski shop in Queenstown," said Portia.

"Don't forget the bar in Wellington and the stint as a tourist guide in Rotorua," Des added.

George chuckled and said to Adam, "To think she very nearly qualified as an accountant, and look at her now."

She looked pretty good to him. Deirdre, however, didn't seem nearly so amused, especially when Cressa turned to Adam and commented, "They just don't understand that people like us don't enjoy being trapped in the same old, same old, do we? We thrive on change, aye?"

It wasn't quite like that for Adam, but this was so not the time to put her right, especially since, with her mother watching, she was seeking support. "Sure. So what are you doing now?"

"I'm a stuntwoman. Dad got me a job on a TV pilot, *The Valkyries*. It's got motorbike chases and broadsword battles between characters in leather gear. All quite mad but loads of fun."

"No kidding. I used to do motorcycle stunts, too." The words just slipped out.

Cressa's incredible eyes widened. "Really?"

"Yeah, but years ago," he said, playing down the experience, "and mainly as a touring show. Very different."

This caused another clamor as all the sisters began asking questions and Deirdre's smile became more and more taut. To his relief, he caught sight of his mother chatting to another group of people across the lawn, and he held up a hand with an apologetic smile.

"Sorry, but I've barely spoken to my mom, and need to say hi to her properly. Nice meeting you all."

BY THE TIME EVENING FELL and the dancing started, Adam was feeling seriously spaced out. He found he had to concentrate to catch what people were saying. Kiwis spoke so damn fast that keeping up was difficult. His body was craving sleep and he was too befuddled now to calculate what time it was back in Texas. Yesterday morning or some such. How great, therefore, when Cressa appeared at his elbow. It was colder now and she was wearing a bright red jacket. Bold with strong lines, it suited her.

"Will you dance with me?"

"With pleasure."

He put his camera down on one of the tables and swept her into his arms. The band was playing "Moon River," probably because of the full moon now laying a silver track across the harbor. Adam was glad the number was a slow one. Drifting like this on the grass, under the trees and stars, a pliant woman pressed against him, it felt good. He hadn't had a chance to catch up with Cressa again before now. He'd only seen her from afar, chatting animatedly in different groups, seeming to know everyone. At one stage he'd spotted her in deep conversation with Jake and Sass. They'd glanced several times in his direction and he'd wondered what they were talking about. Nothing bad, clearly, for here she was, in his arms.

Adam closed his eyes, letting his tired mind relax and his senses take over. He liked her perfume and the softness of her hair. Dreamily, he wound it around and between his fingers. He loved the contrast of the cold night air and the warmth of her body, and his hand slipped up under the hem of her jacket to stroke the sensuous lines of her back. It would be so sweet to melt into the shadows with her and make out. Slow and easy.

Almost trancelike, he danced her to the edge of the crowd, toward the sheltering darkness of trees. He'd been so serious for so long, and Cressa reminded him of what he used to be like.

Tonight he was in a foreign land, among strangers. Tomorrow she'd be gone and he would refocus, get back to his studies. Hell, there was absolutely nothing else to do in Aroha Bay. No distractions, just him and Mom. He'd probably ace the exam, given the empty weeks stretching ahead.

The thought made him smile as he leaned down to rub his cheek, then his lips, on the top of her head. That felt good, too. She raised her face to his, but just as he was about to let his mouth sink onto her beautiful lips, he saw Deirdre only a few feet away, observing the dancers. The way Cressa's mother wasn't looking at them as she sipped her wine let him know she knew exactly what was going on. He swung around with the music so that his back was to her, but already she had knocked some of that delicious, drugged dreaminess out of him.

Cressa smiled up at him. She appeared so full of mischief and wicked promise that he couldn't help smiling back. One night with her would be amazing.

"I've a surprise for you."

"Yeah?" He could hear the husky, lustful hope in his voice and wondered if she did.

"I hope you won't mind. Sass said you'd be delighted. Your mum knows about it and she says that it'll be wonderful."

Suspicion replaced lust. "Really?" His instincts had spotted danger, but his mind couldn't seem to keep up. "What?"

"I told Jake and Sass I'm up here on location for the

next few weeks, and Sass invited me to stay. Now I'll be around to show you the country. Won't that be fun?"

With alarm bells going off in his head, Adam jerked backward, tripped over the root of a tree and stumbled, knocking the glass of red wine out of Deirdre's hand and all down her cream suit.

CHAOS ENSUED as people immediately crowded around, making helpful comments while trying to wipe down the suit. Cressa saw Adam looking wretched as he apologized over and over. She was relieved when Jake carried him off, ostensibly to give a hand bringing out the cake. Adam's mum, Alicia, whisked Deirdre off to the sleep-out to find her a change of clothes. Then came speeches, more champagne and the cutting of the cake.

Through it all, Adam never once glanced her way. Cressa couldn't understand it. When they were dancing, she'd been so sure he was as attracted to her as she was to him. He couldn't have missed the magnetism between them. Or had she really misread the signals so badly?

Over and over again in her mind she replayed the shock on his face when she'd told him she'd be staying. Saw again the panic in his eyes. What the hell? She had to find Sass, tell her staying here was off. But it wasn't easy. The bride and groom were constantly surrounded by people.

Cressa wandered among the tables now showing the wreckage of carousing. Canapes had dried up; empty glasses littered surfaces. Used plates and napkins lay strewn across the tables and some had fallen onto the grass. The dregs of champagne sat flat in the bottles. The celebration was over and her sour feelings about weddings had only been reinforced. For a while she must have been carried away by a misdirected, false sense of romanticism. What a fool. She glanced over to Adam, now standing on the far edge of the lawn. He looked gorgeous and unobtainable. What a waste.

How had she read him so wrong?

Then, to crown her sense of dislocation, she watched as Sass mounted the deck of the sleep-out and lifted her bouquet. Laughing and jostling, all the women gathered below. Des, Portia and Katherine were right in front. Typical. Cressa wouldn't be caught dead in that silly gaggle. Someone started a countdown. "Ten. Nine…"

She spotted Adam's camera lying on the table where he'd left it when they went to dance. She turned it on and flicked through the photos he'd taken of her family. In the darkness of the night, they glowed in bright colors, surprisingly good. Despite her current mood, Cressa smiled. They would all want copies.

"Six. Five…"

She continued clicking on the photos and froze. This one was of her. He'd zoomed in for a close-up of her face. She'd been glancing sideways, laughing at her sisters. The wind had caught her hair, lifting it behind her.

"Two… *One!*"

And the bouquet, caught by a gust, sailed over all the guests to smack Cressa squarely in the back of her head.

CHAPTER THREE

THE NEXT DAY began chaotically. The Curtis family overslept, after having talked and laughed into the small hours of the morning. The rushed start meant hasty cups of tea and battles for the bathroom. Cressa's sisters tripped over one another as they crammed clothes into bags before realizing they'd picked up the wrong bras, hair straighteners and phone chargers. This led to frantic repacking, which was followed by an uproarious brunch at the marina.

Cressa leaned back, cradling her coffee, letting the words wash around her. The sun was warm on her back and shone on the dark and tawny heads of her family. Their faces were animated, hands gesturing to emphasize words. With a teacher mother and an actor father, they'd all learned to make their points forcibly. She smiled, her world complete.

One sister, one brother, one mother.

He'd looked wistful, which was at odds with his bad-boy persona. So many contradictions. She was, she had to admit, intrigued. Images of Adam, memories of his arms around her, his lips in her hair, kept coming back to her and filling her with anticipation. Then she'd recall his look of horror.

"How is Brian?" Her mother's question pulled her back to the present.

Far from playing the jilted groom, Brian had stayed frustratingly faithful and friendly.

"Oh, he's fine. Working mad hours as always." She was careful to sound blasé.

"I thought he must be," said Deirdre. "We haven't spoken to him for a few weeks now, have we, George?"

"Not since he dropped by with that particularly good bottle of wine." Her dad smiled, and she wasn't sure if it was because of the wine or the pleasure of seeing Brian. Cressa might not have gone through with the wedding, but Brian had somehow remained a fixture in her family.

"I caught up with him last Friday," Juliet interjected. "Mike brought him home for dinner. He's looking great but tired. Did you know he's presenting at the conference Mike's gone to this weekend?" She eyed Cressa with a touch of accusation. "He mentioned he hasn't seen much of you, Cressa."

What could she say?

"Filming's busy," she replied.

But Des was already leaning forward, arms crossed on the table. "Why should she? They're not an item anymore."

"He still loves her, despite everything," Katherine said. "Cressa's mad not to see how lucky she is."

"But if she doesn't love him—" Des countered.

"What's not to love?" Juliet said. "He's the most eligible bachelor around."

"It's none of our business," said Mum, as she always did just before going on to deliver her opinion. "However, Cressa, you do need someone steady—if not Brian, then someone like him. Not some wild tearaway, here today, gone tomorrow."

Cressa glanced at her sharply, but Deirdre's sunglasses rendered her face impassive.

Looking mischievous, George covered his wife's hand with his. "Isn't that what your parents said when an impecunious actor strolled into your life?"

They all laughed, then Portia ended the discussion. "We should all butt out. Cressa can lead her life any way she likes after what she's been through."

The uncomfortable silence was broken when their father stood. "I'll get the bill. Then we should hit the road."

Cressa felt squeezed to death by the time her whole family had hugged her before climbing into the van and taking off, hands waving out all the windows. She laughed, waving back with both arms till the vehicle rounded the corner, then she picked up her helmet and made her way to her motorbike. As she switched on the engine, she was aware of a tingle of excitement.

How well her mother knew her. A wild tearaway, here today and gone tomorrow, was exactly what she wanted. She just had to convince him it was what he wanted, too. First, however, she had a phone call to make, and then she was going to drop in on her cousin and his wife. Rob and Moana had gotten to know Sass extremely well, and Cressa wanted as much information about the Walkers as possible. As a Valkyrie, she'd learned never to go into battle without being fully armed.

THE SUN WAS SETTING when Adam opened the door in answer to her knock, mop in one hand, bucket in the other. Cressa suppressed a smile. With his dangerous looks, he should be toting a weapon, not a mop. His hair, as black and glossy as the feathers of an eagle, fell thick and straight down each side of his face. He was wearing jeans and a white T-shirt that made his olive skin appear more tanned than ever. Moana had said his father was Cherokee. Cressa liked that. It made him somehow even more exotic and exciting.

"Hey, good to see you," he said, stepping back to let her enter. "Just finished getting the house in order."

So that's how he intended to play it. His manner was impeccably pitched at the "polite acquaintance" level. As if he had never run his hands up and down her back, causing her to shiver with anticipation. Okay, she could play along—for now.

"Hi." She stepped inside the kitchen. The smell of roast chicken filled the air, and pots were boiling on the stove, though no one seemed to be attending to them. "You didn't have to clean up for me, you know."

He smiled, and his teeth were very white. American dentistry, no doubt. His slanted cheekbones gave his smile a wicked edge.

"I didn't." He sounded apologetic. "I did it because Mom ordered me to."

Cressa laughed. The warrior still taming to his mother's orders. She liked that, too.

"Was there a lot to do? You guys should have taken us up on our offer to help."

Adam dismissed the idea with a wave of one lean hand. "It was no trouble. Rob and Moana came over in the morning, and with the boys here, too, we got most of it done in no time. Sass was commander in chief. Bossy but efficient. To be honest, when they all left at lunchtime, it was a relief."

"Sounds like Juliet. Being the eldest, she thinks of herself more as mother than sister. So, where am I sleeping?"

"Mom's been living in the sleep-out these past couple

of months—Sass put her there to give her some privacy.
So you'll be in the house with me. You've got a choice,
but I expect you'd like Sass and Jake's room. It's the biggest and has a double bed. The twins' room is another
option, but it has bunk beds and is a mess."

He pushed open the door. "Here you are."

But the sight of the double bed, the almost tangible
sense of intimacy, had her backing out.

"You know, I'll take the boys' room."

"Sure," said Adam in his easy Texan way, but
she'd seen his curious glance. She covered up with an
explanation.

"That's where I always used to be. I haven't slept in
the bunks for years. Now I won't have to fight sisters
for the top one."

"You've been here before?" Adam was surprised.

"Yeah, we used to have family holidays here when
I was a kid. That was how Jake got to rent it now, and
why he and Sass invited me to stay. Jake thought I might
like to enjoy the place one last time before the resort
goes in."

She felt sad at the thought of the house being taken
away so the eco-resort could be built, but as Jake had
said with a wry expression, it was time for other people
to share the beauty of Aroha Bay. To have this final
opportunity to experience the serenity of the bay was
wonderful, and she'd have leaped at the chance, anyway.
Adam just happened to be a bonus.

The room at the end of the hall felt like home. She'd
forgotten how lovely it was, with windows on two walls
and a view over the harbor. Teenage detritus was scattered about, but nothing she couldn't chuck into the
cupboard in a couple of minutes.

"It's perfect."

She unzipped her jacket. She saw Adam's eyes follow the movement as he propped a shoulder against the top bunk. So she hadn't been wrong. The currents weren't as edgy as yesterday, but they were definitely running between them, however much he might pretend they weren't.

"Really? Even the artwork?"

The walls were covered in posters of waves and girls in impossibly tiny bikinis. She stuck her hands into her back pockets as she looked around. "Makes a change from the pop posters we used to paper our rooms with. Except for Des. She had this thing for kitten posters. What did you have?"

"I shared a room with my brother, Cole. He's into art, so we had all his drawings on one wall and my posters of motorbikes on the other."

Cole. The one in prison. Moana hadn't known much about why he was there. She'd said the Walker family had lots they chose not to talk about. Adam had mentioned his brother casually, but Cressa decided now was not the time to go into it. Although Adam seemed the same easygoing Texan of the night before, she could sense his defenses were up; his face gave nothing away.

He straightened. "Where're your bags? I'll bring them in."

"Hey, no need. I can manage on my own."

"I'm sure you can, but Mom would kill me if she saw you carrying them by yourself. She's a feminist, but still doesn't see why a gentleman shouldn't be a gentleman."

"Indeed I do not."

They turned at the soft voice, and Alicia came forward to kiss Cressa on the cheek. "Welcome. Sorry I wasn't here to meet you. I was out in the garden. Dinner's nearly ready. We're so pleased you're joining us. We'll eat in the kitchen, since there's just the three of us. It's cozy in there. Adam, you get Cressa's bags while we set the table."

"See what I mean?" Adam raised his hands in humorous resignation and departed. Cressa smiled.

"It's very kind of you to have me, Alicia."

"The pleasure is ours. The house will be so quiet now that Sass and Jake and the boys have gone. I know Adam will appreciate having someone other than his mother around. Wasn't yesterday wonderful?"

Cressa followed her down the hallway to the kitchen just in time to find one of the pots on the stove boiling over.

"Dear me," said Alicia, lifting it off the element and setting it to one side. She opened the oven door. Smoke and the smell of burning chicken filled the room. "Oh, my. That's not good."

Cressa went to set the table, and was astonished to find that the place mats and cutlery were kept exactly where they used to be. It gave her an eerie feeling of déjà vu. As she and Alicia chatted about the wedding, Cressa checked out the older woman. She was as neat as a pin, in white trousers and a blue jersey, and Cressa found it difficult to believe she had been cleaning all day. Her shoulder length hair fell in a silky curtain the way Adam's did. Otherwise, they couldn't look more different. It was as if a dove had given birth to an eaglet. An aura of femininity surrounded Alicia. Her soft voice and graceful movements were a far cry from Deirdre's quick efficiency.

Hard to imagine Alicia an alcoholic. Hard to imagine her the mother of a convict. She'd had a blond husband

and had taken a Cherokee lover. There was a lot more to this woman than her sweet, vague Southern mannerisms might suggest.

Adam came in. "Ah, I'd forgotten the smell of home cooking."

His mother swatted him with the oven mitt. "I was distracted by Cressa's arrival."

Cressa thought about the untended pots and held her tongue, but she and Adam exchanged glances. It was the first time he'd looked her in the eye today, and Cressa immediately found Alicia's cooking methods endearing.

"Now tell me, why are you up here for the filming? Is it just coincidence?" Alicia asked, draining a pot over the sink and disappearing into a cloud of steam.

"Not really. We were going to be on location in the Coromandel, but it got flooded out in the storms last week. I know the assistant director—he's a friend of Dad's—and suggested up here. Our family has been friendly with one of the local farmers for years. He can always do with some cash and his land has everything we need—so here we are."

Alicia turned and smiled at her. "Well, I'm very pleased. It's lovely for Adam to have another young person around. Me, too! What's the show about?"

"It's a pilot for a fantasy apocalypse series. Nuclear holocaust, the collapse of civilization, ongoing battles. Enter the Valkyries, who complicate things when they fall in love with fighters on different sides."

"Sounds like you are enjoying it," said Alicia, collecting the plates from the cupboard.

"Oh, yeah. The Valkyries are great—real kick-butt chicks. The warriors they fall in love with are also seriously cool." Cressa dug in a drawer for serving tongs.

As though he'd read her mind, Adam retrieved them from the dishwasher. "Alas," she added, putting on a woebegone expression. "Only a few more weeks and then I'll have to find a real job again."

Adam and Alicia laughed.

"Are you looking for another stunt gig?" Adam asked as he got a jug of water out of the fridge.

She loved his voice—deep with long, slow vowels. She remembered the huskiness when they'd danced together. Before he'd pulled away.

She shrugged. "No, it's been fun, but now I'm ready for something different." She gazed at Adam. "What about you? Why did you stop doing stunts?"

"I broke my back."

He smiled but glanced away, and the finality in his tone shut down that line of conversation. Was this how the Walkers got around topics they didn't want to talk about?

"And there've been no jobs to tempt you into a career path?"

"Construction suits me for now."

There it was again. You could almost hear the big fat period at the end of his sentence. His black eyes were unfathomable, his long eyelashes shuttering them. Cressa was impressed and intrigued. He smiled easily, but his expression was strangely impassive.

Alicia cut in. "Sometimes it takes some people longer to know what they want. I must confess I was relieved when Adam gave up his horrible show. Construction is much better, even if it isn't the ideal job. You're both still young and have lots of time to find something you love one day."

She smiled brightly at her son as they all took their

seats at the table, but Cressa saw concern in her glance. The same as she'd seen in her own mother's eyes.

"Yeah, people like us aren't in a hurry to get to a final destination. We're enjoying the journey—isn't that right, Adam?"

Before he could answer, there was a knock on the door, and they all turned to see a man through the glass panels.

"Brian!" Cressa exclaimed. "What on earth are you doing here?"

CHAPTER FOUR

ADAM NOTICED CRESSA'S EYES widen, and she hesitated before rising to hug the man. Then they stepped apart and the guy glanced at him with curiosity before extending his hand to Alicia.

"I'm Brian McKenzie. I hope you don't mind me intruding." He smiled at Cressa. "I haven't seen Cressa for a while and wanted to catch up."

Ex-boyfriend or wannabe?

"I'm delighted you did," said his mother. "It's lovely to meet you. I'm Alicia."

"And I'm Adam." He rose and shook Brian's hand. "Just passing, were you?"

Aroha Bay was the end of the road, thirty minutes out of Whangarimu. Brian's rueful smile acknowledged Adam's dig. "Not exactly. Mike and I flew in this morning and Juliet mentioned Cressa was staying here. It's been a long time since I was up this way so I thought I'd use Cressa as an excuse to visit Northland again."

Cressa smiled, but her shoulders were rigid and she didn't say anything. Ex, Adam decided, and wondered why that was. Brian was good-looking in that Harvard kind of way that comes from generations of wealth interbreeding with beauty. His clothes were expensive and his manners seemed nice. All in all, he appeared the perfect package for a woman.

Adam, this isn't easy to write, but I'm leaving you

*for someone else. He's rich and successful and really
nice. You'd like him. I promise he'll make a wonderful
father for Stella. You needn't worry. Please don't try to
find us. It's better for everyone if you let us go.*

Crystal, as usual, had been wrong. He hated that
unknown bastard who, all these years later, still made
him feel inferior. Since then, Adam had also found it
hard dealing with men who were like him—Brian, for
instance.

"You'll stay for dinner, of course," said Alicia.

"I couldn't impose—"

"You aren't imposing. We'd love to have you."

"Well, if you are sure…?" Brian looked at Cressa,
who shrugged, but this time her smile appeared
genuine.

"Of course. I'll lay another place."

Wannabe, Adam decided, noting the expression in
the poor sap's eyes. Poor, successful, rich, *nice* sap. Not
that any of this was his business, of course. He'd woken
this morning with the brain he'd misplaced somewhere
in transit lodged firmly back in place. Cressa's presence
in the house needn't be the disaster he'd foreseen last
night. She'd be out all day working, and he'd be in his
room at night, studying. They'd hardly run into each
other at all. And mealtimes would be fine. She'd be
a buffer between him and his mother, and his mother
would be a buffer between him and Cressa. Simple.

He still writhed to think about Deirdre's suit, but
thank heavens he'd noticed her and been prevented
from taking things too far with her daughter. Now
nothing more than a dance—a close one, granted—lay
between him and Cressa. If she mentioned anything,
he would apologize, blaming jet lag and champagne.
Which was true.

At least, it had all made sense when he'd been lying in bed with only a ceiling to stare at. Now that he had Cressa in front of him, he realized things weren't going to be quite so easy. Her tight jeans and T-shirt showed off her curves. Her hair was in a long braid down her back and he remembered how it had felt sliding through his fingers. Outside the window, her bike sat parked next to his, and they looked pretty good together.

But if he'd required reminding that Cressa was a complication he didn't need in his life right now, Brian's arrival certainly helped to slap his resolve into shape. As Adam struggled to carve the chicken his mom had done her best to kill a second time, Brian produced two bottles of white wine. "I hope you like them. The wine is a new varietal."

"Brian's parents own a vineyard," Cressa explained.

Why was Adam not surprised?

"None for me, thanks," said Alicia, busy serving up the vegetables. "I don't drink."

Adam felt a flare of pride. It would be coming up five months since she'd stopped. Maybe Sass was right and she had changed. Then he watched the way the potatoes bounced as she tipped them into a serving bowl. Her cooking skills, it seemed, were the same as ever.

As Brian poured the wine into the other three glasses, he said with elaborate unconcern, "So, Cressa, I hear you're seeing a French archaeologist?"

"Danish, and no, we finished a few weeks back. The French guy was a tour leader."

"Ah. And wasn't there a skier?"

Adam wondered why Brian would torture himself in this way but supposed it was like having a bad tooth— you just couldn't help prodding it to see if it still hurt.

"Canadian." Cressa smiled. "He was cool, into all that freestyle stuff. You'd have liked him, Adam."

She certainly thought she had him pegged, he decided grimly. People always did. "I've never been skiing." He'd never had the money for it.

"Really?" Both she and Brian spoke together, and exchanged equally surprised looks.

"I'm sure you'd enjoy it," said Brian. "Cressa and I have had some wonderful times together on the slopes."

Nice one. He might have polished manners and a vineyard, but Brian wasn't above getting in the odd jab. It made him a bit more real. But Brian didn't need to concern himself about Adam. For years after his divorce, Adam had kept all his relationships clean and easy and short. These days he was hanging out for something deeper, more permanent. Right at this moment, with his MCAT exam just weeks away, any sort of involvement was out of the question. Whichever way you looked at it, Cressa was a no-go zone.

They settled down to the meal. The extra setting cramped the table and the dinner was past saving, but the wine was excellent, as far as Adam could tell. His budget kept him well out of range of top wines. Alicia stuck to orange juice, and though he saw her glance at the bottle, she showed nothing of the cravings she might be fighting. She was gentle and soft, but she also had a tough core. Funny, he'd forgotten that.

When Brian tried to top up Adam's glass, he covered it. "It's great, but that's enough for me."

"So, Adam, I heard you used to do motorbike stunts, too. How did you get into it?" Brian looked interested, and tried to spear a potato with his fork. Now, how had he heard that? Cressa's family? That would explain his unexpected appearance. The fork pinged off the potato. Surprised, Brian eyed the potato as though seeking a way to break into it. Hammer and chisel, Adam felt tempted to suggest.

"A misspent youth."

"He bought his first motorcycle when he was thirteen," said Alicia, covering for his abrupt answer. "I had no idea, but he got himself a job walking dogs and saved all his money under his mattress. I was appalled when he said he'd bought a bike off his friend's brother."

Cressa looked at him. "Only thirteen? You were a determined little chap."

He could see admiration kindling in her gray-green eyes and for a second he felt tempted, cursing his exam.

"Nothing stops Adam," said Alicia, "once he's got an idea in his head. He'd visit Calvin, his friend, and ride that bike around and around their farm. Bert, Calvin's father, assured me Adam had more natural instincts than any other kid he'd ever met. He knew what he was talking about, having four sons of his own."

She still sounded proud of his riding skills, even though for years they'd caused her nothing but anxiety.

"Yeah, Bert was great. Took me and Cal to all the dirt bike events." Adam laughed. "Now Cal drives an SUV with baby seats in the back."

What had he said? Cressa's face didn't change at all, and neither did Brian's, but Alicia must have felt the sudden stillness because she immediately chimed in. "What do you do, Brian?"

"I'm a doctor."

Adam choked. Then patted his chest and peered reproachfully at the potato on his plate. He so should have guessed! Not content with movie star looks and being rich and *nice,* he had to go be a damn doctor, as well.

"Really," said Alicia. "What branch are you in?"

"I'm a GP, but I'm thinking of specializing in pediatrics. There was this speaker at the conference I've just been at...." And Brian went on to talk about new discoveries in child cancer. Alicia was interested, but Cressa seemed to tune out of the conversation. Was it medicine or children she didn't like? Adam noticed her glancing at her phone several times. Was she waiting for the skier or the archaeologist? Not that it was any of his business.

"Where did you two meet?" Alicia asked after a few minutes, turning to include Cressa.

"Brian is Juliet's husband's best friend."

She said it so offhandedly that Brian looked as if she'd just slapped him.

"I've known Cressa since she was eighteen," he added, staring into her eyes as though daring her to repudiate the fact. He wore his heart on his sleeve as if it were a fashion accessory. Adam couldn't work out whether Brian was the bravest guy he'd met or the stupidest—despite being a doctor.

"Yeah, we went out for a few years, nearly married, but realized the folly of our ways." Cressa was obviously making a big effort to keep her voice light. Against his will, Adam felt a tiny pull of sympathy for Brian. It appeared he wasn't over his folly at all.

"So, Adam." Brian focused on him again. "What line of work are you in these days?"

"Construction."

"Really?" Brian sounded as though he hadn't known, but if the family had talked about Adam's stuntwork, he felt sure Deirdre would have mentioned his current occupation. "Was it hard to get leave to fly out here?"

"I quit the project."

"Hmm. Anything lined up for when you return?" Brian sipped his wine, his eyes on Adam. What was he actually trying to find out?

"Nothing definite." Whatever it was, Adam wasn't going to supply the answer.

Cressa nodded. "Adam's like me. He takes things as they come."

She smiled at him across the table and Adam smiled back. His bad-boy smile that always worked. But he was relying on it for all the wrong reasons and he knew it. Part of him just wanted to rattle Brian's cage. Which wasn't fair—his beef wasn't with this guy at all.

"More potatoes, Adam?" Brian smiled blandly as he passed the dish. Mom's potatoes, a new weapon of war. "I've always had a sneaking envy of anyone with a Peter Pan complex—you know, no commitments, no steady job."

Adam rose to the challenge and put another two potatoes—God help him—on his plate. Equally blandly, he replied, "Well, you only live once." Steam still rose from the bowl as he set it on a mat between them.

"I'm curious, though," Brian said. "Have you never wanted anything a little more permanent, now that you are getting older?"

Cressa rolled her eyes. "Oh, Brian, everything for you always comes down to making things safe and secure, doesn't it?"

He looked at her. "As it turns out, not all my choices prove to be safe."

Her eyes glittered with annoyance, but at that moment

the phone in the living room rang, saving him from a sharp-tongued rebuke.

"That'll be Sass," said Alicia, beginning to rise. "She said she'd call when they arrived."

Adam, though, wasn't about to be deserted in the battle zone, and he pushed his chair back. "I'll get it."

He picked up the receiver, ready to give his sister an earful for catapulting him into this situation. "Hello."

"Adam? It's Deirdre."

He slumped against the wall. "Hey, Deirdre. Look, I am so sorry about the suit. I'll pay for—"

"Not at all. These things happen." He'd never heard someone manage to sound both brisk and glacial. "Is Cressa there?"

"Yeah, we're having dinner with Brian."

"Brian?" Her voice warmed by ten degrees. "Juliet said he might drive up. What a nice gesture, especially as he must be tired after the conference."

"He's a nice guy," Adam offered. He knew Brian's hackles were up only because there was a stray in his territory.

"He is." A slight pause followed, then her voice changed. "He's part of the family. We all adore him."

Adam straightened the picture hanging beside him. "Oh."

"When Cressa comes to her senses, she'll realize they are perfectly suited. Until then, Brian's proving to have the patience of a saint."

She sounded confiding, but Adam could tell when he was being warned off.

"Would you like me to get Cressa?"

"That would be lovely. Thank you, Adam."

Class dismissed, he thought, and went back into the dining room. "Your mom's on the phone."

Cressa rolled her eyes, then glared at Brian as she pointed her finger. "This is your fault. I bet Juliet told her you'd be here. She really wants to talk to you and is only talking to me first to be polite."

Brian laughed. "Rubbish. Your mother is devoted to you all. Now, go. Don't keep her waiting."

He shooed her off and Cressa, mimicking teenage surliness, pushed back her chair with an exaggerated sigh and went through to the other room with slumped shoulders and dragging feet. They all laughed at the performance.

"Perfected by her and her sisters over the years," Brian said.

As is your closeness with Cressa and her family, Adam thought. If he hadn't already decided Cressa was off-limits, if her mother hadn't made it clear he wasn't welcome, he might have felt jealous.

"Actually, I've changed my mind. I'd love some more of that wine, thanks, Brian."

Cressa was back in just a few minutes. "I was right. She really wants to speak to you."

As Brian left the room, her cell phone rang and she pounced on it. "Sorry, Alicia, but I've been waiting for this call."

She exited into the hallway. Adam looked at his mother, who smiled and leaned forward to pat his hand. "I'm so glad you came, Adam. It's lovely to see you again. I've loved being in New Zealand, but I've missed you."

Funny, but he'd missed her and Sass, too, after they'd gone to New Zealand. Following years of seldom seeing one another, the three of them had gotten close while Alicia had been hospitalized with pneumonia and then had entered rehab for her alcoholism. Cole had been supportive, as well, sending letters and sketches from prison to entertain their mom.

"It's great to see you, too," he said, and was surprised at how truly he meant it. She'd fought amazing battles to get this far. He felt a flush of chivalric duty and again silently vowed to look after her any way he could over the next four weeks.

Brian and Cressa arrived back in the kitchen at the same time and took their seats. She was brimming with excitement and turned to Adam.

"You'll never guess."

He was beginning to learn surprises weren't good in New Zealand, and couldn't keep the suspicion out of his voice. "What?"

"I've got you some work on the set for the next few days. It's only a bit part, but it may turn into more. Be ready for an early start tomorrow."

He dropped his knife on the floor with a clatter and, in the few seconds required to retrieve it, tried to gather his scattered wits.

"I don't need any work." It was the best he could think of to say when he straightened.

Cressa leaned forward, eyes dancing. "I know you don't *need* it, but Sass said you'd like it. It'll save you from getting bored. She asked me to see what I could do. So I made a couple of phone calls and the powers that be were really pleased. We're a warrior short because one of the stuntmen had to return to the States for a couple of weeks for his father's funeral." She leaned back, her triumph tangible. "You'll get to meet lots of people and they'll just love you! Isn't that great?"

The same spacey sensation he'd suffered the day before descended on him, the feeling that everything was just out of focus, not quite real. "But," he said, "I'm going to be busy."

Cressa appeared surprised. "Doing what?"

Adam sensed Brian's eyes on him. After their recent skirmishes, no way in hell did he want to admit in front of this guy that he was studying to get into medical school. He glanced at his mother, who appeared curious, a crease of worry between her eyebrows. This was so not the time or the place to tell her, either. Their relationship was too complicated and too fragile at this stage for offhand disclosure. It would kick up old history. So much best left unsaid.

Trapped, Adam uttered the first thing that came into his head. "I've got stuff to do."

He could have kicked himself. Of all the lame excuses available, he'd managed to pick the lamest. Cressa was watching him and he could see questions backing up behind her lips, could feel the ground opening under his feet, so he said the one thing that would make the tense moment go away. "But hey, if it's only a few days, then great. Yeah. Count me in."

The brilliant smile Cressa beamed at him almost made the lie worthwhile, but Adam was too busy wondering how many grooms became widowers within their first month of marriage. Just wait till he got his hands on his well-meaning sister. Damn pain-in-the-Sass.

CHAPTER FIVE

IT WAS MIDNIGHT when Adam decided to call it quits. After all, he thought wryly, tomorrow was an early start. Although he was still pissed with Sass and Cressa, the heat had gone out of his anger as he'd become absorbed in his studies. He leaned back in his chair and scrubbed his face with his hands, tired but satisfied. Despite the upsets of the evening, and the lingering jet lag, he'd still managed to get a few hours' work under his belt. Some days he felt as though he was tilting at the moon. Other times, like now, he felt his goal was almost within his grasp.

He'd spent six long years juggling work and study to get his degree. If he cracked the MCAT in a month's time and did get accepted into medical school, the next decade would be even tougher. He was mad to even contemplate signing away his life like this, but the desire to be a surgeon burned deep and wouldn't let him walk away, no matter how tempted he sometimes was.

Being pinned to the spot by Cressa earlier had left him in a devilish predicament. His gallant arrival in New Zealand to allow his sister to enjoy a long honeymoon should not have backfired on him this way. He had a tingling of uneasy presentiment, but damn it, he had the right to not tell anyone about his crazy dream. If it came off, all well and good, everyone would be delighted and he'd be happy to celebrate with them all.

If not, he'd want to lick his wounds alone, especially away from Alicia. A man ought to be free to make a bid for the stars without the weight of his mother's hopes and anxieties on his shoulders; and he ought to be allowed to fail without the burden of her parental guilt. Ideally, he had to admit, he'd also like to escape having to endure public sympathy and pity. Was that so much to ask? Authors wrote novels in back rooms at midnight; inventors experimented in the hidden shelter of garden sheds. Surely he was entitled to his own privacy.

Why, then, this guilt? Why this sinking feeling because he hoped to preserve his secret for a month? After all, he'd already succeeded for six years. How ironic that he should find himself so close to being outed just when the end was in sight.

And all because of Cressa and Sass and their infernal meddling.

Pushing these thoughts to one side, Adam stretched and became aware that the house was strangely quiet. Where were Brian and Cressa? Had Brian ended up staying the night? After dinner, Adam had left them discussing plans. Thirsty, he now prowled through the house to grab a drink before going to bed. Silence. The door to the master bedroom was shut. He had a fleeting image of Brian and Cressa tucked up in the double bed, which he immediately banished. He grabbed the juice from the fridge, a glass from the cupboard and poured himself a long drink, which he downed at the sink. Craning his neck, he looked out the window. The Porsche had gone.

He put the glass in the dishwasher and closed it quietly so as not to disturb Cressa, then padded to the bathroom. The door to her room stood ajar. He knew he shouldn't, but he couldn't help glancing in. The room was empty. That is, its occupant wasn't there, but her possessions had commandeered the space. Her helmet perched on the desk; her red jacket lay slung over the back of the chair. Her big black boots had been kicked off to one corner. Her bag occupied the lower bunk, its contents strewn across the duvet. An iPod and her cell phone out on the pillow of the top bunk.

Something caught his eye through the window and he moved into the unlit room to look closer. Moonlight illuminated the garden, casting shadows under the trees and turning the harbor to beaten silver. A shadowed silhouette stood by the water's edge. She raised her arms to twist her heavy hair into a knot on top of her head, then waded into the silver water. It was too dark to tell if she wore a wetsuit or not. She got in up to her knees and hesitated. He wasn't surprised. He'd dipped his hand in the water earlier today and it had been freezing. She waded deeper. When the water reached her hips, she slid down, and all he could see was a tiny black head with silver ripples widening about her. She was either brave or crazy.

At the same time she looked very alone in the beautiful scene. The vision stirred something in him. Then she turned and began to wade swiftly out. No wetsuit, then.

He shot out of her room, racing to the bathroom to brush his teeth and get out of her way. Her toiletries bag was already there, toothbrush set in the mug next to his. Her shampoo alongside his. And her towel, thrown over the rail, partially covered his.

He was in bed when he heard soft footsteps go past his room. The shower went on. The water would feel good on icy skin. Smoothing away goose bumps.

Relaxing muscles tensed with cold. Releasing clenched teeth into a sigh of pleasure.

He dropped an arm over his eyes, trying to banish the all-too-vivid images, and groaned. His worries about spending a month alone with his mother seemed laughable compared with the predicament he now faced. *Thank you, Sass!* He should have kept his big mouth shut. He thought back to the clear-headed resolutions he'd made that morning. Clear-headed but, he now realized, hopelessly naive.

Okay. He could cope with the four weeks in New Zealand. He could cope with having a job for a few days. But Cressa was a whole different problem. He'd seen how she was already taking over the house. There was no way he could allow her to hijack his thoughts, his desires and his precious, fast-disappearing time in the same insidious but thorough manner. He could not— would not—allow his body to betray his mind at this stage.

Distance. It was all about keeping the hell away from her. She'd soon get the message.

CHAPTER SIX

"AND ACTION!"

Cressa hurtled down the hillside, through the forest, at a teeth-rattling speed. Trees, tightly packed on either side, swept past in a blur. Cracks of machine gun fire stuttered overhead and a bomb exploded as she shot by, showering her in earth and leaf mold. Her concentration remained zeroed in on the thin path zigzagging downward in front of her. Tree roots, rocks and rotting logs were the real hazards in this sequence.

She hit her skid mark as Jasper leaped out in front of her, brandishing a hand grenade. Gunning her bike, she whirled and plunged down the new track they'd made, barely discernible in the thick undergrowth of ferns and creepers. Her bike was nearly on its nose as she came to the most dangerous part of the stunt. She had to hit the target launch perfectly to sail out over a small bluff and clear the stream. A couple of inches either way would skew her flight and she'd crash into the water or the unforgiving ground.

She saw the mark Adam had left and hit it square on. The bike lifted and for a second she hovered. Sunlight. Stream. Forest. Weightless and floating. Then every bone jarred as she landed with textbook precision. Or rather, Adam's precision. He'd mapped out this run to perfection.

She killed the engine and took off her helmet,

adrenaline fizzing in her blood. She heard scattered applause from some of the onlookers, and Adam stepped out of the shadow of the trees.

"That wasn't the speed we agreed on, Cressa."

Did he have a speedometer in his head? She rolled her eyes. "I landed the stunt. Aren't you pleased?"

He strode over to her bike and grabbed the handle-bars, straddling the front wheel so he could eyeball her. "I'll be *pleased* when you learn to take direction."

"I knew I could do it faster, and I proved that, didn't I?"

Adam pulled the bike nearer so his face was inches from hers. His voice low and angry. "This isn't about proving things, to yourself or anyone else. It's not a game, Cressa. I know for you this is a one-off job, so not that serious, but if you're wanting to test your personal limits, crap like that, do it on your own time. The rest of the people here are professionals."

That stung. "I'm a professional!"

"No," he said, "you're not. You're just playing at being one. This time you were only risking your own sorry ass, but if you push the limits when other people are involved, you could endanger them. Got that?"

Of course she wouldn't endanger anyone. But she didn't have the chance to defend herself. He'd already backed off the bike and walked away. She hated that. Hated people who had the last word. Except yelling after him would seem, well, unprofessional. In the end, he had the final word, because after just a couple of days on the set, he outranked her. She couldn't believe how fast it had happened. The first day he was an extra obeying orders; the second day he was chatting to stunt coordinators; the third day he was managing some of the bike sequences. It wasn't even as though he'd pushed himself forward, but when he talked, they listened.

Initially, Cressa had been pleased, taking an almost proprietary pride in him fitting in so easily. Then she'd had to start accepting direction from him and that had turned out not to be much fun at all. She was used to people listening to her, not the other way round. Plus he had no sense of humor. Her entire life she'd been a clown, but now if she kidded around at work, she got the evil eye. He reminded her of her mother!

Sam, one of the other Valkyrie stuntwomen, strolled over. "Well?"

Cressa did a thumbs-down. "He's pissed because I went a teensy bit faster than he told me to."

"Ah, I thought you'd stepped it up."

"What's the big deal? I could do it far more quickly. I told him at the time, but as always, he just ignored me."

Sam punched Cressa on the arm. "Stop whining. You should know by now—if it can be done slower, he'll do it slower."

"And if I can do it faster, I want to do it faster."

"We're lucky he's so careful. If we fall in these—" Sam indicated the skimpy Roman-army-style tunics they wore "—we'll be skinned alive. Come on, let's get a coffee."

They dropped the bike off with the other two parked in the shade and made their way up the hill to where the forest finished abruptly. A makeshift camp of trailers, awnings and a few portable toilets had been set up in the field.

Bridget, the third Valkyrie stuntwoman, was doing Sudoku at one of the plastic tables by the food trailer. Sam and Cressa got their coffees and joined her.

"Jeez, these costumes are uncomfortable," Sam said as she sat down, trying to arrange the blades of the very short, rubberized armored skirt under her incredibly long, slender thighs.

"Tell me about it," said Bridget, squeezing each side of her ribs to ease her breasts, which were sheathed in the tight faux leather corset. "It's particularly hard on us well-endowed girls."

Cressa laughed. "No sympathy here for your endowments, Bid. They're the talking point of the whole crew."

It was true. Every male eye was drawn to her assets, which brimmed over the tightly laced top.

"Yeah," Bridget replied, "but they still aren't getting me where I want to be."

Cressa followed her gaze to see Jeremy, the sound engineer, was now fiddling with the boom mike. She'd been pining to catch the shy engineer's attention for weeks now. Behind Jeremy, Cressa spotted Adam squatting beside the bikes, checking tires and suspension. Secretly, she was impressed by his single-minded professionalism, which ran like steel beneath his seeming affability. Alpha males were usually center-stage guys. Adam simply slipped in and took control.

"Ask Jeremy out for a drink," Cressa suggested.

Bid sighed. "I tried, but he blushed and stammered out some awful excuse."

"It's because he thinks you're out of his league," said Sam. "You're going to have to show him you are interested in his mind. All he sees is you wrestling buff warriors day in, day out. Of course he feels intimidated." She turned to Cressa and grinned. "I don't imagine Adam feels intimidated. You have a whole different

ZANA BELL 61

set of problems there. How's Operation Texas going at home?"

Sam was older than them and had a predatory approach to relationships. She enjoyed the stalking, the catch. Then she'd walk away in search of a new victim. Cressa found this worldly approach to relationships refreshing, and she was amused by Sam's good-natured, cynical take on life.

"Better than here, I hope," said Bid. "Face it. When Adam's at work, that's his focus."

They had quickly picked up on Cressa's interest in Adam but spoke of it lightly because she hadn't told them about the amazing connection she'd felt when she and Adam first met. It would have sounded stupid, especially as Adam hadn't indicated since, in any way, that he'd felt it, too. In fact, if not for the photo of herself in his camera, she might have thought she'd imagined the whole thing. Her ongoing failure to secure Adam's attention, however, amused Sam, who had turned it into a game. Cressa played along. After all, she prided herself in being able to enjoy relationships without getting too involved or experiencing any of the angst.

Cressa made a face. "He's more terminator than man. When the phone rang yesterday, I ran to answer it wrapped in nothing but a towel. He walked past while I was talking and didn't even try to cop a look."

"You must be doing it wrong," said Sam. "Hey, he's coming over now. Watch and learn from the professionals, little girl." She nodded to Bid. "And action!"

Adam sauntered up to their table. "When you've finished, Hank wants to do the fight scene and then we'll go over the escape run. Okay?"

"Okay," said Sam, smiling up at him. "Why don't you join us for a few minutes." In a way that displayed the full, glorious length of her leg, she pushed the empty chair toward him with her foot.

"Yes, do." Bid leaned on her forearms, maximizing the effect of her tight corset.

"You could do with a break," said Cressa, joining in and arching back to lift her heavy hair, as though the weight of it was too much to bear. "You haven't stopped since the moment you arrived."

Adam looked from Sam to Bid to Cressa, then smiled as he shook his head and slipped into a broad cowboy drawl. "Why, thank y'all for your invitation, but ya think I can't spot trouble at fifty paces? Try Jeremy over there." He grinned at Bid. "He'd just love to sit with you gals. I'll see you in one hour."

With a flip of his hand, he walked away.

Bid rounded on her. "Cressa! I don't want you blabbing to everyone that I fancy Jeremy."

With a small frown, Cressa watched Adam's retreating back. "I didn't. Honest."

How had Adam picked that one up? She'd thought he was completely immersed in his work here.

"In—ter—es—ting. He didn't miss a beat, did he? You've got yourself a real challenge there." She stretched out so both feet now rested on the empty chair, her eyes following Adam. "Maybe I should join in on Operation Texas. What do you think, Cressa? May the best woman win?"

Cressa felt a flush of annoyance with Sam. And with Operation Texas. Which was stupid, because they were only kidding around. She wound her hair up and tied it into a heavy knot at her nape. "Boring. Time for another subject."

Sam laughed. "Okay, I'll take Hank instead."

Hank was the fight coordinator, with the body of a gladiator.

"He's a person, not a conquest," Cressa snapped. She wasn't sure if she was talking about Adam or Hank.

Bid threw her a sidelong glance. "Touchy all of a sudden, aren't you?"

"No. But I'd like to talk about something other than blokes for a change."

"Agreed," said Sam. "I nominate literature. So, what did you think of the ending to *War and Peace?* Did you find it ended on a whimper when you expected a bang?"

"The characterization was what I enjoyed," said Bid. "Robust, yet poignant."

"You can't say that," Sam objected. "That's the same line you used to describe the wine last night. Which was execrable, in any case."

Cressa laughed. "The wine or the line?"

"Both," said Sam.

"Oi!" Bid protested in mock outrage. "That's my most useful stock phrase. You'd be amazed at the number of different conversations I can work it into."

Cressa drained her cup and looked at her friends affectionately, her irritation forgotten. "C'mon, guys. Let's go wrestle."

CHAPTER SEVEN

ADAM WAS SURPRISED Cressa was home that evening for dinner. Maybe it was because it had started raining when they got home. She'd been out every other night, visiting her cousin, going out with the other Valkyries, catching a movie. She couldn't seem to just sit. Couldn't be with her own company. He wondered what that was about.

His mom was happy. "How wonderful to have you join us. I've made chili. There's plenty for everyone."

"Fabulous, thanks," said Cressa, pulling up her chair. "I'm starving."

Tonight her hair was in a long ponytail that fell over her right shoulder. His resolve to hold her at a distance was enjoying only limited success. Yes, he had kept things professional, but he was having to work hard not to look at her too much. In one fight scene he'd gotten a helluva whack on the head from a wooden shield when he'd been distracted by her broadsword and flying leather skirts, her braid swinging in an arc as she ducked and twirled in a beautifully choreographed sequence.

Cressa heaped her plate with rice and his mother's special chili. Adam watched with interest as she took her first mouthful. She coughed, spluttered and grabbed a glass of water. "Wow. That's hot."

Alicia sounded surprised. "Oh, dear, have I put too much spice in?"

She'd been putting in way too much spice for as far back as Adam could remember. Her chili used to lay his friends out flat, and he and Cole had had a running competition to see who could eat most before diving for the water jug.

"No, it's lovely." said Cressa, her voice hoarse as she blinked away the tears. "Great."

Adam smiled. Payback for her insubordination.

"So how was today?" Alicia asked. It was the same question she used to ask every day after school.

"Good."

And it was the same reply he'd always given. It had served its purpose then and it had served its purpose these past few days when only he and his mom had been around. It set a nice, easy, conversational tone that carried them through each meal.

"Good?" Cressa dropped her fork and stared at him. "First he shouted at me for going too fast—"

"I didn't shout."

"Then he got mad at one of the mechanics because a brake line on one of the bikes snapped."

"The fool should have picked it up. He was lucky there wasn't a serious accident."

"And then," said Cressa, still ignoring him, "he stepped onto a rotten log, dislodged a wasp nest and got stung three times." She grinned smugly. "I think it was fate getting him back for being so high-handed."

"High-handed? I was doing my *job*, Cressa. The one you got me."

"Wrong!" She pointed her fork at him. "I got you a nice little number as an insignificant stuntman like the rest of us. It was you who moved in and just took over."

With a so-there toss of her head, she scooped up

another mouthful of chili—and choked. Served her right.

"I haven't taken over, I've simply got some expertise that they are using." He'd meant to sound calm and rational. He was annoyed to hear the so-there in his voice, too.

His mother smiled. "Dear me. Things certainly sound far more eventful today than on previous days."

He cast her a sidelong glance but there was nothing to read in her face except demure interest.

Cressa shook her head as she loaded her fork with a five-to-one ratio of rice to chili. "I simply don't understand how such a nice woman like you, Alicia, could have produced such an infuriating son. I bet his dad was overbearing in that same quiet way."

A stillness fell over the table. Cressa glanced up. "Oh, shit. Have I put my foot in it? Sorry, Alicia."

Alicia's laugh was a shade too tinkling. "Of course not."

Adam wanted to wring Cressa's neck. He and his mom had managed just fine. The two of them had enjoyed perfectly reasonable, friendly chats every night. Cressa was home for one night and already she was upsetting things. Glaring, he said, "We don't talk about him."

Cressa, typically, paid him no attention. She was looking at Alicia. "How come?"

His mother stirred a portion of rice and chili together, not meeting anyone's eyes. "It upsets Adam."

He was taken aback. "No, it doesn't. We don't talk about him because it upsets *you*."

She was surprised. "Why should it upset me?"

"Because..." He floundered. "Well, because you never mention him."

"Because you got so angry the one time I tried to tell you about him. Don't you remember?"

Adam stared at her. "What?"

Alicia put her fork down and faced him. "When you were about six, you asked why you looked different from the rest of us. I tried to explain, but when I got to the part where Dad—Cole and Sass's father—wasn't yours, you covered your ears with your hands and ran screaming from the room."

He had vague memories of that now. Strange, how he'd never remembered before.

She picked up her fork again. "Of course, I completely understood. Terrence, to do him credit, had always treated you exactly the same as the other two. I'll always be grateful to him for that."

Adam thought of their father, tall, blond, good-looking, humorous. They'd all adored him—when he was around, which wasn't that often, even before he took off completely. Adam had wondered a lot over the years how his dad had really felt about having this dark kid foisted upon him, proof to the world that he'd been cuckolded.

"Was I the reason Dad left?" he asked abruptly.

Alicia appeared horrified. "No! Absolutely not. He'd have gone whether you were there or not, Adam. You have to believe that." She paused and added more matter-of-factly, "Some men aren't meant to marry, Adam. Terrence was one of them. He loved being on the rodeo circuit. He was never a 'nine-to-five, come home to the kids' sort of man. Not deep down. We only married because I was pregnant with Sass. Looking back, I see that's the worst reason to get married."

"I couldn't agree more." Cressa was so emphatic that both Adam and Alicia stared at her. "But, Alicia, you still haven't said what Adam's real father was like. Was he all macho and bossy?"

His mother's eyes softened in memory. "No, Adam's father was a modern-day troubadour. A man with a heart full of poems and not a cent in his pockets."

"Wow, he sounds so romantic, whereas Adam—" she looked at him pointedly "—so isn't. How did you guys meet?"

It didn't matter how they met, and it wasn't any of Cressa's damn business. He pushed his plate away and was suddenly aware of how airless the kitchen felt, the heat of the oven fogging up the windows. His mother smiled. "He came to our school to talk about poetry to some of our writing classes."

Poetry! Oh, jeez. Why the hell couldn't he have had a real job, been a truck driver or something? His mom really knew how to pick them.

"And were there sparks the first time you laid eyes on him?" Though she'd asked Alicia the question, Cressa glanced sideways at Adam.

"Why, yes, there were. Funny you should ask. There was this strange electricity between us. Hard to explain."

"I think I know what you mean," said Cressa. "What was his name?"

Adam's stomach hollowed at the question.

"Adahy Wilson. A lot of the time he was just called Andy, but his real name was Adahy. It means 'lives in the woods.'"

"Adahy." He tested the name. "Adahy Wilson."

He must have spoken, because Cressa stared at him. "Don't tell me you never even knew his name."

Alicia cut in. "That's my fault. He never asked, so I never told him. I should have."

Adam was hating this whole conversation, but what the hell, now that Cressa had started poking around, he had a few questions of his own. One in particular that he'd never dared ask. "Did he know about me?"

"No."

At that single word, emotion jagged so sharply that Adam couldn't identify it. Relief? Anger? Disbelief?

Alicia continued. "You see, we only saw each other for a month—Terrence was away. Adahy moved on and I never tried to contact him."

"Why not?"

Alicia brushed her hair off her forehead—a sure sign that she was troubled. "Of course I thought about it. Agonized for a while, but in the end it seemed better not to. Easier." Her eyes met his. "I am sorry, Adam. In later years I came to regret that decision deeply."

Probably one of the things that turned her to drink. He felt anger licking through his body but didn't know whether it was against his mother, his dad, his real father—or Cressa for raising this whole sorry mess in the first place. He had an urge to punch a wall. Which was plain dumb. Why get all het up? What happened was ancient history. Yet now that they'd started talking, he found there was more and more he wanted to know. But it would only upset his mom, he told himself, if he kept badgering her. It wasn't worth it.

Wrestling down all those feelings took a big effort. He felt like he was thirteen again, when he'd first realized Alicia had a drinking problem. But he'd had a lot of practice containing his emotions over the years and now managed a smile and a shrug. "Hey, there's nothing to be sorry about."

She gazed at him for what felt like a minute. "If there's more you'd like to ask about…"

He went for breezy. "Nah. What's passed is past. Right?"

Cressa opened her mouth to reply, but he glared at her so she shut it again and they all ate in silence for the next few minutes.

CRESSA FELT ANOTHER mouthful of chili burn its way down her esophagus and into her stomach. She wondered if she would have any stomach lining left after tonight's dinner. The conversation had been almost as hot. Was this seriously the first time they'd ever talked about Adam's father? She probably shouldn't have lifted the lid on Pandora's box quite so guilelessly, but what was with this family?

Alicia broke the quiet. "What are you two going to do on your day off?"

Cressa realized she was trying to normalize things, so when Adam began to speak, Cressa beat him to it. "I know! You've got 'stuff' to do," she teased, trying to lighten the mood.

"Yeah, that's right."

His tone was mild, but there was something tightly coiled about his body language. Cressa waved her index finger back and forth.

"Nuh-uh. Not all the time. I'm not having you go back to Texas having seen nothing of Northland. I'm going to take the two of you adventuring."

Alicia's smile was regretful. "What a lovely idea, but I've already said I'd go to the movies with Moana. Rob's all lined up to babysit. Take Adam, though."

His face was still set in rigid lines. "Thanks, but no, I'm real busy."

She tilted her head and eyed him. "You have to have some downtime. How about a few hours in the afternoon? That way you can do 'stuff' morning and evening." She leaned forward conspiratorially. "I've got this most amazing secret beach to show you."

For a second she thought he might relent, but then he shook his head. "What?" she added. "Afraid of a little action and adventure? Don't be such a scaredy-cat."

"Scaredy-cat, huh?" He leaned back, drumming his fingers on the table. She mistrusted the look in his eyes. "Tell you what. I'll go if you promise to do exactly what I say at work. Deal?"

The idea burned worse than Alicia's chili. She chewed her lip. "Tomorrow's your last day, right?"

There was a taunt in his voice. "They said more work might be coming up."

Then he went back to finishing his dinner as if he didn't give a damn what she decided. No way would he reveal that he'd already declined their offer. She scowled at his bent head. "Oh, all right! Deal."

He looked up, not bothering to hide his triumph. "Ha! I'm going to have such fun tomorrow."

That coiled tightness was still there, but with a gleam in his eyes, as well. She grinned reluctantly. "Yeah, whatever."

Alicia appeared pleased as she began to stack the bowls. "That sounds like fun. Thank you, Cressa."

"You make it seem like Cressa is taking a child out," Adam grumbled as he removed the bowls from her hands. He was clearly making a big effort to be normal. "Leave the dishes, Mom. I'll do them."

"I'll help." Cressa picked up the empty glasses.

"Don't be silly. You two have both been working all day long, while I've had the nicest time doing absolutely nothing."

"I don't care." Adam dropped a kiss onto his mother's

head. "Go on, out of the kitchen." She protested, but he lifted her off the ground and carried her to the door. "I'm serious. Vamoose."

Laughing, Alicia accepted defeat. Cressa couldn't help smiling. On one level all this niceness between mother and son was pleasant. They were both working so hard to ignore whatever had just happened. On another level, things were still out of whack. Surely they must feel it, too.

As Cressa rinsed the plates and handed them to Adam to stack in the dishwasher, she thought she'd try broaching the subject. "You and your mum seem to get on well."

She gently stressed "seem," but Adam just replied, "Mom's great. A real fighter." He fetched the glasses and serving spoons for Cressa to rinse. "Of course, we had our run-ins when I was a teenager. You know the sort."

She took the spoons and their fingers brushed. Adam moved quickly back to the table.

"No, I don't." she said, flicking her ponytail out of the way. His eyes followed the movement. "Not when I was a teenager, anyway. I mean, you've met my mother. I was too terrified to disobey her."

She began filling the sink to wash the pots. Adam put the last of the crockery into the dishwasher and added soap. "I guess you get your determination from her." He closed the door and turned the dishwasher on, then leaned a hip against the counter and folded his long arms. The kitchen light was bright, emphasizing the hollows of his eyes, the sharp lines of his cheekbones. She could still feel heat simmering beneath his easy manner. *Gangsta in domesticia.* "You appear to have overcome your maternal terror now."

"Meaning?"

"I don't imagine your being a stunt girl thrills her heart."

She chuckled. "Quite the opposite. But she's a fighter, too—she manages to fight her well-intentioned advice back down her throat most of the time." Cressa sighed theatrically. "I'm a terrible disappointment to her."

"Yeah, right. Don't come looking for sympathy from me." He grabbed a tea towel and flicked it at her.

"Ow!" She retaliated with a well-aimed ball of foam that got him right in the forehead.

"Fiend."

He leaped for her hand, which was already scooping up the next missile, and, laughing, forced her to drop the soapsuds back in the sink. His face was very close, his mouth inches from hers. His hand was strong around her wrist and it was as though some of his suppressed energy started feeding straight into her bloodstream, accelerating her heart. She couldn't resist leaning toward him. Their eyes locked and Cressa watched his pupils dilate, felt the pull of attraction and danger. Neither of them moved, and the kitchen seemed very still around them. She could hear the faint crackle of the suds in the sink. Adam's fingers held her wrist as his gaze stayed on her face. His breath hitched, and then very deliberately his long lashes swept slowly, almost reluctantly, down to sever the connection. He dropped her hand and stepped away. His smile was forced as he cleared his throat. "Thanks for helping with the dishes. I'd better get on with stuff."

He disappeared down the hall. Her heart was still thudding, but the sense of anticlimax was strong.

"Scaredy-cat," she muttered.

CHAPTER EIGHT

ADAM CLOSED THE DOOR of his room and rested against it, taking a few deep breaths. He'd so nearly lost it back there. Had wanted to press her hard against the wall, to—

He closed his eyes tight against forbidden images. This tumult of emotion wasn't even about Cressa—well, only some of it was, but then, she'd precipitated the whole wretched mess.

Focus. He rubbed his face with his hands and pulled himself together. He had work to do. He crossed the room, settled down at the scarred desk and opened his books. He picked up a pen, ready to make notes, and stared at the page, but his mind refused to read the words. Instead, he watched as, almost of its own accord, his hand wrote a name. Then added a second name.

Adahy Wilson.
Adam Walker.

As he contemplated them, he realized for the first time where his name had come from. Had Dad known?

"Adahy." He said the name, quietly. He tried it again. "Adahy Wilson. Good ol' Adahy." Hard to imagine now why he hadn't ever asked his mother for the name before. Yet somehow there'd never been the right time. First Dad had taken off, leaving them to move into a trailer home to pay off his debts, and Mom had turned to drink. Then Adam had had his own marriage and divorce, before the accident that had turned his life both upside down and around. Seemed he always had quite enough on his plate without going off on some identity crisis, too.

Above his father's name he wrote *Terrence Walker,* then pondered the names. Adahy the troubadour. What the hell sort of lame job was that? One that didn't make money, that's for sure. Couldn't keep a family, pay for a home. Not that the other man was much better. A rodeo clown! Almost without conscious thought he added to the names:

Terrence Walker: Send in the Clowns.
Adahy Wilson: Lives in the Woods.
Adam Walker/Wilson: ?

How many kids had two dads and both of them deadbeats?

Except he didn't know that Adahy was a deadbeat. The man had never had a chance to prove what sort of parent he would have been. Unlike Adam, who'd blown his only shot at family, at fatherhood. Did Stella ever ask about him? He wished there was some way to tell her he thought about her every single day.

He stared out the window into the blackness of the New Zealand winter night. It was still raining. Then he looked around his room. The hell with study. There was no way he could be cooped up. Not tonight. Not with the enormity of his feelings. He stood up so fast he toppled the chair. After snatching up his jacket, helmet, gloves and keys, he headed down the hall, pulling on his jacket as he went. Cressa was still in the kitchen.

"Adam—" she began.

But he brushed past her and out the door. The rain drummed on his head and he paused, looking up to the sky, letting the raindrops wash over his face. Then he jammed on his helmet, pulled on his gloves and strode across to his bike.

"Adam!"

Cressa was running out the door, helmet bouncing unstrapped on her head as she struggled with the zipper of her red jacket. He mounted the bike and switched on the engine just as she leaped, landing on the pillion behind him. He accelerated away without a word.

He took the driveway too fast and the bike slithered on the wet stones and mud. The unpaved road wasn't much better, but there was something satisfying in pushing the limits, then wrestling the bike back under his control. The twists and turns absorbed his attention. Rain poured down his visor, blurring the world so that all that remained was the thin beam of light showing only the immediate road ahead. Soon they'd be on an asphalt road, with houses and streetlights and speed limits. He didn't want any of that, so he swung right, down a track he'd noticed on his daily commute to the location.

The route was very rough and the bike jolted and jarred, demanding all his concentration. He was going too fast, but damned if he'd slow. Yet through it all he could feel Cressa warm at his back, her arms wrapped around him. She never made a sound; he never felt her arms tighten in terror. The road eventually leveled out and they were at another bay on the ocean side, this one with no houses. He pulled up and killed the engine. The water was black, with white lines of foam marking the waves. The only sounds were the rain on their helmets and the distant slush of the sea. Cressa's arms were still around him.

Gradually, he felt his heart slowing, his breathing becoming regular. There was something about watching a wave coming up to the beach, crashing, then washing back, both following and erasing the wave that had come before it. The waves all looked the same, but no two ever broke in quite the same way.

He lost track of time, but finally the cold stealing through his limbs brought him back to the present. He felt the shiver in Cressa's arms, yet still she hadn't uttered a word. For a mouthy woman, he thought with a grim smile, that must have required some control. He turned on the engine, ready to go back home.

CHAPTER NINE

ADAM CAME INTO the kitchen on Saturday morning looking like every woman's fantasy of a dangerous man: jeans and big boots, black hair spilling over the collar of his leather jacket.

He hadn't said a word when they got home, after the surreal bike ride, and Cressa had gone to bed churned by inexplicable, indefinable tensions. She could still feel his unspoken emotions and could hear him moving around quietly on the other side of their connecting wall. She fell asleep listening to the tapping on the computer, the turning of pages, the soft scrape of his chair against the floor.

The following day at work he'd taken malicious delight in setting her the most painstaking guidelines for every single task, so that by the evening her face ached from smiling with gritted teeth. She was even more annoyed when the stunt coordinator congratulated her on a fine day's work.

Today, however, she'd woken very hopeful of relocating the Adam of that first, incredible meeting. It had been a mistake to invite him into her workplace and she now needed to get him alone to reestablish that connection. It had been real—she was sure of it, though she couldn't understand why he seemed so determined to pretend it had never existed.

"Good morning. I've got everything ready." Cressa

indicated the backpack and tank bag. She straightened and looked at him. "Though I did wonder if you'd try to get out of going."

"I thought about it," he admitted with a slow-burn smile. "When you're around, things seem to spiral out of control. But—" he shrugged "—a deal's a deal. Besides, self-destruction appears to be wired into my DNA."

A curious look filled his eyes, hot but wary. Something hot and not at all wary flared through her in response. She managed to sound casual, however, as she asked, "Can I go with you? My bike's got a loose chain."

"Want me to check it now?"

"No, we should grab the sun while it's here. You know Northland. The sun can disappear anytime. We can sort out the repair later."

"Sure."

He appeared in an amiable mood, so she decided to push her luck. "In that case, will you let me drive? You know I've been dying to try it."

He paused. "O-kay, but any problems and we swap immediately."

"Yes!" Only with difficulty did she manage not to throw her arms around him.

Anticipation sparked as she mounted his bike, keenly aware of the powerful engine beneath her. Adam swung up behind, his thighs running long and lean against hers. He wrapped his arms around her and she felt his chest at her back.

"Ready?" she asked.

"Always." She could hear the smile in his voice.

Heart in her mouth, she turned the key and felt, as well as heard, the roar of 650 horsepower. Of course she wasn't taking on too much. Not at all. She skidded out the back wheel but got it under control again, and they headed off in a swirl of dust, up the rutted track and down the peninsula. It took a few gear changes before she was used to the process, and she felt Adam wince each time. His body, tight to hers, moved in perfect rhythm with the bike. With her.

The green hills spooled past them, and as her confidence grew, the speed increased and they leaned as one into the bends. Once, his hand pressed her thigh. She glanced down and found his finger pointing to an early-flowering kowhai tree glowing brilliant gold halfway down one steep valley. She nodded and he patted her leg in acknowledgment before withdrawing.

The sense of power was heady; huge bike and strong man both in her control. She loved that Adam trusted her enough to let her take him to a secret place on his bike. They veered off onto a dirt road. The going was rough as they jolted and lurched. Once more the back wheel skidded out a bit, but again she wrestled the machine under control. From the shift of Adam's weight, she knew he, too, was compensating, finding the balance.

The last slope down to the beach was particularly steep, and she surrendered to instinct, action and response happening on a subconscious plane. The bike flew down the final jarring drop and she skidded to a halt. The silence when she switched the engine off was loud in her ears. Adam swung from the bike as she removed her gloves and unstrapped her helmet. He also removed gloves and helmet, then looked around. They were at a magic cove, small and secluded, with high cliffs plunging into the jade sea. Beyond the breakers was a tiny island, not much more than a large rocky outcrop, skirted with surf that glistened white under the sun.

"What an amazing spot!" He glanced at her. "Good riding."

"Yeah?" His words evoked a little glow within, but she wasn't going to show it. "You're a remarkably calm passenger."

He ran his fingers through his hair. "Not so calm," he drawled. "I had my eyes shut in prayer all the way."

She began to protest indignantly, but then remembered. "Liar! You pointed out the kowhai tree."

He laughed. "Yeah. Well, some parts weren't as bloodcurdling as others."

"Nah," she said, shrugging off her jacket and flicking her braid free, "you can't fool me. You trusted me."

"Actually, you scared me shitless several times," he admitted. "But for the first time on the bike of that size, you did well." He tugged her braid. "Are all Kiwi girls this crazy?"

She put her hands on her hips, eyed him up and down. "Confident, not crazy. Race you to the island!"

Adam's eyes widened as she pulled off her jersey, then her T-shirt. Underneath she wore her purple bikini.

"You didn't say we were swimming. I don't have any board shorts with me."

"I said we were going to the beach," she told him in a well-duh! tone. "Why? Are Texans afraid of a little cold water?"

That worked. As she undid her fly, he was already ripping off his jacket, T-shirt and boots. He swore as she unzipped her boots and kicked them off while he fumbled with laces.

"This is fricking crazy," he muttered. But as she wriggled out of her jeans, she saw his eyes sweep her body.

She strode over to the bike and ripped wetsuits out of the pannier. "You didn't really think I'd make you swim in freezing water." She tossed him one. "Jake's suit should fit. Sorry, I could only find shorties."

He caught it with one hand. "Thank the Lord for small mercies."

"Thank me," she said. "But I'm still going to beat you."

They fought their way into the wetsuits, laughing as they wrestled neoprene over their shoulders. Then she was zipping her suit as she took off running down the beach. "See you in the water."

In seconds he was in pursuit, and they hit the sea together. Cold knifed her feet and legs. Adam swore, then threw himself headlong into the icy waves. Gritting her teeth, Cressa forced herself to follow him.

They emerged gasping.

"You've got to be kidding me. Does this count as fun here?" Adam's white teeth were clenched, while she shivered convulsively.

"The swim to the island will warm us up."

Their movements were jerky while the water layer inside the wetsuits stole the warmth from their bodies, but gradually it warmed and their muscles began to ease.

"See?" she said.

Adam threw her a baleful look. "See nothing! I'm only swimming easier because my whole body is numb."

She flicked water at him. "Don't be such a baby."

Predictably, he immediately duck-dived, and she spun

in the water, trying to see him. That was impossible with the sun bouncing off the surface, and in seconds she felt a hand curl around her ankle and pull. Grabbing a breath, she surrendered to the icy water. As she sank, she saw the flash of his grin when he rose past her.

Enjoy your victory.

Cressa knew she could hold her breath for what her sisters called a freakishly long time. She swam deeper, grabbed some seaweed as an anchor. Long legs twisted above her. She waited. The legs thrashed. Down he dived again, urgency in his movements. Spotting her, he swerved over. As he used his arms to steady himself in front of her, she grinned, did a thumbs-up and shot to the surface. He rocketed up behind her, but as he broke free, she pressed both hands on his head, bobbing him down again. When he came up the second time, he was spluttering.

"How long can you hold your damn breath? You scared me to death."

She laughed, twirling in the water to stay warm, enjoying the sensation of her usually heavy hair floating weightless around her. "About a minute and a half, but my sisters say it feels like three minutes when you're waiting on the surface."

"Yeah, I'll say." Adam flicked his own wet hair off his face. It fell back sleekly, gleaming in the sunlight.

"Come on," she said. "I've something to show you at the island."

Side by side, they swam against the sea, ducking waves as they went. They weren't exactly racing, but neither of them let up speed, so there was little breath left for talking. Cressa guided him to the rock shelf where it was easy to get out of the water. They scrambled up the steep slopes to the top, where a lone pohutukawa had managed to find purchase amid the sharp stones and tough grasses. Adam reached the summit first, and for a second Cressa paused to enjoy the sight as he stood tall, gazing around. He was pure lean muscle and sinew. Long torso in black neoprene, long arms and long legs gorgeously bronzed and finely muscled. All that construction work, no doubt.

He glanced down and caught her checking him out. His eyebrows rose.

"You remind me of a character in a Bond movie who's sussing out enemy territory," she said.

He gave her a pained look as he extended a hand to her, but just said, "It's incredible here."

She let him pull her up, even though she didn't need help, and waggled her eyebrows. "You'll love this even more."

She led him to the far side, where a small channel foamed and frothed between the island and a wicked outcrop of rock a few yards away. The powerful rush of the incoming swell warring with the equally powerful backwash churned the jade waters into dangerous whirls and eddies.

"We call it the washing machine."

"Yeah, I can understand why."

"You've got to time your jumps. See how there's a very brief lull? Notice the rocks underneath?"

"What? Those vicious ones?"

"Yeah, that's why timing is all-important."

With that, Cressa launched herself into space. It was pure showing off. She'd been doing this since she was ten-years-old. Jake and Rob had taught her. None of her sisters had been game to try it. Neither had Brian. He wasn't a coward—he skied black diamond runs and sailed in storms—but he had a thing about heights. There was the whoosh as she hit the surface, and she immediately relaxed, letting the churning water carry her safely through the channel to pop out on the other side.

Adam peered down at her. "You look like a mermaid from up here," he shouted.

"Are you going to try?" she yelled back.

She had her answer as he disappeared, and seconds later she heard him hit the water. Seeing him in the furious frothing sea was impossible, but she could swear she almost felt him before he bobbed up in front of her, eyes shining.

"That was fantastic!" He kissed her on the nose. "C'mon, let's do it over."

The kiss meant nothing, she told herself as she swam after him. Spontaneous excitement, that's all. Would he do it again?

Disappointingly, he didn't, but they had fun, racing each other up the small island, jumping off and swimming around, laughing and competing. Finally, she called it quits. "I'm getting cold. Let's make this the last one."

"Sure."

She'd noticed that expression on his face at work. Concentration and calculation. He squatted, measuring the rocks and the distance of the drop with his eyes.

Cressa scrambled over to join him. "What are you up to?"

"Nothing."

He grinned up at her with such mischief in his eyes she could suddenly picture him as a kid. "You *are* up to something."

He rose from his haunches, and once again she was aware of how tall he was. "I just want to try something."

His tone was mild, but she eyed him with suspicion. "Adam?"

He went to a rocky ledge and turned around, his heels just off it.

"Adam, no!"

CHAPTER TEN

His white grin was the last thing she saw as he launched himself with extraordinary grace into a back somersault before slicing into the water as neatly as if he'd jumped.

She threw herself after him, and when she emerged from the washing machine's force, she was furious.

"You could've killed yourself!"

He laughed at her. "So, you can dish it out, but you can't take it."

"What do you mean?"

"You're happy to frighten others to death, but you don't like it when positions are reversed."

"But they never are."

He raised an eyebrow and it hit her. What he'd said was true. She was the daredevil, the one everyone gasped over.

"C'mon, I'm starving." Adam started swimming back to shore.

Cressa followed, pondering her extreme reaction. Yes, she'd been afraid for him, but, less nobly, she'd been chagrined, too. She would never do a back flip off the island. Even for a million bucks, she'd never do it.

On shore they stripped off their wetsuits and toweled vigorously to get the circulation going. As Adam bent to dry his legs, Cressa saw a scar running down his spine.

A shorter, second one on his hip disappeared under the line of his black boxer briefs.

"Is that from breaking your back?" She was awed by the length of the scar.

"Yup."

He so clearly didn't want to discuss it, whereas she was dying to find out everything. She'd have to play things light.

"Ah. That explains it." He lifted an eyebrow and she added, "Your obsession with safety. Did it take a long time to recuperate?"

She spread out her towel and he spread his close to hers. "Over a year, with some months in the hospital. Several years before everything was working as it had before."

"What's the scar on your hip?"

"A bone graft. Want a drink?" He was scrabbling through the bag.

"Watch what you're doing—there's a knife inside." She rescued the buns, cheese and tomatoes. "So is that why you gave up doing stunts?"

"Partly. The body wasn't what it had been." He passed her a can, cracked open a Coke and took a sip, eyes on the water. "Neither was the mind."

"You lost your nerve?" No way. Nothing about him indicated that.

He watched her cutting slices of cheese. "I lost my sense of invulnerability. The odds of further crashes in that business finally penetrated my thick skull. I don't intend losing that much time in hospital beds again."

In the bright winter sunlight his pupils were small, but the irises were still very dark. His hair was beginning to lift as it dried.

"Did you ever think you wouldn't walk again?"

He looked back to the waves, sipped again from his can. "For a while I thought I might be a paraplegic."

It was hard to even imagine what that would have felt like. Her words came out sounding like a platitude. "That must have been terrible."

He lay down, propping himself on one elbow. "You know, it was the best thing that could have happened to me. Gave me time to think." His smile was wry. "Lots and lots of time to think."

She handed him the cheese-and-tomato-filled bun. "So what did you think about?"

"Life. The universe."

"No, that was a real question."

"That was a real answer." He bit, chewed and swallowed. She waited him out. "Okay, truthfully? I spent the first weeks being angry with the universe, then angry with myself. Then I wallowed in self-pity for a while and after that..." He shrugged.

"And after that?" she prompted. He was good at evasion, however straight his answers seemed to be.

He smiled. "Then came the meaning of life, the universe and everything." He polished off the remainder of his bun and stretched out flat on his back in the sun. "That feels great."

He closed his eyes and she knew he was signaling the end of that particular conversation. His lashes, slightly crusted with salt, were so long that they cast fanlike shadows on his cheeks. "My kidneys are finally beginning to defrost."

She laughed. "The sea is cold now, but by Christmas it'll be heavenly."

"Sadly, by that time I'll be long gone."

"Do you have to go back?" The question slipped out. One eye opened a slit. "Yeah, I do."

"Why? Hang on, don't tell me. *Stuff*."

"Yeah, that's right." He smiled, opening both eyes and looking at her. "Don't move."

He pulled himself into a sitting position and reached for his camera. She felt self-conscious, sitting cross-legged, wet hair tumbling loose down her back to dry. But it also felt incredibly sexy to have Adam look at her through a viewfinder as he played with the focus. He had great hands. Fingers long, strong and lean like the rest of him, but sensitive and sure on the delicate settings.

"You're beautiful." He said it in such a matter-of-fact way she laughed.

"With this nose?"

She pointed to the offending feature and he snapped a second photo.

"Yeah, with that nose," he said, now focusing the camera on the island. "It gives your face character."

"Character's not beauty."

"It is in my book."

Cressa moved so that she was facing the sea, and leaned back on her hands, stretching her legs out. Sunlight skittered on the water. The sky was deep blue. She turned her head to watch Adam, who was now engrossed in photographing a rock and a flax bush. "You know, if any other guy said that, I'd figure he was coming on to me."

Adam lowered his camera. "You don't hold back, do you? Most girls would just accept the compliment and say thank you."

"I'm not 'most girls.'"

He immediately assumed a lascivious expression and ran his eyes from her feet up to her face, taking his time about it. He was only kidding, but she was cross with herself for finding his perusal a turn-on. "No," he drawled, "you ain't. And isn't this my lucky day, sweetheart. You are one hot lady."

Cressa threw a shell at him. "And you are so full of it." He laughed and she changed the subject. "What do you do with all your photos?"

He busied himself packing the camera away. After a beat he replied, "I put them on Facebook."

"Yeah?" She was surprised. "That doesn't fit."

"What do you mean?"

"You're like the cat that walked by itself. I hadn't picked you as the social network sort of guy."

His eyes remained fixed on his task. "Well, gotta move with the times."

"Why's it so hard for you to answer a question in a straightforward manner?"

He paused and this time their eyes met. She held his gaze. "I wasn't aware that I didn't."

"No? Well, let me tell you, mate, any question that's vaguely personal has you ducking for cover. So let's try again. How come you have a Facebook page?"

"It's for my daughter."

That rocked Cressa. "'Scuse me! Your what?"

"My daughter. There. You wanted to know. I have a Facebook page in case my daughter ever wants to know who her dad is."

"Oh my God." Cressa swung around so she was once more sitting cross-legged facing him. Adam, however, lay back down with an arm over his eyes, as though shielding them from the sun. But she knew better and wasn't going to accept the ploy. "You have a daughter? Why the big secret?"

He shrugged. "It's not. I just don't talk about her."

With half his face covered, she focused on his mouth, learning the shape of his lips. "Why not?"

"There's nothing to say."

Again she waited. Finally he lowered his arm and squinted at her. "Crystal, her mother, ran off with Stella seven years ago. I haven't seen or heard anything of her since. End of story."

He closed his eyes, his mouth a thin line. His body was rigid on the sand. End of conversation.

"So tell me about the Facebook page."

His face hardened. "Don't you ever take a hint?"

"Nope."

For a second he said nothing and she watched the slow rise and fall of his muscled stomach. Saw the thin black hairs running down from his navel to disappear below the band of his boxers. She mistrusted his stillness, mistrusted the tiny lift to his mouth as he swung himself up into sitting, one leg curled in front of him, the other crooked, and he rested his elbow on his knee. His position brought his face closer to hers. Intimacy or challenge? She stared straight into his dark eyes, which glinted in the sun. "I'll answer your question, but then it's my turn."

"No problem. I don't have any secrets."

"Okay, I started on Facebook over a year ago. I post photos because I don't know what to say and because I don't want just anyone reading all about my life—even though it's boring. So I post tags saying where I am, what I'm doing. You know, like 'Hey, Stella, your aunt just got married in New Zealand. It's beautiful here.' Then I put up photos of the beach, that kind of thing." He looked at her dead-on. "Now it's my turn."

"Fire away."

"What happened with Brian?"

She gave her usual explanation. "There's not much to say. He's fabulous. I was young, got swept away.

Panicked when I could see what life with him was going to be like, so I pulled out at the last minute."

Normally, people came to her rescue here, making soothing noises about better discovering sooner than later, about her decision being hard but brave. But Adam pinned her with a dark look. "How last minute?"

She plucked at the edge of her towel. "I left him at the altar. Literally."

Adam gave a low whistle. "Poor guy."

Guilt made her defensive. "He refuses to see it, but it was the best thing for him. I mean—" she laughed "—can you see me as a doctor's wife?"

His expression was difficult to read. "Why not?"

She shrugged. "I'm not the pillar-of-society sort. All that talk of patients and hospitals? I don't think so."

Adam leaned in a bit closer. This time she knew the move wasn't intimate. "You know what? I don't buy that."

She was indignant. No one had ever questioned her before. "What do you mean?"

"I mean, there's one helluva lot more to it than 'Oh hey, I don't want to be a doctor's wife.' What else was there?"

A fluttery, sick feeling kicked in, but she fought it down. "Nothing!"

He raised an eyebrow. "Again, Cressa, we see you can dish it out but can't take it. More fun to rummage through other people's psyches than your own."

She tried for lofty but landed on snappish. "I have no idea what you are talking about."

"No? Okay, here's how it seems to me. You're clearly intelligent, yet you lack focus. You are friendly and out-going, but can't seem to stick with people. You appear to travel light but, lady, you've got baggage all around you."

Her chin went up. "You're just angry because I pushed things about your father."

"Maybe. Though—" he creased his brow "—I may have to thank you for that. It's better to know who your father is." His eyes held hers. "I bet under all your wild-child crap is a strong, amazing woman waiting to come out."

She couldn't tell whether she'd just been insulted or complimented. She could feel the jut of her jaw, her smile both defense and attack. "Thank you, Dr. Freud. So tell me. Did you take my photo to put on your Face-book page?"

She wanted to crack that control of his, that measured and measuring objectivity he was using to create a barrier. She appeared to have succeeded when a slow smile, sexy as all hell, spread across his face. One hand reached up to cup the back of her head, drawing her face inch by tantalizing inch closer to his. He leaned in, his features completely filling her vision. The waves breaking on the shore echoed the beat of her heart. When his face was just millimeters from hers, he paused, their breaths mingling. Then softly, very softly, his mouth brushed hers. For a second she tasted the salt on his lips and then they were gone.

"No," he said, his voice husky, "that photo was for me."

Then the hand holding her head released her, and Adam was standing, picking up his towel in a movement that obscured his lower torso. The scar along his spine was white against his brown skin, healed but clearly visible. He looked down at her, and she blinked up at him, dazed. Disorientated. And burning for more. Adam's smile was wry, his eyes once more objective as they looked into hers.

"When we first met, I admit there was a connection." His eyes strayed to her mouth, then back to her eyes. "But nothing's going to happen. I get that you are all here and now, but you've got me wrong. I'm not like that at all. I have enough on my plate at the moment and I don't have time to be the biker on your list, coming after the skier and the archaeologist, but before whoever the hell next catches your fancy." She began to argue, but he shook his head. "I know what you've been up to and I'm flattered—I really am. But no more games. Okay, Cressa?" His expression was reasonable, but his body was taut.

"Okay."

He eyed her. "What? No arguments?"

"Nope, I heard you. Friends, right?"

"Yeah, friends, for sure." Still, his eyes narrowed as she smiled up at him. She reached out a hand. "Pull me up."

He took it and drew her to her feet. The towel stayed clutched to his midriff.

Friends? Yeah, right. She didn't know whether the day had been a step forward or two steps back, but one thing she was sure of. Their dance hadn't ended, whatever Adam might think. It was only just getting started.

CHAPTER ELEVEN

WINTER RETURNED with a vengeance over the next few days. Temperatures plummeted as impenetrable curtains of rain streamed past the windows. Eiderdowns of cloud hid the hills. Filming was impossible, so Cressa hunkered down with Adam and Alicia. They lit fires in the potbelly stove in the living room and switched on heaters throughout the house. Even so, they needed to bundle up in jerseys and thick socks. Cressa was used to the unrelenting Northland rain and swings in temperature, but her Texan companions weren't.

"What's with houses in New Zealand?" Adam complained on the third day as he paced across the kitchen, where she was making tea. He was wearing a thick, dark blue jersey, hands shoved deep into his jeans pockets, shoulders hunched as he waited for the kettle to boil. She still got a kick out of seeing his exotic features in mundane surroundings, and today he had a prowling restlessness that enhanced his brooding face. "How come they're so damn cold?"

"No regulations." She passed him mugs from the dishwasher. "This is an old house. No insulation. Blame our optimistic nature. We refuse to believe New Zealand winters are that bad."

Watching him put tea bags in the mugs, she tried to work out why he seemed different from anyone else she'd ever met. Partly it was because working out the

real Adam was hard. Her favorite Adam was the man
of their first meeting. He'd had a sizzle in his smile and
promise in his eyes. But she was intrigued, too, by the
wild Adam, who rode like a demon at midnight or back-
flipped into treacherous waters. Work Adam, however,
with his finicky insistence on perfection, was a pain in
the butt, and she just wanted to shake Secretive Adam,
with all his "stuff" shit. She hadn't liked Psychoanalysis
Adam, either, and while she grudgingly admitted that
Affable Adam at mealtimes was good company, he was
also infuriatingly remote.

When she looked at Adam this way, she found there
was a lot about him that wasn't great. So why this growing obsession with him?

Adam put away the box of tea bags. "This weather
is horrible."

His hair flopped forward, and he shoved it back impatiently. She wished she could reach up, smooth it away
from his face.

"You guys have to toughen up." she said briskly. "No
deserts here to dry out in. Alicia's wearing two jerseys,
two pairs of socks and still carries around a hot water
bottle like it's a baby."

As the kettle came to a boil, Adam lifted it. "Poor
Mom. She's always had an aversion to the cold. We both
need some real sun to warm us to our bones."

He poured water into the three mugs and Cressa
crossed to the fridge for the milk. This was another
thing she didn't get. Normally, she liked her relationships crazy and fun filled. With Adam, she caught
herself enjoying the small domestic things they did
together—making tea, washing the dishes, taking out
the rubbish bags. What was with that?

"I was thinking," she said. "How would you like to

go sailing the next fine day off? The Bay of Islands is beautiful. You can't go back to Texas without seeing it."

No one could smile refusal as beautifully as Adam, a lovely mixture of ruefulness and regret. No one could fake it better.

"Thanks, but no."

The finality in his tone was real enough. She was learning to pick her battles, however, and let this one go—for the moment. "You're just grouchy because you've been in your room all day long with nothing to dwell on but the cold. You need something to take your mind off your misery."

He cocked an eyebrow at the "nothing" but let the remark pass, asking, instead, "What do you propose?"

"Monopoly!" She gathered up two of the mugs. "Let's go. Alicia said she'd set the game up while I made tea and dug you out of your lair."

His eyebrow rose farther. "Lair? Hardly. Still…" He eyed her. "What made you think you stood a chance of digging me out?"

"Charm."

"Oh, yeah?" He sounded skeptical.

"All right. I also found chocolate biscuits."

She'd learned early on the Texan was a chocoholic.

"Now you're talking—but unfortunately, I've still got stuff to do. I'll take a couple of cookies with me."

Cressa barred his way. "Oh no, you don't. You need a break."

His eyes narrowed. "Sez who?"

"Sez me." Then she dropped her sergeant-major act. "C'mon, you've been cooped up in that room for two days and two nights. I can't even begin to wonder what the hell you've been doing all that time, but you have to socialize again." She put on her best smile. "I'll let you win."

He laughed. "If I believed that, I'd be one poor fool."

"Well, if I told you the truth, which is that I always win, you'd just turn tail and run."

He sipped his tea, watching her over the cup brim. He had the most fantastic eyelashes. "You are the most manipulative woman I've ever met."

"Thank you. So is that a yes? You'll make Alicia's day."

CRESSA MIGHT HAVE KNOWN that playing Monopoly—usually such a straightforward game of economic dominance—would become something different with the Walkers. Ten minutes into it, Cressa felt she was in an alternative universe. The careful kindness was killing her. There were no howls of triumph at buying a coveted property. No one jeered when she was sent to prison. But when Adam saw his mom had two of the green properties, and offered to give her the third, which he owned, Cressa couldn't stand it any longer.

"Don't just give it, Adam. Sell it. Or play hardball. Don't let her have it at all. Alicia's got the yellows. She'll be able to dominate that corner. Sorry, Alicia, but you know, the whole point of the game is to crush your opponents and *win*."

"Jeez, you're tough," Adam teased.

"I've got four sisters," she retorted. "I've had to be. Not to mention a mother who wouldn't show mercy to a rabbit in a trap if a win was at stake."

"Cressa!" Alicia protested. "Your mother is charming." At the same time, she cast an appraising look in her son's direction.

"I didn't say she wasn't charming—just that she'd trample over all five daughters to win at Monopoly. I'll show you the footmarks she left, if you like. We all play to win, so you'd better be ready for my knife in your backs."

Adam only smiled. Getting a reaction out of him was hard. All loose limbs, he lolled back in his chair, tossing the dice with a lazy wrist. He took the highs and the lows with the same slow grin that melted Cressa down to her core, but at the same time irked her. What would get this guy to engage—not just with the game but with them? When Alicia landed on Mayfair, he refused to accept her money.

"Just give me a free ride the next turn."

Cressa rolled her eyes, but Alicia surprised her. She leaned back and looked at her son. "Cressa's right. Why won't you take my money?"

Cressa paused, dice cupped in her hand, to hear his answer. Alicia seemed to be as relaxed as her son, but her eyes held an expression Cressa had never seen before.

Adam shrugged. "It's just a game."

"I agree," Alicia said. "So answer my question."

Her voice was soft and reasonable, but Cressa wasn't fooled. It seemed that something had finally gotten through to Adam. He glanced uneasily at his mother and scratched the back of his neck. "I just thought—you know."

"No. I don't know, Adam." She settled her hands in her lap, waiting attentively. "Please explain."

Uh-oh, Cressa thought. A *please* in front of a command. That wasn't good. Adam hesitated. He hadn't moved, but somehow his body had shifted from sprawled limbs to tensed readiness. He appeared to be sifting through his mind for an answer, but when it didn't come, Alicia continued in veneer-thin tones of measured logic. "I'm sure you don't mean to, but you are patronizing me."

Adam blinked. "Because I won't accept your money?"

"Exactly."

He held out his hands, palms up. "I don't get what the big deal is."

Oh Adam, thought Cressa. *Don't pretend innocence.* His mom was on to him in a shot. "Have you refused Cressa's money?"

"No, but—"

"If it were Cole or Sass, would you be playing like this?"

"That's different!"

"How?"

Adam turned to Cressa, who just shook her head. "No good looking at me for support. I've already made my family's approach to games very clear."

The smile Alicia gave had a dangerous edge. "What is it, Adam? Are you afraid that if I lose, I'm going to hit the bottle again?"

The only sounds were the drumming of rain on the roof and the cracking in the potbelly stove as a log split open in the flames. Adam blew out a breath in blustering protest. "Of course not."

Alicia's blue eyes pinned her hapless son to his chair. He couldn't meet her gaze. Cressa swirled the dice in the palm of her hand. "I understand where Alicia's coming from, Adam. You don't need to look after us, you know. In fact, your concern reads as a kind of arrogance. It's as though you think that if you play for real, you'll beat us. But I've already told you—I always win."

He glared at her. Watching his cool-dude manner shredding around him was fun.

"Tell you what," she added, leaning forward. "Let's make this interesting. I challenge you. If I beat you, then you have to come sailing with me the next fine day."

"Yeah, right! And what if I beat you?"

"Hmm." She propped her chin on a fist and surveyed him. "That never happens, but in the unlikely event... How about I promise not to hassle you about your 'stuff' ever again? Deal?"

He glanced from his stake of money and properties to hers. She had far more. Well, that was fair enough. She'd been playing the game right from the start. He looked at her and she stared straight back at him. Then he looked at his mother. Alicia's blue eyes twinkled, and Cressa realized she'd been underestimating the American woman. Clearly, she had edges beneath her Southern warmth. Adam's black eyes narrowed and he nodded. "Okay, deal. Pay up, Mom."

Alicia pushed her money over. "Now you're talking."

Adam leaned forward. "So whattaya sitting on the dice for, Cressa? Throw."

Cressa laughed. The game had finally begun.

CHAPTER TWELVE

"I'VE WON?" Astonished, Alicia sat back. "Really? You're both conceding defeat?"

"Mom, all my money's gone and all my properties mortgaged. I'm out."

"I can't see me coming back, either." Cressa gestured at the huge piles of money in front of Alicia. "What's my fifty-seven dollars compared with your millions?"

When she'd called Adam on being too nice, Alicia had had little thought of winning. She wasn't the winning kind. Well, she used to be as a schoolgirl, but that was many years ago.

Her son grinned. "Accept it. You were on fire! For sure, you had a lot of luck, but you were also canny. I never realized how crafty you can be."

Canny. Crafty. How ridiculously proud she felt hearing those two words. "I was, wasn't I?"

"The best player won," said Cressa. "Man, I can't believe it wasn't me. Still—" she smiled smugly "—at least I won our challenge."

Adam stared at her. "What are you talking about? We were both beaten, Cressa."

"Yeah, but that wasn't the deal. The deal was if I beat you or you beat me. I've still got fifty-seven dollars. Amazing, isn't it? That paltry amount loses me the game, but wins me the challenge. You're sailing with me the next fine day, buddy."

Adam appeared so nonplussed Alicia had to bite the inside of her cheek to keep from laughing. She enjoyed seeing Cressa give her son a run for his money. From the time the young Kiwi had arrived, Alicia had been very aware of their attraction. It was there in the laughter they shared and in the crackle as they clashed. Whenever Cressa was in the room, Adam couldn't keep his eyes off her. Alicia understood why. The young woman radiated vibrancy and vitality.

Right now his gaze followed Cressa as she went to put some more wood in the potbelly. Evening was closing in, and as she crouched and opened the door of the stove, the firelight illuminated her features, caught auburn lights in her black hair, which fell loose about her shoulders. Alicia heard her son's sharp intake of breath, then the laugh that was meant to be casual but had a catch in it.

"In that case, I'd better get back to it," he said.

He retreated as he always did when his defenses began cracking, Alicia noticed. Cressa rocked back on her heels, watching his hasty departure. "What do you suppose he gets up to in his room?"

Alicia leaned over and switched on the lamp on the sideboard so she could see to sort the cards and money into piles. "I don't know. He's not saying, so I'm not asking."

Cressa rose, clutching her chest, and pretended to stagger. "Are you a real mother? Do you honestly never pry?"

Alicia couldn't help smiling. Cressa was a wonderful comic. "I used to," she said. "But even as a kid, he'd head off on some secret mission and only tell me about it afterward."

Cressa tipped her head to one side, and her long hair

swung with the movement. "Why? So you couldn't stop him?"

"Partly, but I think he wanted to see how things would pan out. Then he'd know how to play the next scene, if you catch what I mean."

Alicia was uncomfortably aware her nonchalance was disingenuous. Actually, she'd have given her collected works of Shakespeare to learn what he was up to in his room, but no way would she admit this to either of the young people. Cressa would use the admission as ammunition to force Adam to explain himself, whereas Alicia was playing the long game. She'd lost her children's trust years ago. In recent months, she'd finally earned it back with Sass. Now she had to do the same with Adam. That he wouldn't confide in her cut deep. Yet she still had hope they would find their way into a better relationship. All her offspring displayed personality traits common in adult children of alcoholics. She'd done a lot of reading about this since her recovery. Sass had turned out an approval seeker, a workaholic with intimacy issues. Cole had become addicted to excitement, his impulsiveness propelling him into rash actions. Adam, with his over-developed sense of responsibility, was driven by a desire to help people. He instinctively sought out damaged women, like Crystal, to try to rescue them. Alicia knew, too, that under his easygoing manner, he was riddled with low self-esteem, dismissing his achievements and dwelling on failure. She hated to see him short-change himself like that. However, analyzing her children was one thing. Helping them was another. They were all on their own journey.

Alicia watched Cressa pace to the French doors and stare into the pouring rain. It was so dark out she probably couldn't see anything. With Adam gone, her

sparkling humor had turned into a restlessness that ema-
nated from her in palpable waves as she dug her hands
into the back pockets of her cargo pants. She always
dressed in combat wear: khakis or jeans with big boots.
Practical, of course, but Alicia wondered why she never
wore anything feminine, even to the wedding. It would
be interesting to see if she could be coaxed into something softer.

"He's infuriating."

Alicia banged the property cards into a tidy bundle.
"I know."

"He puts on this accommodating exterior, but he
really goes his own sweet way, and nothing's going to
stop him."

That was a fair summation; however, Alicia wasn't
ready to form female alliances. Her first loyalty was to
her son, so she remained quiet.

Cressa swung around and returned to the table, taking
Adam's seat. She was only partially in the light, which
made her eyes glitter. Alicia was careful not to read too
much in their green depths. Cressa picked up the community chest cards, but instead of putting them away,
began shuffling them absent-mindedly. "Can I ask you
something personal?"

Alicia was wary. "Yes, but I hold the right to not
answer."

Cressa had a way of detonating situations.

"Did you love Adam's father?"

"Oh. Well, I don't know." The question flummoxed
her. She'd never asked herself that. Maybe hadn't dared
to. "No, I don't think so." She paused, thought about it.
"If the situation had been different, maybe. There was
definitely a connection. But the timing was wrong. I was
married. I had an affair for all the wrong reasons."

"Like what?"

Alicia stared at the fake money in her hand. "Loneliness, I guess, but also poor self-esteem. Possibly an ugly desire to lash back at my unfaithful husband."

"Oh."

Alicia gave her a sidelong look. "You think that doesn't sound at all romantic."

"I thought it might have been more...you know."

"What? Passions beyond our control, that sort of thing? Oh, at the time I believed it was." She began to sort the money once more. "It's so very easy to talk oneself both into and out of relationships."

"So how can you tell when you've found the right one?"

That made Alicia laugh. "Heavens, I don't know! I'm the very last person to ask. In fact, if you ever find the answer, call me. I'd be interested. Not that it's relevant now. All that relationship stuff is far behind me."

"You're still young," said Cressa, which was charitable of her. Alicia could clearly remember how ancient fifty-one had once seemed.

"Thank you. However, I'm happy as I am, enjoying my freedom since I resigned my job."

Cressa put the community chest cards down, picked up some houses and began stacking them end on end. It struck Alicia that this was symbolic of the young woman's life. She was full of action but didn't seem to achieve much in the long run.

"Don't you get lonely? I mean, Adam and I aren't much company a lot of the time."

Alicia did feel alone often. She missed Sass and Jake and the boys. Being part of a family again for a while had been fun. But she wasn't going to indulge in self-pity. There had been too much of that in the past, along with self-loathing. "At the risk of sounding cli-chéd, I'm actually finding it very therapeutic to get to know myself again."

"Is that because you aren't—I mean, you're getting over…that is, getting better?"

Part of Alicia winced, but another part appreciated Cressa's clumsy attempt to acknowledge the elephant in the room. Adam was still tiptoeing around the issue, pretending it wasn't there, which was why Alicia had ambushed him in the game. It had erupted out of frustration of being continually treated with kid gloves. She loved that he cared, but she ached for some real communication.

"Yes, since I stopped drinking, I've found I can think clearly again." She put the lid on the box. "Of course, it does mean I have to face up to my many failures." Cressa began to demur, but Alicia shook her head. "No, I'm past platitudes and pretenses. I did okay for my kids. I kept them housed and fed and clothed. I wasn't there enough for them emotionally, though, I realize that. But something went right." She smiled. "I've got the best children a mother could hope for. They're all fine adults."

The tragedy was her boys couldn't see that yet. They were both wrestling demons. With Jake's help, Sass had overcome hers.

"Yeah, Sass seems amazing. Adam's pretty cool, too." Then, as if she'd said too much, Cressa abruptly changed the subject again. "So, what will you do when you get back to the States?"

"Truthfully? I don't have a clue." Alicia laughed,

suddenly feeling young and mischievous. "I haven't been this free since I got pregnant at nineteen."

"And had to get married. I remember you telling me the other night. You know," said Cressa, not making eye contact, "that's why I landed up nearly marrying Brian."

That went some way to explaining this young woman. "What happened?" Alicia asked, trying to sound both gentle and matter-of-fact.

"I miscarried." She said the words boldly.

"Oh, my dear." Alicia put out a hand, but Cressa pulled back out of the light.

"These things happen. No biggie. Best thing, really. Can't imagine being a mother and tied down. Instead of like now—" she gave a bright smile "—when I can go where life takes me."

"That's good," Alicia said cautiously, not sure how to read this conversation.

"It's great, I can tell you. Everything's an adventure. I'm always meeting new people, having new experiences."

She spoke with raffish confidence and Alicia could see why her son was fascinated. But she felt the stirrings of unease for Adam.

"Well, now," she said. "That does sound very free."

Cressa leaned forward, so the light of the lamp fell fully on her face. "What is it?"

"What do you mean?" Alicia played ignorant.

"There's something you're not saying."

She was no fool, this young woman. At the beginning of the conversation their friendly politeness had slipped comfortably into familiarity. But somehow, in the past few minutes, she and Cressa had jumped over weeks of getting-to-know-yous. Alicia hesitated, tempted to pull back and spare Cressa, but her urge to protect Adam was too strong.

"I was just thinking how being free and being lost can sometimes look the same."

CHAPTER THIRTEEN

THE STORM WORSENED in the following hours, rain lashing the house, the howling wind whipping the trees. Immersed in his studies, Adam didn't pay it much mind, but nearing midnight a different noise caught his attention. It sounded like a faint shout. There seemed to be a distant banging, but nothing else penetrated the wind and the rain, so he went back to his books. Then he heard it again. He cocked his head. Perhaps his tiredness was giving him hallucinations. He'd been studying all day apart from meals and the time-out to play Monopoly. His eyes were aching and his back was stiff. Maybe this was the equivalent of aural exhaustion.

The third time the noise definitely sounded like his name. Distant but urgent. Alicia would have gone to bed hours ago. Leaping to his feet, he called out, "Cressa?"

The house was very quiet as he tore through it. In the kitchen the yell was louder and more distinct, as was the sound of banging metal. "Adam, help!"

Wrenching the back door open, he peered into the wild night. It was pitch-black out and impossible to see through the torrential rain. "Cressa," he bellowed.

"Adam!" He heard strained relief in her voice. "Quick, I'm going to fall."

He began running toward the garage, where the sound was coming from. As he drew closer, he could make out a figure swinging from the gutter at the tallest peak of the high roof. Above her he could see a heavy sheet of corrugated metal flapping freely on two sides. A big gust would rip it off.

"Cressa, hang on!"

Images of her falling jolted his heart as he raced across the yard, skidding through mud, splashing into deep puddles, dashing the rain from his eyes. He hardly noticed he was drenched in seconds.

"My fingers are slipping."

He was right under her when she fell, flattening them both into the mud.

"Oh, my God, Adam." She immediately scrambled off him. "Are you okay? Have I killed you?"

She'd knocked the wind out of him. He tried to suck in oxygen, but his lungs refused to cooperate. Light exploded in front of his eyes. Then the light steadied and he realized Cressa was aiming a flashlight at his face. He went to yell at her, coughed instead, and blessed air flowed into his body again.

"What the hell were you up to?" His question came out as a croak.

Rain poured down her face, and her hair hung in rat tails. She grinned. "Thank heavens! I'm so *relieved* to hear you speak. I was just rehearsing my 'Alicia, I'm terribly sorry, but I just killed your son' speech."

She helped him get to his feet. Still shaken, he tried to collect shattered thoughts. "What about you? Are you okay?"

"I'm fine. You provided a nice soft landing."

He grunted. He had a lot of words in his head—most of them not nice at all—but he wasn't yet up to shouting more than the necessary. "What the hell were you doing?" That was better. Severity was there and volume was returning, too. Another five minutes and he'd be able to give her a piece of his mind.

"I was trying to fix the roof. Look." She shouted above the noise of the wind and gestured upward.

"I saw that. But *alone?* Why didn't you come and get me?"

She held out her hands. "For a few nails? I'm perfectly capable, you know."

He wanted to shake her. "Clearly, you're not." They had to shout because of the storm. He'd have been shouting anyway.

"The ladder slipped."

She made it sound as though it wasn't her fault at all.

"Don't they teach you anything in school about safety in the workplace?"

She wouldn't look at him and he decided to save the rest of his harangue for later. He was cold, wet and furious. "Where're the damned hammer and nails?"

"I'll do it. You just hold the ladder."

He glared at her so sternly that she shut up and instead turned the flashlight on the mud and soaked grass around their feet. The fallen ladder was nearby. Something glistened; he bent and retrieved the hammer. The nails took a few minutes longer. He raised the ladder and felt it being violently buffeted. Anger surged. She could have killed herself with her foolhardiness. Damn woman and her damn silly notions.

She didn't say a word as she held the ladder, and he felt grim satisfaction when he saw in the glimmer of the flashlight that she at least looked a little chastened. The job itself took only a few minutes, though brute force was required to wrestle down the piece of metal and bang the first holding nail in. Did she honestly think she'd have the strength or the reach to do such a job on her own?

Pounding with the hammer vented some of his feelings. The last nail got a couple of extra whacks to assuage some of his desire to throttle her. In silence he descended the ladder and put it away. In silence they trudged back to the kitchen. There was no point in racing. She was wearing an oversize raincoat, while he was already saturated.

At the door she kicked off her big boots. His sneakers were soaked and he realized the soles could have been treacherously slippery. He'd been so livid he hadn't stopped to consider. No way would he admit that, however. The moral high ground was his territory and he intended to keep his flag firmly hoisted above it.

She shrugged out of her raincoat and flicked a sodden lock of hair back from her face. "You have the bathroom first."

"No," he said. "You."

She disappeared down the hall without argument. Her submissiveness ought to have placated him, but he didn't trust it. He filled the kettle and put it on. Then, not wanting to track mud and water through the house, he stripped in the kitchen, found a small towel and wrapped it around himself. It didn't quite reach, which meant he couldn't tuck it in and had to hold both ends with one hand. He was busy loading his clothes one-armed into the washing machine when she materialized in jeans and a huge sweater, toweling her long hair.

"Your turn."

Her cheeks were rosy from the heat of the shower. Her eyes were huge. Delayed shock, he decided. She must have been terrified, hanging from the gutter in the pouring rain. He took a step forward.

"That is one devilishly sexy outfit, Texas."

Muttering an oath, he stalked out of the room with as much dignity as a man can muster clutching an inadequate towel.

SHOWERED AND SUITABLY attired, he returned to the kitchen to discover Cressa had hot chocolate laced with whiskey waiting for him. She was curled up on the sofa in the living room, her head tilted toward the potbelly, letting the heat dry her hair. The lighting was subdued, since she'd only switched on one lamp, and the air smelled of warm apple essence shampoo. As he took a seat on the opposite end of the sofa, she passed him the cup and gave him her most disarming smile.

"I'm truly sorry."

Maintaining his wrath was difficult. Besides, a lot of it had already been washed away in the heat of the shower.

"Yeah." He couldn't let her off completely, though. To sell the moral high ground for a hot chocolate and a smile was too cheap a price. "But a finer example of irrational, pigheaded, not to forget downright ignorant thinking is hard to imagine."

Her eyes narrowed. "I have fixed roofs before, I'll have you know."

"In the rain?"

"Well, no, but—"

"In the wind? With no one to hold the ladder?"

Talking about it brought back visions of her small figure dangling in the wind. Good thing she had such strong fingers to hang on with. A litany of possible injuries flashed through his mind and he took another swig of his drink.

"It was a bit…" She trailed off.

"Foolish?" he suggested. "Rash? Idiotic?"

She tucked her feet tighter under her. In the muted light her eyes seemed filled with mists and dreams. He looked at his mug. How much whiskey had she put into the thing? Had fright unlocked some scary poetry DNA, sequencing courtesy of Adahy? The very idea made him shudder.

She pushed her hair back, tilted her head and gazed at him. "You're right. No excuses. I was stupid. It's just that I saw the piece of metal flapping as I was about to go to bed, and thought it would only take a couple of minutes to fix. I couldn't very well leave it."

"Again, why didn't you come and get me?"

"I don't like being...helpless. You know, weak. Dependent."

He stared at her. "Are you serious? You equate someone holding a ladder with dependency?"

She squirmed. "Not when you put it like that. Are you going to be angry with me for the rest of the night? I suppose you have a right to be. I can't think of any other damsel in distress who flattened her knight in shining armor."

"Hardly a knight."

"You did break my fall."

"True."

"I'm glad the sheet's nailed down tight." She drew in a breath and added, "You did a much better job than I'd have done."

He eyed her over his cup. "I did, but I bet that magnanimity cost you one helluva lot."

Cressa laughed. He loved her laugh. "It burned all the way up my throat."

His eyes fell to that throat, soft and white, disappearing under the woolen sweater.

"You did well to find all the gear," he said grudgingly.

"You forget—I spent summers here. We used to explore all the nooks and crannies." She looked around the room with affection. "It's good staying here. These walls have enjoyed a lot of laughter. Being back is kinda weird, though."

"What, with just me and Mom?"

"No, it's not that." She paused, then gave a self-conscious smile. "It's me, I guess. Strange being back as an adult is what I meant. It reminds me of being a child again. I remember all the games we used to play, the dreams we used to have."

"So what did you used to dream of?"

They were both talking in low voices, though there was no need to. Outside the rain and wind lashed, but he and Cressa were cocooned in warmth. She lifted her hair and shook it to help dry it. To do so, she had to arch slightly. Adam wondered if she did that deliberately. "I don't know, lots of things. Sailing around the world was probably my greatest dream."

"So why aren't you doing that?"

"Because—" Cressa broke off. "I don't know," she added slowly, as if trying to find the answer to a profound question. Then she shrugged and looked back at him. "What about you? What did you dream about when you were a kid?"

She cradled an ankle in one hand. It was a slender ankle at the end of a beautifully toned leg. She kept herself in great shape. He knew what her body looked like really well now. Had seen it in a bikini, had seen it in skimpy warrior gear, knew it in pants and sweats, knew it in the mornings when she stood yawning by the coffeepot with just an oversize T-shirt and fluffy slippers on. But he didn't know the feel of it. His hands had yet to learn the textures of skin and hair and—

He realized he was staring. "Me? Oh, I don't know. Working in a circus was right up there at one stage."

"The circus? Really? Trapeze or lion tamer?"

He loved the mischief in her face. The scent of warm apple made him want to draw closer, to rub his face in her hair.

"Trapeze."

The word sounded as if he'd dragged it out. He found it hard to think with senses rapidly overriding brain.

"So why aren't you doing that now?"

The question was gently teasing, but it snapped his mind back into his body, and Adam realized he couldn't do this. Couldn't sit in the softly lit room, Cressa an arm's reach away, and trade confidences. He knew the game so well—hey, he and Cole had invented half the rules. It would be madness to addle his concentration only weeks from his exam, and for what—a meaningless fling? He drained his mug.

"Dreams change." He stood, destroying the insidious web of intimacy. "It's late. We should get to bed."

She laid a hand on his arm. "Why the rush? Stay a bit longer."

If he did, they both understood what would happen. Fantasies of what Cressa was offering right here, right now, spun vividly. He'd be a fool to leave. He should take it then walk away. That's what she wanted. What any red-blooded male wanted.

He just wanted more.

CHAPTER FOURTEEN

TYPICAL NORTHLAND, by the next day the weather had cleared and filming resumed. Cressa's days were long and she scarcely saw Adam, who made an appearance on the site only one day, to help swell the number of extras and to consult over some of the stunts. The rest of the time, as far as she could tell, he was closeted in his room except for his long runs.

Despite the punishing work schedule, she filled her evenings socializing with the film crew and talking on the phone to her sisters. But no matter how much she tried to keep busy, she still found herself thinking far too much about Adam—which was ridiculous, because she wasn't the sort who got fixated on one guy.

She wasn't like Bridget. She was pleased for her friend, though. Bid had finally plucked up the courage to ask Jeremy out, and now they were in the first flush of infatuated love. Cressa thought it sweet, but Sam made vomiting noises if Bridget went on too long about Jeremy's virtues. Sam had started up a hot affair with Hank, but while their lovemaking sounded impressively physical, her heart remained unattached. Neither she nor Bid rated Cressa's chances with Adam anymore. If it hadn't happened by now, they advised, look for someone new.

Trouble was, Cressa didn't want someone new. All she wanted was one stubborn-as-hell, hot, sexy Texan.

She simply didn't understand him. That night she'd seen the hunger in his eyes, a hunger that matched hers. She'd never met a guy with so much self-control. He wanted it; she wanted it. No strings. Wasn't that what guys dreamed about? All she needed was to get him alone for a few hours. On a boat...

When her next day off finally came round, the fickle Northland weather was right on her side, sunny and very windy. In high spirits she banged on Adam's door. "Leaving in one hour. Don't forget to bring a change of clothes."

She sang as she packed the bags of food and changes of clothing. Alicia strolled into the kitchen, a blouse in her hands.

"My, but you are happy today."

"I adore sailing, and it's been months since I was out on the water. I haven't been on *Takapu* for years. She's my uncle's boat. He taught all of us how to sail her."

Since their chat, she'd felt closer to Alicia in some ways, though that comment about her being lost had hurt at the time. On reflection, she realized she had to forgive Alicia. The woman was a mother, so no wonder she'd sounded like Cressa's own mum. They simply didn't understand where Cressa was coming from. Alicia held out the blouse. "This is a bit young for me. I wondered if you'd like to have it."

Cressa stopped short, beer cans suspended above the ice chest. "Really?"

Alicia smiled. "Really."

The blouse was peasant-style, with a drawstring neck and long sleeves gathered into cuffs. Embroidered flowers wreathed the neckline. It was way too beautiful for a scruffy type like her.

She took it, but said, "I don't think I can carry off

something as lovely as this. I'm just not…" And she indicated her cutoff jeans and hoodie.

Alicia smiled. "It'll look lovely with your long hair. Besides, it might be useful today to help stop sunburn."

"Oh no! It's far too nice for that." She draped the blouse against her body and could feel herself weakening.

"It was made to be worn. I'll be sad if you don't accept it."

"Well, in that case, thank you!" Cressa laughed as she hugged Alicia. "I'll feel like a princess when I wear it."

"It's my pleasure. Now, take care of my son. Don't drown him."

Alicia had been entertained when she'd learned about the roof escapade, though she'd again sounded like a typical mother when she'd commented that as a child, Cressa must have been as much of a worry as Adam had been. A good thing she said that, though. Cressa and Adam had rolled their eyes at each other, and for that split second, they'd connected again.

"He'd better obey me. I'm captain today, and any subordination will have him walking the plank."

"I heard that!" Adam sauntered into the kitchen. "Brace yourself. I've never met a captain not in need of a little mutiny."

He whipped her over his shoulder in a fireman's lift. She shrieked and pummeled his back. "Put me down!"

He just laughed.

"Do you know what captains do to mutinous crew?" she demanded.

"Threats? Oh, bring it on, baby." He spun around so hard her braid swung wildly.

"You're in an exceptionally good mood, too, Adam." Alicia sounded amused.

"Yeah. It's the prospect of getting out for a bit," he admitted. "I've been going a bit stir-crazy these past two days."

"Self-inflicted, so no sympathy." Cressa tried to kick him, but the action was futile. Adam had her legs in a vise grip. But she knew how to outwit him. "Actually, the view's great from this angle." She patted his butt. Immediately she was on her feet again.

"That's better." She pulled her hoodie down, smoothed her hair. "So how many captains have you met, anyway?"

"Including you? One. I've never been on a boat before."

"You must be kidding. I can't believe it! You are in for such a treat. You'll love it!"

SHE WAS RIGHT. The sails, the sheets, the instruments and the small galley enchanted Adam, though he eyed the tiny head with suspicion. He bounded barefoot around the deck like an old salt and was quick to pick up the basic principles of sailing, even if he couldn't read wind direction very well and was initially over-exuberant on the tiller. She loved watching the way he moved, light and fast. Loved the flex of muscles when he stripped off his shirt and hauled up the anchor. Loved the reach of his long arms as they pulled up the sail. Loved, especially, the moment he looped an arm around the mast as if it were a friend, and flung his head back to draw in a deep, blissful breath. His scar ran clean and uncompromising down his olive-brown back. It ought to have marred the perfection of honed muscle and sinew, but strangely, it enhanced it. His legs looked longer than ever, encased in black jeans. The jeans were incongruous on a boat, but less incongruous than a Texan biker dressed in surf shorts.

He turned to her, dark eyes glistening. "This is go-oo-d." He drew out the last word as though it had a couple of syllables in the middle. "Thanks. I feel as if I can breathe properly for the first time in months."

They flew down the long reach of Te Huna Inlet, the conditions proving windier than Cressa had expected. Years had passed since she'd sailed in the Bay of Islands, and seeing the familiar green hills and islands, the countless coves with white sands, was glorious. Adam dropped into the cockpit next to her, bracing himself with his feet as *Takapu* heeled at a steep angle, her sails fat with wind.

"This is incredible," he said. "Bay of Islands. Well named."

She trimmed the tiller, wondering if she'd been rash in hoisting the boat's sail, the large genoa. "Yeah, there are more than a hundred and forty of them. Over there is Urupukapuka Island. Zane Gray used to go there for deep-sea fishing."

"You're kidding! I've read all his books." He touched her lightly on the nose. "This is fun. Thanks."

She resisted the impulse to lick his finger. "'Sa pleasure. It's nice to share it with someone."

With Adam.

He began asking all about the history of the region, the geographical features. At one point she laughed.

"What?" he asked.

"I hadn't expected you to be interested in such things."

He smiled, but his eyes went guarded. "Why not?"

She shrugged. "You're more Action Man."

"All plastic muscle and nothing between the ears?"

"No! I meant as in an outdoorsy type."

"So are you."

"Ah, but deep down nerd qualities lurk."

His eyes followed a seagull. "Maybe we all have an inner nerd."

"Maybe." Another large gray cloud scudded overhead. That wind was definitely picking up. "I think we'd better drop the jenny."

"That's the front sail?"

"You're learning fast. If you can release that rope—" she pointed to the sheet "—from the cleat and go forward, you'll be able to pull her down. Okay?"

He followed instructions, but the sail didn't give. Adam shaded his eyes and squinted up the mast. "It might be caught."

She brushed a strand of hair out her eyes. "Damn! The halyard's jammed."

She gazed across the water to see a large gust rippling the surface as it came toward them.

"I can climb up and free it," Adam said.

"Are you sure?"

"Are you kidding me?" he demanded.

She pretended to cringe. "You're right. Sorry. That would be great."

He shinnied up the mast and began fiddling. She brushed her hair out of her eyes, glanced forward and saw black rocks ahead. She'd completely forgotten about the reef. At high tide it was submerged, but with the tide going out, its vicious serrations were visible.

"Adam, we've gotta jibe," she bellowed above the sound of wind and flapping sails.

"Gotta what?" he called back.

She had no time to explain.

"Hang on tight!"

As she yelled, she sheeted in the main, hauled on the tiller and ducked. There was a bang as the boom snapped over her head. Adam gave a startled cry and she watched the mast swing with sickening suddenness in a vast arc as the boat lurched, tipping to the other side. He clung like a monkey as the mast reached far out over the water. Cressa fought to steady the *Takapu* and bring her onto the next tack. She was filled with visions of Adam being catapulted, smashed or drowned, but he was still clasping the mast as it slowly rose to a vertical position. In seconds, he was back on the deck, and pulled the genoa down a second before the gust struck. The boat heeled wildly, but they were sailing on course again, reef behind them. Cressa's heart was still racing, though, and when he dropped back into the cockpit, she was stricken.

"Oh, Adam, I'm so sorry. I'm so very sorry. I—"

"What do you mean? That was fantastic."

She stared at him in disbelief. His eyes were brilliant in his dark face. "I nearly killed you. For a second time."

He laughed, putting his hand to his chest. "Yeah, heart attack material, all right. But hey, did you see that? It was amazing!"

He was high on adrenaline, and as relief kicked in, she started laughing. "Oh, man," she said, swiping at her eyes with the back of her hand. "I thought I'd killed you."

"Nah. If I'd fallen in, you'd have come and gotten me."

She sobered. "I shouldn't have let you climb the mast without a harness."

"Are you kidding?" He grinned. "When the mast whipped like that—hey, it was the most incredible rush I've ever had. They should make a ride like that at Disneyland."

This made her laugh again. "Not everyone is as crazy as you. Still, I shouldn't have put you in danger."

He gave her a funny look. "Cressa, I'm a steelworker."

She stared at him blankly.

"My job. Construction. I'm a steelworker. I do the high-rise stuff."

"What—skyscrapers?" Light began to dawn. "Are you one of those lunatics who teeter out on the beams hundreds of feet in the air? Who eat lunch sitting with feet dangling over the most terrible drops?"

"That's me. A lunatic. Though it's not so dangerous if you keep your wits about you and use common sense. We aren't a bunch of cowboys up there. Hard hats are professionals who know the risks and work around them."

She found this new aspect of him hard to take in. "I thought you were, you know, building houses."

He shrugged. "Yeah, well..."

Her eyes narrowed. "Alicia doesn't know, does she?"

"No, she doesn't, and you'd better not tell her. She'd just worry."

"Unbelievable. There she is, thrilled you aren't doing stunts, happy you're going safely to work each day." Cressa shook her head as she leaned on the tiller and gazed at him. His black hair was blowing back, leaving his face stark and strong. Wrestling huge steel girders high up in the sky—no wonder he was in such fantastic shape. "Why do you do it?"

"It's far better money than working on the ground. Besides, I enjoy it. It's not a big deal. It's just a job."

Except it wasn't. Once again he'd shattered her pre-conceptions. Just when she thought she was getting to know him, he revealed another side to his personality. For him, though, the topic was closed.

"I'm hungry. When's lunch?"

"Minutes away."

She steered them into a small cove on one of the islands, out of the wind. Adam went forward, but as he was dropping anchor, something in the water caught his attention. "What the hell?"

She heard a splash as he vaulted over the side of the boat into the sea.

CHAPTER FIFTEEN

CRESSA LEAPED FOR THE railing. "Adam?"

"Here."

Then she saw he was swimming toward three dolphins circling the boat. She immediately stripped to her bikini and jumped in, too. The water was pure ice, and she gasped as Adam arrived beside her. "This is mad. We ought to have wetsuits."

"I know," he said, shivering violently, eyes alight with excitement. "But I wasn't sure how long these guys would stick around. Now where are they?"

He spun in the water, and as if on cue, a huge gray shape rose beside him. Cressa yelped. Even though she'd swum with dolphins ten years earlier, she'd forgotten how enormous they were up close. And how spellbinding. The water around them churned as the dolphins wove around them and one another, coming near enough to touch. She forgot to be cold, forgot to be scared. Adam laughed in delight.

"This is incredible."

This communion with wild creatures in their own habitat felt almost spiritual. Cressa had grown up in the water, but all of a sudden she was vividly aware that she was in their world. The largest dolphin rose and sank again, his muscular flank passing inches in front of her face. His skin was rough, she saw, scarred and nicked all over. A livid scar ran across his brow, as long as the one down Adam's back. Somehow this made him seem more real. He, too, had battled. Suffered. Lived to fight another day.

As he surfaced again, he paused. Mesmerized, Cressa stared straight into his eye. He only glimpsed her world as he jumped out of the water, but he knew intimately his own underwater mountains and valleys, caverns and canyons. Places she'd never go.

As the dolphin held her gaze, the surrounding scene faded. Sea and sky melded together, and the sounds of water against boat and Adam's soft splashes went mute. Just she and the dolphin existed. Intelligence glistened in that eye, and it was as if he could see right inside her. Could see all that had happened, but made no judgment. Still he held her gaze, going deeper and deeper into her core. She felt hot tears brimming in her eyes. Felt her chest, her throat, constrict. The dolphin seemed to be nodding and smiling at her, and she found herself nodding and smiling, too.

Then he was gone. All the dolphins were gone, and she was shivering and brushing her tears hastily aside as Adam said, "Oh, wow. I can't believe it. That was the most mind-blowing experience of my life."

Back in the cockpit, they stumbled on numbed feet as they pulled towels out of bags, giggling as they collided, in the grip of almost hysterical euphoria.

"Damn pants," Adam muttered. Having wrestled the button and fly open with icy fingers, he was hopping on one leg as he fought to peel the jeans off the other. He lost balance and sat with a bump. "Ow!"

Cressa laughed at him, but said, "Here, let me help," as she grabbed the cuffs and pulled. The wet material was heavy and obdurate, and her hands were so cold she couldn't get a grip, but the jeans suddenly slipped off in a rush and she toppled backward. It was Adam's turn to laugh.

"Dumb and dumber. But thanks."

Then she got tangled with towels and wet hair that had come loose in the water, so Adam said, "Here, I'll help." He wrapped the towel around her while she held her hair on top of her head, and he rubbed feeling back into her arms, her shoulders. It was glorious to be enveloped in the warmth of the rough towel, and as circulation returned, so too, did her senses. She became conscious of his brown torso close to her face, his arms enfolding her as he toweled her back vigorously. It was like being a kid again, except she hadn't had thoughts like this when she was a kid. He smelled clean and salty. She wanted to lean into him, rub against him, arching like a cat.

He knelt to rub her legs, but here the efficient rubbing faltered. His movements became slower as the towel shifted from calves and shins to her thighs. His face was directly in line with her bikini bottoms. The rubbing slowed almost to stroking. She could feel the shape of his hands through the towel.

He swallowed. His hands paused. Their light pressure on the backs of her thighs zinged all nerve endings in her body, sending them into an agony of anticipation. For a second she and Adam both remained absolutely still. Then he was getting to his feet, clearing his throat.

"Warmer?" His voice was husky and he didn't look at her.

"Mmm." She had to clear her throat, too. "Thanks."

She went down into the cabin to get some clothes. To work out what was happening. Why had he pulled back? Was she misreading signals again? He constantly left her off balance—she, who was usually so sure of things.

She wrapped a sarong around her waist, pulled on Alicia's top and went halfway up the ladder, then paused, feeling suddenly self-conscious to be in something so feminine. The sun was hot through the muslin.

Adam turned to her. "You look nice."

His tone was light, but the expression in his black eyes hollowed her stomach. He'd tied a towel around his waist. Nope, she wasn't misreading signals at all. Well, two could be off balance, Adam Walker.

"Thanks."

She leaned over to check a cleat that didn't need checking, so that the neck of her top gaped softly. "Lunch?"

"What?" Adam blinked, cleared his throat once more and became intensely interested in rubbing his thumb over some worn varnish on the tiller. "Lunch? Oh, yeah. Right. Good idea."

Smiling to herself, she went back down to the galley.

ADAM ATE A GOOD LUNCH, the sea air having sharpened his already healthy appetite. He wished other appetites could be so easily assuaged. Maybe if he and she just did it, then it would be out of their systems. Cressa made it perfectly plain all she wanted was fun.

With the sea, the sun, the wind, the open spaces, he felt alive again. Not that he was backing down on his study, but he was stale. Stale and tired. Tired of chemistry and physics and essays. As far back as he could remember, they'd dominated his life. Surely a guy could take some time for fun. Have his reward for hard work. Especially with Cressa putting out all those signals.

When they set sail again, the enormous gusts had

dropped to a steady wind and the waves had flattened. Clouds were massing low on the horizon, but the sun was warm. He lay on his back, staring up at the sky, feeling full and lazy. The cramped walls of his bedroom seemed a million miles away. "What's with New Zealand and clouds? How come you never have a cloudless sky?"

"Aotearoa," said Cressa.

"Say what?"

"Aotearoa, Land of the Long White Cloud, the Maori name for New Zealand. Pretty, isn't it?"

Damn, but she looked pretty herself, dressed in that blouse, with her hair loosely tied in a ponytail. He could make out the hazy outline of her low-cut bikini top under the blouse that had just one ribbon at the neckline....

"Land of the Long White Cloud. Sums it up. That would make Texas Land of the Long Straight Road, I guess."

She laughed as she leaned forward to adjust a sheet. Her sarong fell open, revealing her leg. Why did he continue to resist? He'd have fun. She'd have fun. She could add him to her tally. The skier, the archaeologist, the Texan. Why the hell not?

Lying down was beginning to make him strangely dizzy, so he sat up and dangled his legs into the cockpit, scant inches from her. "Cressa, what's the real reason you left Brian?"

She was taken aback. "Where did that come from?"

"You never gave me a straight answer. He seems perfect."

In a Yale kind of way.

The boat was rolling over the water's surface now, instead of bouncing as it had in the morning. Adam discovered he preferred the rougher ride. Cressa's arm rested on the tiller. Tendrils of her hair floated on the breeze. The only sound was the shushing of the water below them. "He does everything perfectly. Would you want to marry someone like that?"

He smiled. "My ex-wife was anything *but* perfect."

Cressa didn't buy his cynical tone. "Yet you loved her."

It was not a question.

"Yeah, I did." He coiled a sheet and laid it down. He liked the precision of sailing. "So what happened?"

She adjusted the tiller, correcting their course. "There's not much to say, really."

"Okay. Give me the salient points only."

He loved those half smiles of hers. They made him want to kiss her. He remembered her lips, soft and salty against his.

"Salient points? Well, we went out while I was at university. He'd already graduated. Everyone thought I was the luckiest girl to have him—I did myself. Our relationship was picture-perfect. Except, though I enjoyed accountancy, I couldn't imagine being a suit, stuck in some big firm in downtown Auckland. And then…"

She leaned over to scratch an ankle. Through the thin material of the sarong he could see her thigh. He could almost feel its shape beneath his hands. As she straightened, she saw him watching her. Her eyes darkened and he caught that speculative glint in her eyes. Damn. If she made one of her moves now…

"So then?" he quickly prompted.

She resumed her position at the tiller, their course unchanged. Her eyes fixed on the horizon. "Then I found I was pregnant."

So there it was, finally, the reef under her apparently smooth waters. He'd been so sure one existed.

"Brian immediately proposed." She sounded outraged, then looked at Adam, head to one side. "Oh, man, you did the same, didn't you?"

"Why do you make it sound like it's the weirdest thing a guy can do?"

"A wedding's not always the solution."

He gave a short laugh. "So I learned."

"Next thing I knew, Mum and Brian were planning the most beautiful wedding, complete with veil and a white dress with an appropriately full skirt to disguise the bump."

Adam wondered if Crystal would have felt more married if she'd had a wedding like the one Cressa had fled.

Cressa continued, "Suddenly, I hadn't just chosen the wrong career—I seemed to have fallen into the wrong life." She paused and stared out over the water. "I didn't dare tell anyone. It sounded so stupid. A great husband, a great job, a baby. What more could any girl wish for?"

She stopped speaking, focused on the waters in front of the boat. The hand not holding the tiller was braced on the seat beside him. Adam covered it with his. Knowing what had to come next, he couldn't look at that stern, empty profile, so he, too, focused on the horizon. The way it tilted slowly up and down made him queasy.

"I miscarried at twenty-two weeks." Adam squeezed her hand, but she pulled away. "These things happen." Her voice was brusque. "Brian still wanted to marry, so plans went ahead, and well, you know the rest."

"Running away was understandable. You needed space to grieve—"

She whirled on him. "Grieve? I was *relieved,* damn it. Everyone was treading around me on eggshells, ready with handkerchiefs and homilies, and there I was, thanking my lucky stars for my narrow escape. Can't you understand?"

He wanted to but something was still missing. Her tone was adamant but there was pain in her eyes. Pain she wasn't going to admit to. "Understand? About the marriage, sure. But not the baby. Crystal was a huge mistake, but Stella wasn't. She was the best thing that ever happened to me."

Cressa's eyes blazed on either side of her indomitable nose. "My problem is no one gets it! No one *wants* to get it. I just don't believe in the picket fence, the happily-ever-after. Is that such a crime?"

The crime was that at this critical moment of confession and sharing and closeness, Adam was finding it hard to ignore the deadly slow, rolling motion.

"Whoa," he said, leaning back, hands up in surrender. "You've made it clear what you want. Freedom and sailing off into the sunset, right?"

She eyed him. "It sounds trite when you say it like that, but yeah, along those lines."

"Though why the hell you'd want to live on one of these things—"

He barely made it to the railing in time before he was thoroughly and horribly sick.

CHAPTER SIXTEEN

ADAM RECOVERED THE MINUTE his feet were on land again. Cressa had assured him lots of sailors got seasick, but he knew he'd put a serious dent into her image of him. He told himself this was a good thing. The Adam in her head was nothing like the Adam he really was.

Driving home through the darkness, they talked about movies, saying which ten they'd take to a desert island. There were no overlaps, which just went to show how different they were. Then he found an ancient CD in the glove compartment.

"Ah, your theme song." And he put on "Girls Just Want to Have Fun" full volume.

"Corny!" Cressa leaned forward and turned down the sound. "And what's so wrong with that, any way?"

"Nothing. Nothing at all."

The country road was dark and winding. It felt as if they were in their own little world, just the two of them. Cressa wasn't driving her usual shit-or-bust style, and he was suddenly aware of her glancing sideways at him.

"So, a steelworker, eh? Walking across the beams so far off the ground must give you a rush. What's it like?"

Oh, man. This was going to feed her already too lively imagination. "You boil in summer and freeze in winter. Mostly you don't think of the height at all."

His prosaic answer didn't dampen her interest.

"It must be amazing, though—you'd have the most incredible views. What sort of safety gear do you use?"

He kept his eyes on the road ahead. "We don't. Harnesses are as much a liability as a help. There are safety nets, but the chances of hitting one when you fall are very slim."

"Wow. So you are literally risking your life every single working day." She looked at him again, and even in the dark he could see the admiration in her eyes, hear the awe in her voice. "I don't know anyone else who'd have the courage to do that. You must have absolutely no fear."

"Oh, I feel fear, believe me. Just not with heights."

She barely heard him. "Do you remember the other night? You said your dreams had changed. But you know what? I reckon being a steelworker is not so different from being a trapeze artist, though it's a lot more dangerous."

All of a sudden, he knew this couldn't continue. Somehow his secret had turned into a lie. It was making fools of them both. He had to put her straight once and for all. The truth would kill whatever it was she felt for him, but that would be all to the good. She'd stop pursuing, and then he wouldn't have to keep fighting temptations that were fast becoming uncontrollable.

"Cressa, you've got it wrong. You've got me wrong. My dreams did change." He wound down the window and the cold wind hit him in the face, sharpening his resolve. He turned to her. "I do steelwork because it pays well—real well—and because it gives me flexibility to pursue my true goal." He drew in a deep breath. "I'm studying to be a doctor. I'm saving to pay my way through medical school."

She laughed. "Yeah, right. A Brian in Texan leathers."

Then she glanced at him. "Oh, my God, are you serious? You are. But a doctor?" She shook her head as if to clear her ears. "How? Why?"

That was the trouble with women. Too many questions. If Cressa were a guy, she'd have said, "Medicine, huh. No kidding. So who do you think'll win the Rose Bowl this year?"

Adam looked back at the road. It was pitch-black, in the middle of nowhere. "I told you that after my accident I had a year in and out of hospital."

"Yup. Life, the universe and—oh. That was it? Becoming a doctor was the answer to the universe?" She was kidding, of course, but he could hear her underlying disbelief.

"It is the answer to *my* universe. I want to fix people. I want to be a surgeon."

The Jeep swerved off the road and he slammed his hands against the dashboard. "Cressa! What the hell?"

The vehicle bumped onto the rough verge, the headlights now crazily lighting the trees immediately in front of them. Then she switched off the engine, plunging them into darkness. It was quiet, too. He could hear the crickets in the grass.

"I need to get things straight." She leaned her arm on the steering wheel to face him. "This is the 'stuff' that's been occupying you day and night these past weeks?" She was incredulous. "You're studying?"

"Yeah, for my MCAT."

"Your what?"

"It's an exam that gets you into medical school. I'm taking it in a month."

Funny, how the dim light accentuated her features— large eyes, strong nose, wide mouth. She looked every bit as fierce and resolute as the Valkyrie she played. "A doctor? Of all professions, you want to be a doctor! I can't believe it." Her voice was rising, and she stared at him as though trying to read a different answer in his face. "It just doesn't fit with the—" her hand made circles in the air "—the whole biker dude thing."

There wasn't anything to say to that, so he didn't.

"I feel so…misled, *played*. That's it!" She drew herself up the SUV door, skewering him with a glare. "I feel played and deceived. You've been deceiving us all."

He shifted in his seat. If this was how someone he'd known only a few weeks was taking it, no way in hell would he tell his mother. "Now, don't get all riled. It didn't start like that. I never lied as such. I just left stuff out."

"*Stuff?*" she shrieked. Damn, he should have chosen a different word. "Stuff! All that mystery. I thought you were engaged in something secret, something big. Espionage, nefarious business deals—the white slave trade, maybe. And all the time you were studying to be a *doctor.*" She spit the word.

He tried a joke. "You sound disappointed I'm not a master criminal."

Big mistake.

"Don't be bloody ridiculous," she exclaimed. "It's just that you seemed so supercool. I never thought your secret would be something as ordinary as becoming a *doctor.*"

She made it sound like a swearword, and something snapped for him. "Grow up, Cressa," he said. "Right from the start you've had me wrong. You made assumptions. You had all these fantasies. Well, tough if I don't live up to them. This is me. This is who I am. A guy who has this dumb dream to be a doctor. Which is why

I don't have time for you and your games right at this minute. Why don't you go live out your own fantasies, instead of foisting them on others."

"Oh, I so can't just sit here and take this crap." She flung open her door and jumped out. "You made a fool out of me." And she slammed the door so hard the Jeep shook.

He leaped out his side and intercepted her in front of the vehicle, catching her by the shoulders. "I never made a fool of you. You did that all on your own."

Realizing his fingers were digging in, he let go and stood back, but still his eyes nailed hers.

"Is that so?" she hissed, advancing. "Excuse me, but are you going to deny your own little fantasies that first dance we had?"

Her accusation stopped him short. She pressed home her advantage. "What about the night after the roof incident? Was that all in my imagination?"

He stayed silent on the grounds that anything he said could incriminate. Her hands clamped her hips like a vise. "And today. What would have happened if you hadn't vomited? Have I really been making everything up in my fevered imagination?"

"Ah, shit. No, you haven't." He slumped against the SUV, its hood still hot under his hands. "There *is* something between us."

"Maybe if you'd been straight with me from the start, I wouldn't have been so confused by your mixed messages. I'd have been spared the humiliation of pushing things, believing there might be something special to explore."

He lifted his hands. "Okay, yeah, you're right. That's why I told you tonight. I couldn't stand it any longer that not saying anything had slipped into lying to you. Now you know."

"Yes," she said gruffly, "I do."

"Can we get back in the Jeep now?"

In silence they climbed in, but she hadn't finished. She was a woman; of course she hadn't. "I don't get why wanting to go into medicine is such a big secret."

He tried to hold her unwavering gaze but looked away first. "It's not a secret as such. I don't broadcast it, but my friends know. Some of the people I work with know. The only ones I specifically haven't told are my family."

Cressa slumped against her door. Her eyes hadn't left his face. "Because…?" She drew out the word.

"Look, I hardly ever see them. We mostly come together in crisis moments—my accident, Cole's arrest and court case, Mom's illness. There's never been a good time to raise the subject. We aren't exactly the Christmas and Thanksgiving sort of family."

"Given your mum's cooking, I'm not surprised."

They both laughed and the tension between them lightened a little. Cressa was marginally less stern when she returned to her interrogation.

"I still don't get why you wouldn't just tell us."

"'Us'! That's just it," he said, aggrieved. "I'm in a foreign country. No one here gives a damn what I do, so before you happened along, 'us' was going to be just Mom and me. We may have a dysfunctional relationship in your opinion, but hey, it works. She's getting better by the day and I don't say anything that will upset her. But you appeared—" he stabbed a finger at her "—and disrupted those dynamics. You are so damn meddling."

She shoved his finger aside. "Nice try, Walker, but you can't pin any of this on me. I came to stay with a perfectly nice, ordinary family, only to discover in-nocent questions cause skeletons to dance in their cupboards."

"A recovering alcoholic and her biker son are not your ordinary family," he said dryly.

"No, but you present like one. Although," she went on more thoughtfully, "I doubt there are any ordinary families. Usually once you start getting into people's lives, they are never as straightforward as they seem on the surface."

He wondered about her family. Five sisters, an ambi-tious mother, an actor father. What were the dynamics there? The big difference was that something held them together. They sure did talk a lot, what with all those phone calls. Maybe that was part of it. It certainly wasn't just a question of love. Hell, he loved Mom, Sass and Cole. He'd loved Crystal and Stella. The Walkers just didn't have the knack of togetherness. They'd all been trying more, though, these past six months. Maybe that's what Sass and Mom had been working on here, learning to be family. Was that what Sass had been trying to tell him at the wedding?

He became aware of Cressa watching him. "What?"

"I was just thinking about you being the 'biker son.'" She made quote marks in the air. "You're buying into your own publicity. The more I get to know you, Adam, the more I realize you are not the person you show to the world. The skeletons don't need to come out of the cupboard—you do."

"And thank *you*, Dr. Freud."

"Furthermore, I think you should tell Alicia."

"No." He shook his head. "I don't want to raise her hopes. She'll be all excited and happy for me and then when—if—I fail, she'll start blaming herself, and who knows what that would trigger."

Cressa pressed her fingertips to her temples. "Back up. Who says you'll fail?"

His eyes had grown accustomed to the blackness now and he could see her features more clearly—the glint of green in the dark depths of her eyes, the curve of her bottom lip, the line of her throat, all framed by the billowing cloud of hair she'd taken down once on dry land. Perhaps because he knew the opportunity would never come again, he almost couldn't resist leaning forward and kissing her. But now that he'd started, he felt he had to make a full and frank confession. She had to know the truth about him.

"Because, Cressa, that's what I do. I fail." He looked at her so she'd grasp that his words were for real. "I'm really good at failing. I fail at the most important things in life and it puts Mom through hell. She was upset when I dropped out of school. She got drunk at my wedding and cried with my divorce. She couldn't visit me in the hospital without saying it was all her fault for not having been a better parent. And when Cole—" Adam shook his head. "I'm not risking putting her in a tailspin if I fail again."

"That's crazy! That was all in the past."

He folded his arms across his chest. "Would you like to put your mother through your wedding drama again? Could you look her in the eye a second time and say, 'Oh, made a mistake again. Another wedding's off.'"

"That's not the same because—" Cressa broke off. She gazed into the darkness, then turned back to him with a rueful grin. "You're right. I'd walk over live coals rather than face Ma with something like that."

He wasn't done. There was one final admission. "To

be honest, it's not just Mom. When my stunt went wrong, I crashed in front of a thousand people. I had to face our friends when Crystal took off. All that sympathy, that pity. That false cheeriness." He shook his head at the memories. "Just this once, I'd prefer to fail in private."

Cressa's eyes were steady on his face. "Oh, yeah, I remember that only too well. After the ba—the wedding fiasco," she continued smoothly, "people not knowing whether to talk about it or not was a nightmare. I'd never have gotten through it if it hadn't been for my family. Even Mum was supportive, though I knew how awful it was for her, especially being so sure I'd just made the biggest mistake of my life."

She straightened in her seat and switched on the ignition, the lights exploding the darkness. With a clash of gears and the roar of acceleration, she had the Jeep back on the road.

"So, Adam," she said, her tone conversational now, "to make things clear. You'd like me to back off and us both to ignore this attraction between us."

"Yeah, I can't afford any distractions just—"

"Say no more." She threw him a bright, friendly smile. "Now that I understand what the hell is going on, I promise to leave you in peace for the rest of your stay."

It was what he'd wanted all along. He ought to have felt relieved. Instead he felt deflated. "Great. Thanks for understanding."

"But you have to admit—" she changed gears "—it might have been fantastic. *We* could have been fantastic."

CHAPTER SEVENTEEN

CRESSA HAD MADE her promise in good faith. Now that she understood him, there was really nothing left to explore. A relationship might have been fun, but hey, there were always new and interesting guys, fresh adventures.

She soon discovered, however, that the day's sailing had shaken her philosophy of life, exacerbating her restlessness and causing her to rethink her values. Snatches of conversations reverberated in her head: "…being free and being lost can sometimes look the same." "…under your wild-child act is a strong woman wanting to get out." "…go live out your own fantasies."

Adam was pursuing his dream with a single-mindedness she couldn't help admiring. It was one thing to let fate fill her sails, but perhaps it was time to take the tiller.

Trawling the internet took some time, but the search came up gold. She sat back in her chair and stared at the screen in disbelief. There it was, the dream job. Crew wanted for a tall ship used for chartering. Fate seemed to be handing it to her on a platter. There remained, of course, the small problem of applications from around the world; they would be flying in. The job was a long shot. The longest shot. But what if she got it? Just imagining Adam's expression when she told him brought a smile to her lips as she opened her résumé file.

Adam. She was thinking of him again. Despite all her efforts not to, she'd given him quite a lot of thought. Now that her initial shock had worn off, she could see that his desire to be a doctor made sense. He had the focus and precision necessary for operations, and kept a cool head under pressure. He already worked life-and-death situations and he was certainly bossy enough to be a surgeon. And what better goal than to fix people?

At least he'd finally been honest. She knew where she stood and that was great. Everything was out in the open, rules clearly defined. Life could go on as it had before Adam roared into her life. So this agitation that she woke up with was inexplicable, as was the disturbed night she'd spent. She was usually such a good sleeper.

Monday she was due on the set, so she dropped from the top bunk as she did every morning and ambled down the dark hallway to the kitchen, where she put on the kettle. Usually she did her stretches while waiting for it to boil, but this morning she paced restlessly to the living room, where she leaned a shoulder on the French door, looking out.

The harbor waters were motionless, a dark pewter under a sky freckled with stars, although dawn was not far off. Matariki—the Seven Sisters—stood out bright and bold. It had been there every morning, but normally she was too keen to get on with the day to stop and look. The stillness had an almost breathless quality to it, the beauty an aching loneliness that tugged at her. A memory of the dolphin flashed. How distant that euphoria now seemed. She gazed toward the sand spit at the far end of the bay. The fairy terns would be returning in spring, but she wouldn't be here to greet them.

The thought saddened her, which was silly, because she could come back anytime to visit over the summer.

The strange, wafting emptiness followed her to work. On the way she spotted her first lamb of the season. In the long, low, early-morning sunshine it ran to its mother on wobbly legs, and the sight made her tearful, then cross. She needed to pull herself together. Once at work, everything would be fine. The other two Valkyries were always good at making her laugh.

Sam and Bridget were oblivious to her odd mood, however, caught up in their own relationships.

"Jeremy is such a romantic," Bid sighed as they sat in makeup. "Over the weekend he took me away to an exclusive hideaway up at Russell. Chilled champagne was waiting for us in the room and the food was out of this world. I felt like a princess."

"Hank and I went skydiving," said Sam. "It was incredible. Afterward—" she leered lasciviously "—the sex was triple X."

Bid looked pained. "Sam, don't you ever feel anything but lust for a man?"

"No, sweetie. I leave all the romantic sighing and crying to people like you." Sam blinked as the false eyelashes were applied, and batted them several times at her reflection. "Life's too short for all that he-said, she-said analysis of what in the end is just a case of what all animals do best. What did you do on the weekend, Cressa?"

"We went sailing," she mumbled as best she could while lipstick was applied.

"Oh, yeah? Anything happen?"

They both waited, but Cressa wasn't in the mood for confidences. Her feelings fell somewhere between those of Bid and Sam, but for the life of her, she wasn't quite sure where.

"Adam threw up."

That got a laugh, but she knew she was being mean. The story of him at the top of the mast could easily be talked up. The revelation that he was a steelworker would impress. Then there was the small fact of his wanting to be a doctor. She could just imagine the storm of discussion that would spark. In many ways she could see where he was coming from. It would make people view him differently. Her mother, for instance. And failure would alter viewpoints yet again.

People judged; that's just what they did. Mind you, the Walkers didn't pull their punches, either, when it came to analyzing her rather than sorting out their own problems. They were wrong, of course, about her life. She'd stared the alternative in the face and hadn't wanted it. She'd chosen her path. Adam had chosen his. They just happened to be going in opposite directions. Which was fine. Hers was the fun route, she thought defiantly as she strode out of Makeup to do battle.

Strenuous activity was just what she needed to snap herself out of her silliness, and that day she threw herself into the action, slicing and dicing her opponents with bloodcurdling yells. She kicked Dave, menacing with chains and a machete, hard in the gut. He folded with immaculate timing, his wire jerking him up in the air as though flung by the force of her blow. Packing a punch like that could go to a girl's head. On cue, Mike ran up behind her and she skewered him with an underarm blow, then whirled around, felling him with a chop to the head before racing to rescue Sam from three assailants.

She was breathing hard at the end when Dave walked

over. "Crikey, Cressa. You nearly winded me with that kick."

"Yeah," said Hank, rubbing his skull. "Watch it with those swords, okay?"

"Okay." She ought to be repentant, but somehow she wasn't. She couldn't wait for the next battle scene to begin.

BE CAREFUL what you wish for.

Adam tapped his pen on the blank sheet of paper in front of him. He was supposed to be writing an essay under timed conditions, but instead he found himself checking his watch. It was late afternoon; Cressa should be home soon. For the past half an hour he'd been listening for the sound of her engine. Not that he'd go out and talk to her or anything.

The past three days, they hadn't exchanged a word or look that could be interpreted in any other way but friendly consideration. But, he had discovered, for him this pact or standoff or whatever it was had come too late. Cressa was already lodged in his consciousness like a burr. When she was out the house, he waited for her to return. When she was home, he knew exactly where she was every minute, could picture what she was doing. Even when he was studying, he caught himself daydreaming like a schoolboy in the throes of his first crush.

How wonderfully straightforward his carnal yearnings of their first meeting now seemed. He should have taken her to the trees then and there, Deirdre be damned, before everything became so complicated.

We could have been fantastic.

Now he'd never know, and that prospect ate him up. On the surface, Cressa seemed unaffected by their new understanding, though at night as he lay in his single bed, feet dangling over the end, he listened to her toss and turn on the creaking bunk. She came home physically exhausted, but went out again each evening, caught up in a new frenetic whirl of socializing. Looking for the next man already? The few times their paths crossed, she was bright and breezy. The only clues that all might not be perfect in Cressaland were some lines of tiredness in her face. Once or twice he thought he saw shadows in her eyes, but that was probably the effect of sun and cloud outside.

There it was. His head reared. Her motorbike. She'd have a shower, phone someone in the family and then go out again. That's what she'd done every other evening this week. He watched her park the bike. She didn't have her usual jaunty swing. He leaned forward to watch more closely as she walked to the door. What was wrong with her?

Her?

With a groan he bent over and beat his forehead against the desk. What was wrong with *him!*

OVER DINNER, her face was drawn.

"Are you all right, Cressa?" Alicia asked.

"Of course." Cressa's smile was brittle. She had two vertical lines between her eyes. Adam was annoyed to find himself yearning to lean forward and smooth them away. When they all stood up at the end of the meal, Cressa groaned involuntarily and pressed the heel of her hand hard into her lower back.

He frowned. "What's up? Have you pulled a muscle?"

"It's nothing. I was a bit energetic in the sword fight today, that's all."

She reached for the plates, but breathed sharply and bit her lip.

"Here, I'll massage it."

Cressa straightened. He could see she was making an effort not to grimace. "I told you, it's nothing. Don't worry."

The same stupid fear of appearing weak that had left her dangling from the garage roof. How had she put it? Being dependent.

Ridiculous. He could help her, if only she'd let him. Concern made him gruff. "We need to get it sorted out or you won't be much good tomorrow."

Alicia cut in. "Yes, let Adam help. Even as a twelve-year-old he gave the best shoulder rubs in the world. Do you remember how I used to call you my little healer?"

He caught Cressa's eyes and saw humor flash before they both quickly looked away. "Yeah, I remember."

He came around and ran a hand—a purely professional hand—down her back. "Here?"

"A bit lower. Oh, yeah, right there." She gave another groan, half agony, half pleasure, which hit him in the solar plexus. He knew that touching her would be exquisite torture for both of them. He ought to say right now that treating her was beyond his skill. He ought to walk away. Yet how could he? He wanted to fix people. This was his *calling,* one half of his brain argued. The other half leered. Calling, indeed.

He lifted the glorious weight of her hair and ran his hand down her spine, feeling bone and knots of muscle. Tension riddled her back, but he didn't think it was all from one pulled muscle. While his mind analyzed, he was aware, too, of curves and the soft skin at the top of her neck. He yearned to lean forward and touch it

with his lips. At the same time he wanted to carry her
to her bed and force her to have a good night's sleep.
She looked exhausted. "This whole back needs work.
It would be better if you were sitting for this."

CRESSA DIDN'T PROTEST. She'd really overdone it today
and the ride home had been hell. Adam had her straddle
a seat while he fetched a pillow, which he placed over
the back of the chair. "You should have gotten this seen
to on the set."

"I didn't want to fuss. I'm just a bit stiff. It'll pass."

"You can't afford to seize up."

She was dropping with fatigue, having driven herself
too hard, but how else to escape the vulnerability and
confusion of feelings haunting her? Fragments of the
past had strayed though her memory, fleeting but un-
settling. The ghostly tug of emotions she thought she'd
signed off on years ago returned. Sometimes she found
her hand drifting toward the secret compartment of her
wallet, but she still couldn't bring herself to look at the
photograph she'd kept there for over two years.

Adam's hands began moving across her shoulders,
pinpointing knots of pain and kneading them into surrender. Perhaps he was using her as a way to brush up
on his anatomy. They shouldn't be doing this, though.
How could she maintain her bright detachment when she
could feel herself melting into the pillow? Even without oil, without nakedness, Adam was transporting her
into a world where touch reigned. Those long capable
fingers finding the exact spots of pain and easing them
felt so good. What could they do, she wondered, if their
whole mission was to give her pleasure? A longing far
deeper than any previous arousal settled deep in her
core, and her universe narrowed to where there was

only physical sensation. She was barely aware of Alicia leaving the room; her thoughts focused on his fingers as they learned her body, unlocking its secrets.

And then the phone rang in the living room. Alicia answered. "Oh, hi, Katherine."

Adam swore softly.

A short exchange of pleasantries ensued before Alicia walked in, phone to her ear. "She's right here. Nice talking to you." She passed the phone over.

"Keep it short," Adam ordered. "We haven't finished and you look exhausted."

Cressa laughed. "Short? We're talking Katherine here!"

He growled and pushed her head back down, so her voice came out muffled. "Hey, Katherine, what's up?"

"I've broken up with Dirk," her sister sobbed. "He's been cheating on me, the bastard."

Cressa sat bolt upright and shook off Adam's hands. "Oh, my God." She covered the receiver and mouthed over her shoulder, "Sorry, emergency." He grimaced, but she gave an exaggerated what-can-I-do shrug, so with a shake of his head, he left the room. Cressa leaned back over the pillow, already missing those long, devastating fingers. "Okay, how did you find out?"

PORTIA ARRIVED at Katherine's home in answer to a distraught text message and picked up the extension. Several hours passed as the three of them went over and over what a pig he was and how good that Katherine at last knew the truth. She swung between tears and fury, then watery laughter, as Cressa described various tortures, beginning with keeping Dirk locked up in a room until he'd watched every one of Ingmar Bergman's movies. Dirk was a *Die Hard* man.

Alicia passed, waving good-night, and Cressa finally hung up, having promised to tell Juliet. Katherine couldn't face sharing the news with her elder sister, who'd never trusted him. That conversation took another age, as Juliet had always *known* Dirk was a no good son of a bitch. They raved for a bit, then moved on to Juliet's problems at the office. Cressa was curled up on the sofa, dropping with fatigue, when Adam materialized in front of her, frowning and tapping his watch. His peremptory concern touched her and she nodded, holding up splayed fingers to indicate she'd finish in five. He disappeared and she heard him in the bathroom, cleaning his teeth. He puttered around the house, turning out lights, and returned in front of her. Ten minutes had elapsed, and for the past three, she'd been making unsuccessful attempts to stem her big sister's tirade.

The phone was snatched from her hand. "Juliet? Hey, it's Adam here. How are you…? Great! …Yeah, I gather there's been problems with Katherine. That's too bad." His tone was the perfect pitch of friendliness and brisk sympathy. "But, Juliet, here's the thing. Cressa's had a really tough day and she's got a dawn start tomorrow so she needs to get some sleep. I'm sure you understand…." There was a pause as Adam stood, head cocked. "Yeah… yeah…oh, for sure… Yeah. 'Night, Juliet… Yeah… Juliet, I'm hanging up now. Good night."

He disconnected. Cressa was awed.

"No one's ever hung up on Juliet."

"No? Well, she says good-night. Now, off to bed."

At that moment the phone rang. Cressa snatched it back. "Hello."

"Cressa!" It was Portia, brimming with laughter. "Did Adam just hang up on Juliet? She was so taken aback she was almost lost for words. That's *almost*. She's talking to Katherine about it now, and I don't think she's drawn breath yet."

Adam snatched the phone back. "Who's this? Portia? Get off the damn phone. Cressa's got to get to bed. *¿Comprende?* She'll talk to you tomorrow."

He hung up and glared at Cressa, who was torn between indignation and laughter. "You've got to learn to be tougher."

Indignation won. "They're my *sisters!* But now you've really done it. This'll set them off for another hour."

On cue, the phone rang again and she grabbed it out of his hand. "Desdemona! I guess you've heard all about it. Yeah, I know, it's sweet of him to take care of me." Adam looked so nauseated she couldn't resist. "Yeah, really sweet. I guess it's a Texan thing." She slid her back down the wall to settle in for another long chat.

Adam flung both hands in the air, disappeared down the hall with an oath and banged his bedroom door closed.

Another half hour went by before Cressa finally dragged herself to bed. The irritating thing was Adam was right. She should have been in bed two hours ago. Despite her exhaustion, her vivid, tangled thoughts kept her awake. Her back felt much better, but she moved restlessly, aching for more of Adam's touch. Aching for Adam.

CHAPTER EIGHTEEN

THE FOLLOWING DAY, Cressa stood in the shadows of the trees, watching a scene between Gina, the actress she doubled for, and one of her two warrior lovers. Ellis Powers projected smoldering intensity that would burn up the screen as he declared his undying love and demanded the Valkyrie relinquish the other warrior. Gina's refusal to do so would catapult Ellis into behaving like a demon on the battlefield before being slain. The moment was pivotal because Ellis would then become one of the Undead and haunt Gina forever. He could come to her, but they would never again be able to touch, to kiss, to make love. The Valkyrie would be forever tormented with regret. There was something in this scene that plugged straight into Cressa's heart.

But Gina was off the mark. Cressa couldn't understand it. The role was an actor's dream. Instinctively, Cressa reared her head, eyes narrowing, chest rising as Gina refused to belong to any one man. The speech was searing scorn, yet Gina sounded hollow.

"Cut!" Ed, the director, bounded up to the actors. "Gina, what the hell? You sound like a robot. C'mon, Ellis is acting his pants off and you have all the animation of a mannequin."

Gina pressed a hand to her forehead. "Sorry, Ed. I have such a headache I can hardly think."

Ed sighed but flapped a hand impatiently to an

assistant. "Get some pain meds." He turned back to Gina. "Go rest while we shoot the Messching massacre."

The massacre proved to be one of the most difficult scenes of all and took a very long time to get on film. The choreography was brilliant and Ed was a genius, but he demanded everything from his cast; and he did take after take to capture the vision he held in his mind. Cressa was breathing hard and sweating under the mud and fake blood by the time he was finally happy. Mercifully, her back had held up well—thanks to Adam.

"Corpses, don't move," Ed yelled through the hailer. "We'll do the death scene. Someone get Gina. The light's perfect."

It was late afternoon. The sun, molten orange, squeezed between the heavy dark clouds weighing down the horizon. Shadows were long and black. The carnage of the battle scene in the mud seemed suddenly eerie. A boy ran up, with a don't-shoot-the-messenger expression on his face. "Gina's gone home."

"What?" Ed turned puce. "Why?"

"She's got a migraine."

"Oh, for crissakes!" Ed threw up his hands and beseeched the heavens. "Why, oh why, am I plagued by diva actresses?" His eyes fell on Cressa. "You up for it, Cressa? All you need to do is hunt among the bodies, find Ellis and fall to your knees. You reckon you can do it?"

"Yeah, sure." Cressa handed her water bottle to Sam and was shown the marks she had to hit. Couldn't be simpler. A walk in the park.

Except it wasn't. She heard "Action!" but as she stepped onto the field, something happened to her. She was aware of several extras searching the bodies as she was, but something in the setting sun, the long shadows presaging night, the grimed and bloodied corpses, felt real. She walked to her first mark, bent over a body. Not Ellis. She straightened, scanned the field. Surely he'd be walking toward her any minute, fierce yet euphoric at having survived another battle. Nothing. An out-flung hand caught her eye and she hurried to the corpse. But as she turned the head, using a hank of hair, she saw it wasn't Ellis. Mark winked, and on one level she noted it, but on another, she was under a spell. She dropped the head and leaned back on her haunches, relieved, yet feeling gathering dread. Ellis ought to be looking for the wounded, ought to be rallying the men. That's what he always did. Where the hell was he?

She rose, and her movements became more frantic as she moved from body to body, sometimes noticing at a glance it was not Ellis, sometimes having to squat to check. Over by the trees she saw two bodies locked in death. Dread slowed her as she picked her way through the fallen warriors. Then she stopped, right on her mark. It was Ellis; she was sure of it. Her heart seized. He'd declared his love and she had flung it back in his face. That couldn't be their final conversation. It couldn't be. She took his broad shoulders and, with an effort, rolled his dead body over to look at his face.

The sun was very low now, but there was no mistaking his features, which appeared serene in death. This was the end. There would never be a future for them. Grief and loss such as she'd never felt in her life welled up and engulfed her as she slowly brushed his hair off his forehead. In death he looked perfect. He could have been asleep, but she knew that however much she willed it, she could never ever wake him. Tears spilled down her face as she wrapped her arms around his great barrel chest in a final embrace.

"And cut!"

Her fallen warrior folded his arms around her and copped a feel. "Great stuff, Cressa." Then he squinted. "My God, are those real tears?"

She scrubbed them off with the back of her hand as she struggled into a sitting position, disorientated and lost. She managed to laugh. "Nah. It's something I've always been able to do," she lied.

Ellis sat up, too, cleaning the mud from his hair. "I hope that's that for the day. I need a really long shower." He slanted her his best warrior smolder. "Fancy joining me?"

"Nice invitation, but she can't." Adam was suddenly, miraculously, there, pulling her to her feet. "We've got to get home."

Ellis waggled his eyebrows. "Like that, is it?"

Normally, Cressa would have been able to say something sharp and funny, but a whole part of her was filled with agony. She couldn't transition into this world, and she followed Adam to the trailer.

"What are you doing here?" Everything felt surreal.

He smiled grimly. "I was worried about your back. Worried about you. Decided to come over and check up on you."

"Great work," Ed yelled. Cressa gave an automatic smile.

"Go, girl!" Sam thumped her on the shoulder, but for once Cressa couldn't do the Valkyrie thing. She was grateful when Adam shoved her into the trailer.

"Get your stuff and I'll take you home."

She turned and forgot what she was going to say as her eyes met his. He put his hand to her cheek and with his thumb rubbed away the tear tracks. "Go," he said in a softer voice. "I'm here."

She went straight into the bathroom to splash water on her face. "Get a grip," she muttered. "It's only a stupid movie."

But the haunting sense of loss made her nauseous, and when she looked at her reflection, she understood Adam's concern. Her face was white, her eyes huge and tragic. "He's a *character,* for heaven's sake," she told herself. "Just a character."

She struggled out of her costume and pulled on her jeans, T-shirt, jersey and jacket. Still she felt cold and couldn't stop shivering.

"You decent?" Adam called from outside.

"Yeah."

He stuck his head in the door. "I've locked your bike up in the shed. You'll ride home with me."

She wanted to argue but couldn't find the words, the energy. He jammed on her helmet, did up her chin strap and helped her with her gloves. She followed him to the bike. Maybe she was getting a migraine, too, because nothing felt real. She climbed up behind Adam, and as he switched on the engine and took off, she leaned her helmet against his back, her arms wrapped around him. He felt reassuringly alive and strong.

Closing her eyes, she surrendered to the movement of the bike, grateful for the roar of the motor, which broke through the bubble of silence that had enveloped her. Though she and Adam were both wearing jackets, she could have sworn she felt his heat warming her through her clothes, to her bones, and thawing out her frozen core. And then she found she was crying, racking sobs that reverberated in her helmet.

Adam covered her hand with his. She clung to his

fingers for a second, then let him go. He went back to steering the bike.

Over and over, she saw the dead face, knew that she could never awaken it, and she cried the tears that she'd never allowed herself to shed.

The violence of her reaction shocked her. She couldn't believe she'd so nearly melted down in front of them all. Adam had saved her from humiliation. She pressed harder into his back, grateful that he didn't stop and make a fuss. Gradually, her sobs quietened into shuddering breaths, which finally smoothed into a strange sort of peace. Eyes closed, she relaxed into Adam's strong body, content for once to submit. He would take her home.

CHAPTER NINETEEN

IT WAS SUNDAY and Adam was fed up. He'd already been awake for hours, plugging away at organic chemistry, but progress was slow. What the hell was he trying to prove, anyway? Cressa was right. He was Action Man. Being cooped up in this small room while outside another glorious day beckoned went against every strand of his DNA.

Cressa's door opened. She was awake at last. It was nearly lunchtime, for heaven's sake. But then, she'd only gotten in around 4:00 a.m.

He didn't have to look out to picture her, hair gloriously rumpled, face soft with sleep. She'd be heading to the kitchen in a T-shirt that revealed legs and tantalizing outlines but little else. He heard the kettle being flipped on, and pictured her leaning against the counter, lifting her hair back with both hands, then moving into a full stretch, arching her spine and reaching her arms upward. She'd drop her head toward one shoulder, then the other to ease her neck. After that she'd move to the window to look out. She was always ready for the new day.

Apart from his mom, Sass and Crystal, Adam had never known a woman's early-morning routines so intimately. He'd had lots of girlfriends, but none had ever really gone past that first excitement when staying in bed all day was a way better option than getting up.

He moved over to his own window and gazed out.

The drizzle had lifted and sunlight glinted on the wet grass. Alicia was out there, planting a vegetable garden. She appeared happy, but putting all that energy into a garden that would turn into a building site for a resort in a year's time seemed kind of pointless. It was funny to see her growing into this nature person. Maybe she was where he got his love of the outdoors from, and not good ol' Adahy.

It was strange, but he was getting used to the idea of having a father now. A biological father. Maybe Adahy had had other kids. Maybe Adam had some other half brothers, half sisters somewhere. Much as he hated to admit it, he was getting sort of curious to know more about his old man. It was as though knowing Adahy's name had suddenly made him real, and Adam was slowly coming to terms with that.

The kettle clicked off and he heard the fridge door opening. Cressa was a whole other problem, one he sure as hell wasn't coming to terms with. The really irritating thing was that he and Cressa were playing by *his* rules. Still, no man on earth was created to live under the same roof as a sexy, stubborn woman without having fantasies.

That whole meltdown thing seemed to have released or fixed whatever had been going on with her. Yesterday she'd been back to her bold, teasing self. Not a trace of the weeping woman who'd whisked herself off to have a shower the instant they'd gotten home, and reemerged an hour later in outrageously tight clothes, to go off drinking with the Valkyries. The thought of her letting loose at a nightclub—oh, he so didn't need this crap.

There were ten days left before he headed back to Texas. Time was running out in all sorts of ways. His glance fell to his desk. What madness made him think he would succeed in getting into med school? He'd be better off obeying genetics, scooping Cressa up on his bike and whisking her off to a beautiful cove to see exactly how much substance lay behind all her seductive promises.

He sighed and hauled himself off the wall. No point in going there.

At that moment, he caught the unmistakable throb of a Porsche engine. *Son of a bitch.* Which was unfair. Brian was a great guy. Deirdre had a point; Adam could see where she was coming from now. Cressa had serious shit to sort out, needed a guy who could ground her. Who better than Brian? The doctor probably had his own secret cove planned for today.

But when the passenger door of the Porsche opened, Desdemona spilled out, looking like a curly-haired breed of lion cub. He'd liked her at the wedding; now she rocketed in his estimation. With her around, Brian was hamstrung!

Cressa had obviously heard the car, because she shot out of the house—yup, in that T-shirt—and the sisters bear-hugged, talking and laughing. Adam wondered if Brian was enjoying the spectacle, too. Des's voice carried clearly. "You gotta get dressed, Cressa. Come on, it's an amazing day. Spring is almost here!"

Brian also gave Cressa a hug. Ex-fiancé, father of her baby, he had every right. It was none of Adam's business.

Minutes later there was a rap on his door.

"Adam?" It was Desdemona.

He crossed to the door and feigned surprise. "Hey, Des. Whatcha doing up here?"

Des rose on tiptoe to kiss his cheek. "Hi, it's good to see you." With her honey-brown eyes, tawny hair and

Curtis nose, she looked all the more like a lion cub close up, cute but just a bit dangerous. He bet she caused all sorts of havoc in the jungle. "Brian wanted to go for a drive so I invited myself along. Come and say hi to him."

How could he refuse? Brian and Cressa were chatting in the kitchen. Brian put out his hand. "Hi, Adam, nice to see you again."

Adam shook it. "Likewise."

Didn't matter that both of them were lying.

Cressa appeared surprised. "Did you agree? I told her not to ask."

"Agree to what? I just came out to say hi." He turned to Des. "What's going on?"

She smiled. "I wanted support to help persuade you. We need a fourth for tennis, but Cressa said you're not to be disturbed."

"Sorry, you've picked the wrong man. I've never played in my life."

Brian couldn't keep the surprise off his face, but Desdemona was happy. "Yay! I suck at tennis, so that will even things up. I'll be Brian's partner, and you can be Cressa's. Don't worry, she's really good."

"It would be fun," said Cressa.

"C'mon, Adam, don't abandon me to these two sports freaks," Des beseeched.

Funnily enough, it was Brian who clinched the deal. "Look, if Adam doesn't want to play, we won't force him. The three of us can still play. No problem."

No problem having Cressa to himself all afternoon.

"Actually, a break would be great." Adam's smile had as many teeth as a serrated knife. "I'd enjoy it."

Twenty minutes later, standing in front of the sagging net on a tennis court out in the country, and surrounded by a field of curious cows, Adam realized he should have cut and run while he could. He may have put a temporary spoke into Brian's works, but the good doctor, he was sure, was about to savor exquisite revenge. They'd found an array of old tennis rackets in the garage, but as the rookie, Adam had been given the one with the largest head and only one broken string. He flourished it a few times. Defeat and humiliation were already pulling up ringside seats.

"Nah," said Cressa. "Not like that. You'll send the ball to the moon at that angle. You've watched tennis, I take it."

"I'm more a doer than a spectator, but I know the general principles. See the ball, hit it. Simple."

"Ye-ah. Let me just show you how to hold your wrist."

It was nice having her hand over his, correcting his hold. It was not so nice once they began warming up.

"Yes!" said Cressa, as Adam whacked the ball, all brute strength and no style. "Mind your wrist, though," she added as they watched it soar over the perimeter fence. They all had to pile into the field to search for it.

"Look out for cowpats," Cressa warned at the exact moment Desdemona squealed and began wiping her foot vigorously on the grass.

Adam altered his aim for the next couple of shots, only to discover that the net, though old, held strong. Brian, of course, was superb. His shots all had the thwack of ball hitting the center of the racket. Adam's hits were more like twangs. Bring in a banjo and he'd have his own Appalachian band going. Brian's serves were poetry in motion, but lethal as cannon shot. He was also competitive, for all his modesty and good-sport laughter. Clearly, he wanted to beat Adam as much as Adam wanted to beat him.

Cressa was an excellent player and more competitive than Adam and Brian combined. She laughed, too, but Adam saw fierce determination in her eyes. Power underscored her elegant style and her shots were speedy, accurate and as deadly as Brian's. She and Brian were well matched. Desdemona was his slight consolation. She specialized in high, lollipop hits that were surprisingly tough to return. Their height made it difficult to guess exactly where they'd land, and the soft balls meant that gauging their bounce was challenging. A lot of the time the balls went wide. Plus Des didn't run, leaving Brian to sprint around the court, trying to return shots she'd missed.

"Shall we start the game?" Cressa asked.

"If Adam feels he's ready," Brian said.

"Yeah, sure," he said. *Not.*

Brian—and Desdemona—won first service.

"Watch out for his service. It's a killer," Cressa warned in a muted voice.

Brian's first shot whistled low over the net and nicked nicely into the corner. Cressa was right there and powered it back at Desdemona, who swiped and missed.

"Get it, Brian," she yelled, and he raced across the court, managing to parry it before the second bounce. Adam saw the ball coming and hit with all his strength. Desdemona ducked as the ball shot past her head and into the perimeter fence.

"Fifteen-love," announced Brian.

"Sorry," Adam said.

"Don't apologize," said Cressa.

"That was a good return, Cressa," Brian called.

"Yeah, it's funny being on the receiving end again,"

she shouted back. To Adam she said, "We used to be partners at the tennis club. We played all the time."

Partners. Tennis club. Oh, Lordy. Adam knew he was way out of his league.

He readied himself for Brian's serve, shifting from foot to foot the way Brian did—a panther waiting to pounce. He watched the doctor throw the ball into the air and rise on his toes, arm outstretched. For a second it was a freeze-frame shot, a moment of potential and power and professionalism. Then real time kicked in. Brian punched the sucker with turbo-charge zeal and the ball whizzed so fast Adam heard rather than saw it before it bounced.

"Out!" There was satisfaction in Cressa's voice.

He narrowed his eyes. No way was this doctor going to beat him. He did the shuffling thing with his feet again. It really didn't help. Brian's full weight came down behind his serve and this time Adam managed to get a racket to it. The shock reverberated up the handle and he only just held on to it. His return bounced out.

"Sorry."

"Don't apologize."

Surreptitiously, he shifted his racket to his left hand and flexed his fingers. They were still in spasm. This was going to be a long competition.

He and Cressa lost the first game. They lost the second one, too. They won Desdemona's service because none of her serves went in. Then it was his turn to serve.

He aimed his racket at the far end of the court like a gun. Brian was in his sights, light on his feet and looking as though he'd been born with a racket in his hand. He had it all—job, wealth, looks, car, personality. Adam could taste the old, sour bile of failure and wished he could take Brian into his world. How would he cope up on the girders fifty stories high?

Then suddenly, it was blindingly clear. Brian would never enter his world, while Adam was killing himself to scramble into Brian's. It would always be that way. If Adam got into medical school, he'd always feel inferior to the Brians. But only if he gave them that power.

Adam tossed the ball high in the air, rose on his toes and came down with his full weight behind it. The ball was satisfyingly fast but hopelessly wide. He narrowed his eyes, shifted his sights from Brian to the inside corner, and by some miracle cracked a brilliant serve that caught Brian napping.

"Ye-e-s-s!" Cressa raised both arms in a victory salute.

"Good shot!" said Brian, unable to keep the surprise out of his voice.

"Oh, man," said Desdemona.

From there, things got easier. Adam stopped seeing the racket as an alien thing and began to get the rhythm of playing. The score evened out, two all. Desdemona took more interest, even running sometimes, and, like Adam, made some valiant shots. The magic, however, remained between Cressa and Brian. Adam might be her partner, but Cressa and Brian knew instinctively where the other would place the next ball, moving to the correct position even before the shot was taken. It hurt, almost physically, to watch. Matched in power and grace, they seemed to work together in a choreographed performance. The only faltering came with their partners' haphazard hits. Still, Adam wouldn't quit. Texans never did.

The score crept up: 3-2, 3-3, 3-4, 4-4, 5-4, 5-5. The light by this stage was failing, the sun very low in the sky. Long shadows cast by the trees in the field caused confusion. There was no time for a second set. Everything hinged on the final point.

Brian was serving to Adam, whose senses went on high alert. The evening breeze was cool on his cheek. Part of his brain noted the bird overhead, the cows that had ambled to the fence to watch. Most of his mind, however, was concentrated on Brian. He could feel his opponent's unrelenting desire to win.

Brian hit the ball.

It came so fast Adam barely had time to swipe at it. By some fluke he hit the ball—not elegantly, but it was in and bouncing near Desdemona. The girl gasped and whacked it. The ball rose higher and higher. All four stood, necks craned, to determine its trajectory.

"Mine!" yelled Cressa, running backward.

But she was too slow. The ball bounced and lifted high once more. In vain she leaped and tried to get it, but the ball passed over the racket to land just inside the line.

"Yes!" shouted Desdemona. "Yes. Did you see that, Brian? I won!"

She began doing a victory dance but was swept off her feet by her partner, who enveloped her in a bear hug.

"You were brilliant." Brian gave her a big kiss on the cheek.

"Sorry," said Cressa.

"Don't apologize," said Adam, and he grinned. She looked so annoyed that her little sister had beat her. He nudged her with his shoulder and she smiled reluctantly. Their eyes caught and Cressa burst out laughing. Her laughter was infectious and he joined in, loving the way she could laugh at herself, loving her laughter in the face of defeat. Loving the way her hair fell like a dark waterfall with her head tipped back like that. Loving so that it was an ache and a joy at the same time.

Still laughing, Cressa looked at him again, sharing the joke. But something of his thoughts must have shown on his face, because her laughter died and her eyes darkened, as they'd done the first time he'd met her. He heard her breath catch, and his heart missed a beat.

Brian hurdled the net and ran up, hand outstretched. "Good game." He regarded Adam. "For a first timer, you played remarkably well. Once you get a bit more practice, I'll really have to watch my back."

That was the problem with Brian. Someone as generous and well, yes, as *nice* as him was hard to hate.

Then Brian turned to Cressa, and the expression in his eyes softened. "It was fun to play together again."

Glancing past Brian, Adam saw Desdemona watching her partner and her sister shake hands. Brian and Cressa made a great-looking couple. Des was smiling, but Adam could swear her shoulders slumped a little.

CHAPTER TWENTY

WHEN BRIAN AND DES DROVE away, Adam went back into his room. Even though he'd put on a good old Texan show of friendliness after the game, Cressa had sensed his underlying tension. She felt it herself. Something had sparked on the court, but Adam Bloody Walker was once again pretending it didn't exist. She heard his door click shut, so she took her laptop into the living room and fired it up. She'd been checking emails every day, yet when she saw that finally a message was waiting for her, she hesitated before opening it. This was the first time she'd really cared about whether she got the job or not. Heart tripping, she clicked on it.

The message was brief and to the point. They had liked her application. Would she be available for an interview on Monday?

Would she! Thank heavens she had only the odd scene left to shoot. Tomorrow was clear. She could feel fate billowing in her sails as she wrote to confirm, yes, she could indeed be in Auckland.

She'd just pressed Send when Adam appeared at the door, his expression stormy.

"We have to talk. Now."

He grabbed her by the wrist, hauled her out of her chair and marched down to the beach. Cressa was almost forced to trot to keep up with him. She ought to be fighting him, of course, telling him to unhand her, but her heart was too busy racing in a rather thrilling manner.

When they were at the water's edge, he dropped her wrist and rounded on her. "It's not working."

"What's not?"

"I'm not," he growled. "I sit at my desk, but all I can hear is your voice in my head. I listen for your damn motorbike to pull up in the evening. At night I hear you in bed. It is driving me crazy. *You*—" he pointed accusingly "—are driving me crazy."

She smiled—she couldn't help it. But she tried to sound sympathetic. "Oh, my." She'd done a credible imitation of Alicia. Adam, however, did not seem to be in the mood for clever mimicry. With a growl he backed her against a tree and slammed one hand against the trunk.

"For the last time I want to try to understand. Remind me why you ran out on Brian. I get the bit about the baby, the predictable future, but what about Brian himself?"

The night was clear and cold, the stars bright in the sky. The black waters carried the sheen of the moon. Adam's face, only inches from hers, was angles and planes. His cheeks and slanted eyes were dark hollows, his brow, nose and cheekbones sharply defined.

She struggled to keep her voice natural. "What do you mean?"

"I saw you at tennis today. You guys play well together. You are matched. You can read each other's moves. And he loves you, Cressa. He adores you. Surely, if you wanted to, you could sort things out with him. I want to know what the hell is wrong with him. I bet that's a question he asks himself every night."

She gave her usual answer. "Nothing." But as Adam

continued to glare at her with predatory eyes, she suddenly snapped. "Nothing! It's me, okay. Brian is as perfect as everyone thinks. I love him, I admire him—I really do. He's fantastic, kind, considerate, smart. He's every woman's fantasy."

Adam drew in a breath and stepped away, jamming his hands into his back pockets. "So what *is* your problem?"

Cressa pulled herself up and looked him dead in the eye. "I'm not *in* love with him."

"Oh, jeez." Adam turned away. "Women."

Anger washed over her. How many times did she have to justify her decision to her family, to Adam? To herself. She grabbed him by the arm. "Oh, no, you don't. You don't get to dismiss my feelings like that. You brought me out here. You wanted to know." She jabbed him in the chest with her forefinger. "You'll bloody stay to listen. You think I didn't anguish about it for months, wondering what on earth was wrong with me? I didn't stop our wedding on a whim. I stopped it because I was overwhelmed by the heart-wrenching panic that I was doing the wrong thing. Can't you understand? Haven't you ever thought something was crazy but you did it anyway, even though it defied all rational explanation?"

He stood absolutely still for a second, silhouetted against the harbor waters. A muscle ticked in his jaw.

"Yeah," he said, in a voice broken and husky. "Oh, yeah, I know all about that feeling, and the hell with it!"

He seized her by both arms and crushed his mouth to hers. There was no tenderness, no soft teasing—just need and demand. The suddenness took her by surprise, but Cressa wasn't going to argue, and she opened her mouth in response. He gave a small half laugh, half groan and released her arms to pull her hard against him. She wrapped herself into his embrace and they sank into a kiss that deepened and lengthened till the stars spun and blurred in the sky above them.

Then he eased back. "I've been wanting to do that since the moment we met."

She chuckled. "You may not have noticed, but I've been wanting it, too."

He laughed softly and leaned his forehead against hers. "You've been an awful distraction, Cressa Curtis. Being so close to you day in, day out, has near killed me. These past few days have been a special kind of torture."

"For me, too." She felt light and happy and very lustful as she ran a hand up under his sweater and T-shirt to find the warm flesh of his stomach. He shivered.

"Cold hands?"

"No."

Her palms strayed up his chest, tracing the muscled lines of rib, feeling the thin trail of hairs. Her fingers reached his nipples just as his head dipped to find her mouth again. Then his hands, large and warm, were under her sweater, caressing chilled flesh till her need ran fiery and she gave a small moan.

"It's too cold out here." Adam's voice was hoarse in her ear. "I've waited so long I'm going to enjoy you properly." He grabbed her hand and ran her up to the house. Something in her broke free as he yanked her into Jake's bedroom and tried to unzip her jacket. The zipper caught, Adam swore and she laughed as her fingers wrestled with his to free it. And that's how they undressed, hindering each other as they struggled to help, stripping awkwardly, hopping with boots and socks, her turtleneck getting caught up with her hair so that he had to tug the top off as though she were a child. And all the time they laughed and kissed, and copped feels that only heightened their desire and their clumsiness. Finally, they tumbled into cold sheets, a tangle of limbs and lips, needs and desires.

As Adam began his exploration of her body with mouth and hands, she felt heat, like a lit fuse, streak through her blood, inflaming her senses. He was the oxygen to her fire and she needed him inside her. He entered her, and in a blinding white flash point, they climaxed.

They fell back, panting, slick with sweat. For a second they lay there. Cressa, dazed with the intensity, felt maybe she should say something funny to lighten things. She began to speak, but Adam rolled over and placed a finger to her lips as he began to explore her body again.

He took his time, starting with the palms of her hands. She'd never known how many exquisite nerve endings were there. He made her moan when he licked the inside of her elbow, nuzzled the soft skin behind her ear. Tongue and mouth sought all the delicate trigger points while his hands slowly traced her contours.

Turning to him, she began her own exploration. She traced the scar up his back, the bands of muscle across his belly, the long line of his throat.

She inhaled deeply. It was all pheromones, of course, but somehow he seemed to smell of vast skies and wide prairies.

Time dissolved as they discovered the intimate triggers of pleasure and excitement. With needs building, breath quickening, Adam slipped inside. He thrust deep, then with almost unbearably slow strokes he controlled her urgency until they were moving together in a rhythm that built inexorably, swifter and swifter, to a shattering conclusion.

Spent, Cressa snuggled into him. "I told you we'd be fantastic," she murmured, and fell asleep almost immediately.

ADAM LAY ON HIS BACK with one arm around Cressa, the other tucked behind his head. All his desires and needs were for the moment satiated, and their lovemaking—sex—had been amazing. But now he closed his eyes, listening to her rhythmic breathing. Her compact body, strong and curvy, warmed him down one side. He felt cold down the other.

Haven't you ever thought something was crazy, but you did it anyway, even though it defied all rational explanation?

Oh, God, yes.

Just when he was reaching for his own almost unobtainable goal, he'd allowed base instincts to pull him out of the game. Was she his way of sabotaging himself? The excuse he needed to let himself off the hook?

He glanced down. Her hair spread like a blanket, covering them both. Her small, competent hand lay curled on his chest. Their lovemaking had been even more incredible than his wildest dreams. What harm could there be in just letting rip these last few days?

Except he wanted more. He hadn't told her that. He knew any hint of commitment and she'd be off. Couldn't he just play it her way? The here and now—that was all that was on offer. Which was a crying shame. She was playing in the shallows, when a whole ocean stretched in front of her. Courage came in different shapes and forms. He wondered when she'd realize this.

The thing was, when Cressa finally decided to risk commitment to a man, to a job—to life—she'd be unstoppable. Given her brains, her drive, her personality, she'd be the most amazing woman.

Pity he wouldn't be around to see it.

With a sigh, he tightened his arm around her and couldn't help a smile. Tonight had been extraordinary. Damned if he was going to regret it! He thought back to the tennis game—the power and elegance in her serve, her determination to win. He remembered the times she'd wafted by in just a towel, the lazy, teasing come-on in her green eyes. Her leaps into the churning cauldron. Her gentleness with his mom. He hadn't stood a chance. Hell, he ought to be awarded an endurance medal for having held out against her for so long.

Now he was poised at the top of a roller coaster. The ride would end in a tangled wreck, of course, but for the moment it seemed almost—very nearly, in fact—worth the price he would ultimately have to pay.

CHAPTER TWENTY-ONE

ALICIA WALKED INTO THE kitchen and found Adam assembling eggs and bacon to cook.

"Hey, Mom, pull up a chair. I'll make breakfast for the two of us. Cressa's gone out."

Alicia didn't like big breakfasts, but she'd never turn down an invitation from Adam. "Wonderful. Where did Cressa go? I thought this was her day off."

There was something different about him this morning.

"Auckland. She was very mysterious. Wouldn't say why."

"Ah." They exchanged glances.

"I know," Adam said wryly, "Cressa's surprises are always a little alarming."

He didn't look alarmed, however. Happiness hummed in the air like an electric current. "Adam?"

"Yeah?"

He had such a goofy grin that Alicia burst out laughing. "So that's it. Well, it's been a long time coming."

He cracked the eggs with a flourish worthy of a magician. "Tell me about it! But it was—great." The bacon sizzled as he put the slices into the frying pan. "Really great."

For the first time his careful kindness had been overridden, and Alicia felt a wave of gratitude toward Cressa. Would this be their first real conversation?

"I'm so glad for you, for the two of you. I haven't seen you this happy since the bicycle you got at Christmas when you were eight."

"That was the best Christmas *ever*. And this is even better than that." He grinned and she recognized its mixture of mischief and apology. He'd always smiled like that when he and Cole had been caught misbehaving. "Oops. Probably too much information."

"I can cope."

What she wanted to do was fling her arms around him, share in his joy, but she felt prickling unease. He looked somehow naked in his happiness. Cressa had taken a blowtorch to his defenses and burned them away. It might be the best or cruelest thing she'd ever done in her heedless young life.

So hard to know what to say next. Adam, typical male, focused on the task at hand and didn't notice the silence. Warnings bubbled to Alicia's lips, but she managed to bite them back. He wasn't her baby boy any longer.

"Here you are." He placed two plates on the table and drew up a chair.

The bacon was fried to a crisp and the eggs a bit runny. Really, she needed to teach the boy to cook.

"That's wonderful, thank you."

He tucked in with a hearty appetite.

"So," she said, keeping her tone light, "does this change plans?"

"You know," he said, "I have no idea. I've still got to go back to the States—I've got commitments." He was just a touch too casual as he added, "I'm wondering about inviting Cressa to visit for a bit."

No advice, Alicia reminded herself. "Will she go?"

He stopped eating and gazed at her. "I don't know. What do you think?"

"Is that a genuine question?"

He sounded surprised. "Yeah. Of course."

She beamed at him. "I think this is the first time in your life that you've asked for my opinion."

"I must be growing up or growing senile. So what do you think?"

How much should she say? "I think you could get her there. Getting her to stay, if that's what you're planning, is something quite different."

"I know. It's just…" He looked away. Shadows had left his face this morning. Now they returned.

"Just?"

"Just that she may be the one. You know, the one I want to live the rest of my life with."

Oh, Adam, she wanted to say. *Be careful. Guard your heart.* Until Cressa confronted her past, it would always eat up the present. Surely he wouldn't try to form a bond with another woman incapable of commitment. Adam blamed himself for the failure of his marriage, but Crystal had been a damaged young thing—probably the result of her own family. Oh, what harm parents did to their kids. Alicia had always meant well for her children, but it hadn't been enough.

Adam was watching her. "What do you think?"

In the past she'd have spilled all her fears over him, believing he had to fully understand the danger he was putting himself into.

"Truthfully?"

"Of course."

She lifted her shoulders. "I think you'd be risking your heart, with the odds heavily against you." He opened his mouth as if to argue, but she raised her hand.

"However, seeing as you risk your life day after day on construction sites, I don't see that this will stop you."

He appeared sucker punched. "You know? How?"

She rose and began gathering their empty plates as she said casually, "I saw it on your Facebook page. I checked it after Cressa told me about it. You posted a photograph to show Stella what Houston looked like from up high. There was only one way you could have gotten a shot like that."

Adam opened the dishwasher. "Why didn't you say anything about it?"

He sounded aggrieved, almost accusatory. Taking the wind out of her son's sails was quite fun. "What's to say? It's your life. Now, I must get going."

"Gardening?"

"Yes, later. First, I've got some writing to do."

He paused and glanced up at her. "Writing?"

"Yes, I have a blog."

"Blog?" he said, in much the same dazed, scandalized way he might have said, "Porn site." Oh, it was good fun indeed to blindside him twice in as many minutes. "I had no idea you were so computer savvy."

How very male, she thought fondly, to consider the technical stuff first, the real stuff after. She waited. The query came as an afterthought. "What sort of things do you write on your blog?"

"This and that." She tucked her hair behind her ears. "It began as therapy, something I shared with my loop of recovering alcoholics. They enjoyed my writing so much they encouraged me to set up a blog. I started out keeping a record about the first hundred days of being alcohol-free. Writing about how it felt, how I began coming to terms with what I had been and what I wanted to be. Then, when I got here with Sass, I included bits about my life in Aroha Bay—planting a garden, learning about a new country. I started with only one or two followers, but they grew. When my hundred days were up, people asked for a year. So…" She shrugged and smiled.

Adam leaned back against the kitchen counter, arms crossed over his chest; he looked half amused, half incredulous. "I just can't believe you haven't mentioned it in all this time." His tone turned accusing. "Does Sass know?"

"Of course she knows." Alicia saw his eyes narrow. "We *talk*, Adam. Things get shared when people talk."

"So why did you keep it a secret from me?"

"I didn't as such. You never seemed interested in what I was doing with my time, never asked." She saw that shaft hit home. "Did you assume I spent every minute of the day in the garden?"

"Well, no, I…" He floundered.

"Of course, you have been very busy," she conceded. "What with Cressa and 'stuff.'"

She watched as his eyes flickered away, and her heart filled with misgivings. What had he gotten himself into? In some ways he'd turned into an amazing adult, but he did take the most appalling risks. She hastily blocked images of debts and shady deals. *Dear God, don't let it be gambling, like Terrence*. Determined to keep the conversation light to the end, she patted his cheek as she prepared to leave. "We all have 'stuff,' Adam. However bad it is, I am always here for you."

She left, feeling she had given him quite enough to think about.

ADAM WENT INTO HIS ROOM. He needed to go over some math today, but curiosity won out and he typed Alicia

Walker into Google. Her blog popped up immediately. Steps to Freedom: a recovering alcoholic's diary. He read a few entries. They were good, although he probably shouldn't be so surprised. After all, she was an English teacher. But often they were funny as well, with wry, understated humor running through them. There were also some that talked frankly about the cravings she fought, the times of despair and loneliness. Mostly, however, her writing was filled with the quiet joy of a new life, symbolized by her planting the garden.

She had quite a following, too, and readers' comments were almost always positive: "Your blog gives me hope." "I have started growing a few potted plants in my apartment." There were some negative ones. "It's easy to run away to a new life. What if you were still caught in the routines of your old life?"

She'd answered that honestly. "I don't know. Becoming involved with my children again has made an enormous difference. Without them, life has little meaning for me. What about those of you who are succeeding in turning your lives around without having to literally move to the ends of the earth? Thoughts?"

Suggestions and support had flooded in. Adam liked the way she wasn't trying to be an expert; she just wanted to get people talking. *Things get shared when people talk.* Cressa was a talker. She approached every topic fearlessly—except her baby and her marriage. He might not be a talker, but even he could see something was still wrong there. He didn't like to admit it, but maybe his mother was right; maybe they all needed to talk more.

Movement outside his window caught his eye, and leaning sideways, he saw his mother up on a ladder, struggling to free a tree from some sort of creeper. He watched her snipping, then wrestling with what looked like long, springy ropes all tied up together. Some jerked free; others required more snips, and then she could drop a big knot of creepers down from the branches. She'd run out of any within arm's reach soon, though. They were going to run out of time soon, too. This was as good a time as any, he thought, and went out to help her.

ALICIA WAS SURPRISED to hear Adam's voice. "Hey, Mom, need a hand?"

She batted her hair out of her eyes with the back of her wrist, the gardening gloves rough on her forehead. He was standing below her, looking up. From this angle he was foreshortened and she realized this was the first time in many years that she'd been able to look down on him.

"That would be wonderful. This jasmine is a nightmare. If you can free this tree, I can start on that poor bush over there, though I'm not sure it's going to survive." She descended the ladder and handed Adam the large snippers.

In the beginning, they worked in silence. She heard Adam cuss a few times as he fought some of the fat, snaking ropes. "What did you say this stuff was?"

"Jasmine," she repeated. "Remember I used to keep some in a tub outside by the steps?"

"Oh, yeah, I remember. It smelled nice at night."

"That's the one. Except here it's become this weed that's taken over everything." She gestured to the bushes buried under the weight of the jasmine. "I can't bear to see it smothering all the other plants."

The task seemed symbolic, somehow—freeing bushes that had struggled for light, that were bowed under the weight of this invader. Even the tallest trees weren't safe from the jasmine. It would make a good topic for her blog. She heard Adam give a sigh of satisfaction and another large tangle dropped from the branches above. She wondered what had brought him outside.

"It's good to see you enjoying the sun while it lasts." The weather was always a safe topic.

"Yeah, it's nice to get out." Adam grabbed a branch above his head and swung himself up off the ladder into the tree. "This jasmine is a bitch. The limbs are riddled with it."

"I know. It's amazing to see such a pretty plant become such a darn menace. You can see the poor bushes over there that it's already killed. Still, there's something very cathartic in getting rid of it."

"Another topic for your blog?" Adam asked, teasing.

Startled, she laughed. "Why, yes, that's exactly what I was thinking, as a matter of fact."

He paused and glanced down. "You write well, Mom."

Alicia was surprised at how much his words meant. "Thank you, Adam."

She tugged, another heavy weight of jasmine came away in her hand and she smiled. Some things didn't need words.

They continued to work in silence for a bit.

Freeing the shrubs was one thing, she discovered; trying to dig the jasmine with its wickedly effective root system, out of the ground, was quite another. Which was another nice metaphor—one, she thought, that might help Cressa.

Adam had climbed higher, and it was hard to see him when she looked up. The sun was right in her eyes.

His voice floated down. "Mom, you know the stuff I've been doing?"

The snippers in her hand stilled. "Yes."

"It's study. I'm studying."

"Oh? What for?" She was pleased to hit the right note of casual interest, and began clipping again.

"I'm hoping to get into medical school next year."

"You *what?*" Shocked, she snipped the tip of her garden glove right off and gave a little shriek.

"Mom, are you okay?"

No blood. Whew. She glanced up to see Adam peering at her through a cloud of greenery, his face upside down.

"Fine. Your news caught me off guard, that's all. But Adam, honey, you need a degree first."

He grinned. "Mom, I've got a degree. I've been shut up in my room studying for my MCAT. I'm hoping to get into medical school now."

"Are you serious?" she said slowly. "A doctor?"

"Yes." He added, with all the resolution of a man making a deathbed confession, "Eventually, I plan to be a surgeon."

Then he pulled himself upright, and she heard rustling as he went back to chopping jasmine as though the topic was over and done with. In his dreams!

"Adam Walker. You come down out of that tree this instant."

Any other time, she'd have enjoyed watching him, lithe and athletic, swing through the branches and drop the last ten feet to land lightly on the grass. He smiled again, intending, no doubt, to be placatory, but he was no fool and she saw the way his eyelashes swept down. Another gesture he used to do when she'd caught him at some new piece of mischief.

Waving the pruning shears under his nose, she said, "Would you kindly explain?"

He shrugged. "I've been doing part-time study since I got out of hospital."

"You've been working on a degree all this time?" He smiled again. The smile drove her over the edge. "All these years!" she repeated, her voice rising as anger began smoldering deep inside her. "Do you have any idea what you've been putting me through? I can't believe you did this to me!"

And she punched him on the arm. It was the first time she'd ever raised a hand to one of her children. Fortunately, the pruning shears were in her other hand. Her fist pinged off his biceps.

He reared back. "Whoa, Mom. Physical violence. What the hell? I thought you'd be pleased. Some parents give their kids cars when they graduate."

"*Pleased?* I can't decide whether to hug you or throttle you."

Only a child could tilt your world like this in just a few seconds. She needed a drink.

He held both hands out low, as if calming a rabid dog. "Settle, Mom. Just settle."

"All these years I've been worrying about you becoming more isolated, more secretive. I was terrified you were up to something dreadful, that you'd lost your way. And here you were doing something marvelous. Why on earth has it taken you this long to tell me?"

"I didn't want to worry you."

She cast eyes and hands heavenward. "I'm a parent. Worry is part of the job description. It would be nice to know, however, what it is I should be worrying about. You cannot imagine how wild some of my fears for you have been: Drugs! Gambling! Business deals gone bad.

When all I needed to be worrying about was whether you'd fall to your death every time you went to work or whether you'd fail an assignment."

He had the temerity to grin as he led her over to the garden bench nearby. They sat side by side. "Sorry to disappoint. Cressa had the same feeling of being let down when she heard I wasn't up to nefarious doings."

That hurt. "Cressa knows?"

He rubbed his knuckles with the palm of his other hand, realizing he'd put his foot in it again. "Yeah, I had to tell her. It felt as though things were getting dishonest."

"Didn't it feel that way with me?" Alicia managed not to make the question sound too plaintive.

"I thought, seeing as we don't talk that much—" he gave her another sideways, under-the-lashes glance "—least said and all that."

She was feeling shaky, the craving for a margarita very strong. She ought to be thrilled. She was! But the weight of her failure sat heavy on her shoulders. That Adam might not trust her with bad news was one thing, but to shut her out of good news, too...

"Why?" she asked. "Why couldn't you just say it? Especially over these past few months. It might have helped so much."

"Yeah? I wasn't sure." His forearms rested on his thighs and he stared at his hands, clasped between his knees. "I didn't want to get your hopes up. Didn't want you to be disappointed if I fail."

His reluctance to say the words, his awkwardness, alerted her.

"Did you think I'd crumble, start drinking again if you did?" He stayed silent. "Oh, my God, you *did*."

What little faith he'd had in her. It was her fault that

he didn't. But it was worse than that. Slowly, inexorably, the realization dawned on her. *She* was jasmine. Her love and her fears had been the jasmine in her son's life. Small wonder he'd stayed away these later years. She had smothered him, nearly killed their relationship. The craving for alcohol was very, very strong.

Then she lifted her head, saw the bush she'd been working on. All the jasmine had been ripped off it, and though the plant was misshapen, with some love and judicious pruning it would be fine in a year or two. The miracle of nature was regeneration.

"Oh, Adam." She looped an arm over his strong shoulders. "I'd like to promise that I'm not going to start drinking again, but I don't dare. However, I can promise you that if I do, it will be entirely my own fault and have nothing to do with you. You are not responsible for my actions. Understand?"

He hesitated, but then turned and looked at her, straight at her. "Okay. And understand, if you start again, I'll be there for you again."

"That," she said frankly, "is such an awful prospect that I don't ever intend to slide back. You should be leading your own life, not worrying about mine. Besides, you'll be far too busy studying to worry about any of my dramas."

"If I pass."

"You will."

"You don't know that, Mom." His voice was low.

He was right. Her words had no meaning. So often encouragement was born not out of knowledge or understanding but out of well-meaning ignorance. She had no idea what chance he stood. "It's true," she said.

"I don't. I don't even know if I'll manage to stay off the booze. We can only give things our best shot. That's all one can do in life."

CHAPTER TWENTY-TWO

WHEN CRESSA'S MOTORBIKE pulled up, Adam was at the door to greet her. She leaped into his arms, wrapping her legs around his waist and her hands around his neck. "Adam! It's been the most incredible day."

She felt so good. He kissed her on the nose. "Tell me about it! I've felt amazing all day."

"Oh, yeah. That, too. But wait till you hear. I've got my dream job and it's all thanks to you." She pulled his face close and crushed his mouth under hers.

He stepped back and sat down heavily on one of the chairs, with Cressa in his lap. "A job? That's fantastic." He felt a little dazed. "And because of *me?*"

"Do you remember asking me why I wasn't following my dreams?"

"Sort of. You'd put a lot of whiskey into my drink. It was probably a stupid thing to ask."

"No, it wasn't." She looked earnestly into his face. Today her eyes were more gray than green. "You were right. I did need to be proactive. So I found this job on the 'net."

"The perfect job?" He wondered if his voice sounded as hollow as he felt. "But you didn't say anything about it."

"I didn't want to jinx it. You of all people should understand." She leaned back, fingers laced behind his neck, her voice teasing. "What? You can dish it out, but you can't take it?"

"Yeah, you're right." He tried to sound enthusiastic. "So, tell me about it."

"She's a beautiful old boat—the *Maria Louisa,* ninety feet, three masts, over a hundred-years-old. I've just spent the day on her. She was in that TV series *Pirates* some years back. You didn't see it? It was one of my favorites when I was a teenager. Now she's a charter boat and cruises around the world. This year is the Pacific. Later, they'll probably take her up to the Arctic Circle for the summer. Sailors kill to work on her, but they've given *me* a position as crew. Said I'd fit right in! We set sail on the ninth. Isn't that just amazing?"

The same day as his MCAT.

"That's amazing, all right."

"You should meet the captain. He's a yachting legend. He's done the Whitbread Round the World four times. I'm just going to learn so much, working with him. And it's all because of you! I have you to thank for it! You and Alicia. She also said something that really shot home and made me think."

Thanks, Mom! Way to go.

Cressa squeezed him to death, plastering kisses all over his face. Then she broke off, eyes sparkling.

"Oh, and another surprise."

He struggled not to wince. "Really?"

"Yes, except I don't know what it is, either. I went to visit Mum and she says we have to be down in Auckland on Thursday. She's arranged a birthday treat for me. Crafty old bird checked that I'm not required on set. She says we need smart clothes. I wonder if Alicia would like to go shopping with me. She's been dropping some broad hints about wanting to see me in something more feminine."

"'Smart clothes'?" said Adam. Then, "'We'?"

Cressa grinned. "I told her we're an item, so you'd be coming."

"I'll bet that thrilled her."

"Cut the sarcasm." Cressa leaned forward, and this time gave him a kiss that sped up his heart and slowed time. When she pulled away, he felt light-headed. "She said that was fine."

Adam knew then that Deirdre had sounded less than enthusiastic. He wrapped his arms around Cressa and drew her back in for another kiss, this time sliding his hand up under her top to find warm, firm flesh.

She gave a happy sigh. "I can't wait to show you off."

He loved the weight of her pressed into his hips. Loved the brush of her hair against his hands. Loved her Texas-sage eyes, her kissable mouth, her indomitable nose.

Her indomitable spirit.

Despite having been hit over the head twice with the worst possible news, he couldn't help smiling. "Your birthday, huh? You didn't tell me. I haven't bought you a present."

"Hmm." She tipped her head to one side. "Then you'll just have to be my love slave for a week."

"Hey, it's not my birthday." She laughed and he added casually, "I guess the whole family will be there? Brian, too?"

"Yes, of course. It'll be great to see them all again."

A whole evening with Deirdre *and* Brian.

"You know, it might be best if I didn't come. I don't

want to cause problems." Then, even though it hurt, he added, "It's not like we're a long-term thing."

Cressa pulled his head toward her and kissed him deep and slow, a kiss that burned away all thought—at least for the moment. "Stoopid," she said when they broke off. "If we've only got a short time, then we have to make every moment count."

"I couldn't agree more," he said as he carried her off to the bedroom.

ON THURSDAY NIGHT in Auckland he realized he should have known he wouldn't like any surprise Deirdre had organized. He took another slug of champagne. He needed it to get through the long hours that stretched in front of him. Opera! He looked around the foyer of the Aotea Center. It was jam-packed with excited theatergoers standing in groups, sipping from glasses, laughing, sharing anecdotes about people and places he'd never heard of.

"The Pearl Fishers!" Cressa exclaimed for about the fifteenth time. "I can't believe it! I've always wanted to see it." Adam had never even heard of it. She gave her mother a squeeze. "You are brilliant, Mum."

They made a striking picture, Deirdre in dark green, Cressa in the flame-red sheath she'd bought that morning. Alicia had gone shopping with her and Cressa had returned full of misgivings, saying she'd never worn a dress like it before. When she'd put it on, though, she must have read his thoughts, because she blushed and shut up in the most un-Cressa way. The dress was asymmetrical, with a diamante buckle holding the single shoulder strap up. Adam was looking forward to undoing it. Looking forward to— Ah, no! Get a grip. No such thoughts. Not here. Not in front of her *mother*.

He'd never noticed a resemblance between Deirdre and Cressa, but as they beamed at each other, he saw that Cressa's wide smile, her pouty lower lip, came from Deirdre. The observation was unsettlingly intimate, almost as though he'd kissed this woman who chatted graciously and froze him out so successfully.

Cressa slipped her arm through his and smiled up. "There's this aria that I've loved since I was a kid. I've been dying to see this opera my whole life."

His whole life he'd never dreamed of going to an opera. His smile was stiff, but damned if he was going to spoil this night for Cressa. "Yeah, that's really something." He glanced at Deirdre, feeling her gaze upon him. He wished George, who'd been swept away to another group, would return. He liked the guy, and what's more, George seemed to like him. But then, George liked everyone.

"Cressa!" Desdemona's voice carried over the chatter as she bounded up to wrap her sister in a huge hug. "Happy birthday. Oh, my, is that a dress you're wearing? You look like a *girl*."

Cressa hugged her back. "Is that a dress you're almost wearing?"

Des looked stunning in a shimmering gold number— what there was of it. It was very short and had hardly any back to it, just enough to cover her cute little ass. Deirdre closed her eyes in horror, but the men all around appreciated it. Then Des threw her arms around him. "Adam. I'm so glad you came."

Her delight was genuine, but it seemed out of proportion.

Suddenly, they were all there, the sisters and Juliet's husband, Mike, with lots of greetings and hugs and excited chatter. One big, happy family. Adam stood on the edge, his smile growing more and more fixed. Not that they were excluding him. All the sisters had kissed him, and Mike had shaken his hand with a firm grasp and a friendly face. Everyone asked him about his work on the film, and how his mother was. It was Adam's fault he felt awkward. They couldn't have been nicer. Their very niceness made him feel all the more alienated.

He was relieved when the bell rang and they made their way to their seats. As he entered the theater, though, he realized the night had just gotten a whole lot longer.

It turned out there was a lot to enjoy. The costumes were great and Adam enjoyed looking at the sets, seeing how they worked. The orchestra was cool. The singers were probably good as far as opera singers went. Cressa said they were magnificent. The story was okay, too. But if Cressa had been hoping for a scene out of *Pretty Woman,* he couldn't oblige. Opera didn't speak to his soul. Maybe he didn't have one. The soprano was meant to be dazzling, but when she did her solo, the top notes did bad things to his fillings. Still, it could have been worse. It could have been ballet. And at intermission, he could have another glass of champagne.

Intermission, however, proved even more painful. As they came back into the foyer, Brian pounced. "Cressa, happy birthday."

He pressed a small box into her hand. She opened it and exclaimed, "Oh, Brian, it's beautiful."

It was a pendant made out of some green stone.

"Look, Adam." She held it up for him to see. "It's made from pounamu. This is a koru."

"It symbolizes new beginnings," said Brian. "Peace and harmony." He smiled at her. "I got Wirimu to carve it especially for you."

Her eyes filled with tears. "Wirimu? Oh, Brian, you know how much I've always wanted one of his. Thank you." Putting her hand on his arm, she leaned up to kiss his cheek. She had the casual intimacy of a woman treating a man's body as an extension of her own, and Adam took another swig of champagne.

"My pleasure," said Brian, looking into her eyes. He knew the secrets of Cressa's body far better than Adam did.

"Hey, Brian," said Desdemona, "your tie's crooked."

She moved forward to straighten it, and the moment was broken just as their party was engulfed. It turned out Auckland wasn't a city—it was a village. And every person in the whole theater seemed to know Cressa. She was besieged on all sides, laughing, exclaiming, answering a million questions of "Where have you been?" and "Why haven't we seen you around for so long?"

Of course she introduced Adam to everyone and kept her arm entwined through his, but his face grew sore with grinning. He felt more like an accessory than a person. Brian was a couple of paces away, but somehow he was far more Cressa's escort than Adam was. Brian knew everyone, too, and chatted easily.

"Yeah, the skiing at Cadrona was fantastic, wasn't it, but you know, I'm a Treble Cone man. We had one day—powder snow, clear skies. It was fantastic.... This summer? Thought I'd take the yacht up to the Bay of Islands. Maybe go north from there to Whangaroa... Oh, the Evanses, as well? Excellent. We can all meet up."

People and places Adam had never heard of, sports he'd never tried. This was so not his world. And there in the center of it was Cressa, vibrant and burning like a flame amid the black suits and dark colors of the women's dresses. Perfectly at home, yet distinctly her own person. Adam felt foreign—no, alien. This was so not his place, not his people. They were all doctors and lawyers and business moguls. He was just a dropout who had a dream of becoming one of them.

He took another mouthful of champagne and tried to view them objectively. These were the grown-up version of the kids at school he'd openly derided and secretly feared. The geeks made good. Boys who couldn't hit a baseball to save themselves now ran companies that employed the guys who'd hit home runs. Girls whose eyes used to follow him down school corridors now checked him out with friendly but detached appraisal.

Who the hell did he think he was to even contemplate trying to join this elite set? What if everything did work out as planned and he did succeed? Then what? Would he have to learn to talk about opera and skiing and sailing? He was a kid from a trailer park, for crissakes. No, that wasn't quite fair. Mom would fit right in here. She'd grown up in this sort of world. She'd only left because of Dad. His debts had condemned her to a life outside the one she'd always known.

Adam sipped his champagne and watched Deirdre laughing with some other women. Mom ought to have friends like that.

No wonder Deirdre didn't like him. She thought he could do to Cressa what his dad had done to his mom. Of course, Adam was nothing like him, wasn't even his son. But if he failed, what then? What the hell would he have to offer someone like Cressa? Steelworkers didn't belong here.

He looked over at Brian. He'd have hit home runs *and* topped his exams. Someone made a comment, and Brian and Cressa laughed at exactly the same moment, then exchanged glances that shouted of a thousand nights together, a history long and deep.

Feeling eyes on him, Adam turned and caught Deirdre contemplating him. Her gaze locked with his. It was as if she'd read his thoughts as he'd watched Cressa and Brian. *They belong,* her expression seemed to say, *and you don't.* There was no malice in her face. Facts were just facts. She gave a slight nod before turning when a woman at her elbow greeted her.

Adam looked away and saw Desdemona leaning against a pillar, arms folded against her chest, champagne glass in her hand. Her expression was stormy; her animation had vanished. She was watching Cressa and Brian. It wasn't surprising. They were the most charismatic couple in the room.

Adam crossed over to stand next to Des. "It's a bitch, isn't it?"

She glanced up at him, her honey-brown eyes wide. "You know?"

"Yeah, it's fairly obvious."

"Is it?" She thought about it. "I guess. But my family doesn't see it."

"No, they've still got their own story in their heads."

She bit her lip, then gave a defiant toss of her tawny curls. "I'm not too young!"

Adam looked down. She was every man's fantasy, with her plunging neckline, clinging gold dress, wild hair, inviting lips. Didn't Brian realize it was all a bid for his attention? "No, you're not. But…" Adam paused. "You're still the kid sister."

"In some ways I'm older than Cressa," she argued. "I've always known what I wanted."

He smiled ruefully. "Then you're lucky. I'm only just beginning to know what I want."

His gaze strayed back to Cressa. Des sipped her champagne, eyes now mischievous over the brim of her glass. She was incredibly dangerous without fully realizing it. "I'm so pleased you guys are together."

"For now. It won't help you much, though. I'm going to be gone soon and Cressa will be sailing off into the sunset."

Des tilted her head and looked at him. "That's a shame. I think you are the best bloke for her, and that's not just because of Brian. They were all wrong. I can't believe I'm the only one who can see that."

"What makes you think that? They look pretty good together from here." He hadn't meant to sound so sour.

Des glanced over and winced as Brian touched Cressa on her arm to point someone out. Still, Des sounded very definite when she added, "They're too similar and too different."

"Oh, right. Whereas Cressa and I...?"

Des appeared exasperated and said, as though it were patently obvious, "Are completely different and exactly the same."

Adam gave her a slight bow and exaggerated his drawl. "Well, thank you, Miss Desdemona, for that lucid explanation. I can't think how it escaped me before."

They both laughed and Adam saw Brian glance in their direction. For a second he could have sworn he saw irritation on that good-natured face.

"Don't give up," he said to Des. "Brian is more interested in you than he might realize."

"Really?" The hope in her face touched him. Her next words touched him more. "Thanks, Adam. You're the first person who's ever understood. I feel like I've finally got someone on my side."

Strangely, he felt the same. She grabbed his arm and tugged. "Come on, we'd better get back to the family."

As they joined the group, the Curtises all smiled and Juliet made space for him. "Hey, Adam, Cressa was just telling us about you on the mast. I wish I'd been there to see it."

"Did she also tell you I threw up?"

"Yeah, we heard all about that, too," Katherine said. "I know exactly how you felt. When the boat is in that greasy, slow roll…" She shuddered. "Such a pity you aren't staying. Then there'd be two of us begging for shore in those conditions."

The conversation roared on, as it did with the Curtises, leaving Adam to muse that if circumstances had been different, if he hadn't had to return to Texas, if Cressa hadn't been about to sail away, he could have found a place in this exuberant family. He was surprised by the depth of his regret.

CHAPTER TWENTY-THREE

THE FAMILY GATHERING after the opera was chaotic and wonderful. Cressa propped a shoulder against the doorjamb of the living room, watching everyone. Dad was deep in conversation with Mike. Brian was helping Deirdre with drinks. Juliet and Katherine had Adam buttonholed, and were no doubt giving him the third degree. Cressa wondered if she should rescue him, but he looked to be doing fine.

He'd taken off his jacket and tie. Tonight he could have been either an Italian count or a South American bandit, with his combination of dark looks, innate lean elegance and edge of danger. She'd worried about him at the opera—he'd retreated behind his defensive walls. Now he'd reemerged and seemed to be enjoying himself. He said something, and both Katherine and Juliet laughed.

"He's a keeper." Des's voice behind her made her jump.

Cross at being caught ogling her date, Cressa replied, "Don't be ridiculous. He goes back to the States in a few days."

"That's too bad." Des leaned against the wall.

"You seemed to be getting on well together at the opera." Cressa heard an edge in her voice, but Des, who was usually quick to know when she'd annoyed her sisters, surprisingly didn't appear to notice. Instead, she just smiled.

"Yeah, it's impossible not to fall for Adam, isn't it? When he turns those dark eyes on you..." She gave a theatrical little shiver, and even though Des was kidding, Cressa felt a spark of possessiveness.

"What were you talking about?"

Des shrugged. "Nothing special."

Was she avoiding the question? Cressa took one look at her sister's artless expression and knew that she was, but before she could pursue the matter, Portia said, "Budge out of the way. Cake coming through."

They both moved from the doorway, and Portia carried a huge chocolate cake alight with candles to the coffee table. Dad got everyone singing "Happy Birthday," and Cressa had tears in her eyes when they finished.

"Oh, you shouldn't have. But I'm glad you did."

Laughter followed and Dad raised his glass. "To Cressa and her wonderful new job. May it lead her on many adventures."

Everyone said, "Hear, hear," and drank to her.

"Thanks, Dad. Thanks all of you." Tears brimmed. "I love you all. You're the world to me." She raised her own glass to them. "Here's to the best of parents and sisters and brother-in-law and friends. I'm going to miss you all so much." With a pang, she realized how true this was. Her family was the weft in the fabric of her life. Of course, once she set sail, the people on the boat would become a new sort of family, even though the turnover in crews could be high, she'd heard.

Her eyes sought Adam. He was there in the background, the formal attire accentuating his height and not disguising the strength of his shoulders. The smile he sent her across the room and the dark look in his eyes were so intimate that despite her lovely family, she suddenly wanted nothing more than to drag him upstairs to her old room. To where she and Brian used to stay.

She glanced at her ex-fiancé. He must have witnessed this exchange, because although he smiled at her, the smile had that twist she knew so well. Oh, she so didn't want to hurt him. Didn't want the burden of his love. Then that moment was over and the world began moving again. Deirdre pressed a knife into her hand. "Make a wish. Though of course your dream has already come true with this job of yours."

Her mother didn't sound hugely thrilled about the job, but then, she never approved of Cressa's choices. Still, it was nice of her to have baked a cake.

Cressa said, "Oh, Mum, I'm too old for that." But as she poised the knife over the heart of the cake, a wish flared unexpected and urgent. *Make me know what truly I want.*

There was laughter and chatter as everyone crowded in to get a piece of cake. Adam insisted Deirdre take a piece before he did, and Cressa was relieved to see Des cross over to Brian and say something that made him laugh. Those two had always shared a special bond. Brian used to say that if he could pick any kid sister in the world, it would be Des. Dad cornered Adam in conversation just as Juliet said to her, "I can see why you like him. He's gorgeous."

Cressa put on a lascivious smile. "Yeah, he's hot!"

Juliet nodded. "I'll say. Oops, better not let Mike hear me." More seriously she added, "That wasn't what I meant, though. I mean, he's actually really nice." There was a note of surprise in her voice.

Katherine joined them. "I know—you don't expect such a great-looking guy to be so sweet."

The sisters always muscled in on one another's conversations. "Sweet?" Juliet wrinkled her nose. "He's too macho for sweet, but he's…" she paused, head to one side "…considerate, interested. And that accent." Juliet sighed. "Like rich chocolate sauce poured slowly over ice cream."

"Hey, he's *my* boyfriend—keep your mitts off. Though it does give me a few ideas…." They dissolved into peals of laughter.

"Oh, man, don't put images into my head," said Katherine. "I haven't had any fun since Dirk the Jerk."

"Tell me about it. Mike's night calls at the hospital are beyond a joke." Juliet sounded rueful. "But seriously, Cressa, Adam's fabulous."

"Yeah, we really enjoyed getting to know him."

"So did Des." There it was again. That edge. Surely Cressa wasn't jealous of her own sister. She added quickly, "It's a Walker thing. Alicia has it, too—Southern charm."

"It's more than charm, though—that's the point," said Katherine. "Adam really makes you feel he's listening. He'd make a great lawyer."

"Or doctor," said Juliet. "Wonderful bedside manner. Yeah, he's really fab, Cressa. Too bad you guys have to separate just when you've gotten together."

Cressa gazed at Adam and her dad as they chattered away. It really was too bad. Impulsively, she found herself saying, "You know, it's weird, but I'm really sorry he's leaving. I'm even kinda sorry this job came up when it did. I'd have liked to know him better."

Katherine eyed her. "Wow, that's quite a change for

you. Since Brian, you've become an aficionado of the short-term relationship."

"It's probably because you aren't able to control this relationship the way you usually do," Juliet offered.

"What do you mean? I'm not a control freak!"

Her sisters exchanged looks and snorted with laughter.

"No insight," said Juliet.

"None," Katherine agreed.

"Stop cackling and explain."

"Cressa, you've been in the driver's seat with every relationship."

"Even with Brian," Juliet interjected.

"But you both love Brian and think we should get back together," Cressa stated.

Her sisters exchanged looks again.

"We used to," said Juliet. "I mean, you can't find a better man than Brian."

"But after talking to Adam," Katherine added, "we can see you guys might be more suited."

Cressa shook her head. "Ten minutes' chat and he has you both eating out his hand. How easy can you get?"

"Us easy? We've been watching you making googly eyes at him all evening. You've got it bad, Cressa."

"Got what bad?" she demanded.

"Lo-o-o-ve," Juliet drew out the word. "You are head over heels, girl."

"Rubbish!" She saw them eye one another knowingly. "I'm so not. Not at all, so you can wipe those smirks off your faces."

"Methinks she doth protest too much," said Juliet.

"Methinks, too," Katherine agreed, and they went into such paroxysms of laughter that Cressa left them for more sensible, less-annoying company.

ADAM FOUND DES in a corner, ostensibly choosing a CD but in truth looking glum. She'd already knocked a couple of glasses of wine back way too fast, he'd noticed.

"Brooding's not going to help."

"I know, but look at him." She gestured to where Brian and Cressa were chatting. "He's still besotted."

"I've been thinking, and you wanna know what?"

Des was wary. "I'm not sure. Will it hurt?"

"Only if you don't take my advice."

She heaved a huge sigh. "Go on, then."

"You should tell him."

Des choked on the wine she was sipping. "'Scuse me?"

He patted her back. "You heard me. Tell him."

"Yeah, right. I sidle up to Brian and tell him I love him. That I always have. Just like that."

"Why not? Doesn't seem your current game plan is working. What is it, by the way?"

She drew herself up. "I'm making myself indispensable." Her slight slurring undercut her dignity.

"Yeah—as a younger sister." She winced and Adam nodded. "You've got to shock him out of his role of big brother."

"By telling him I love him. Simple as that."

Adam ignored her sarcasm. "Any man would be bowled over to have a gorgeous woman declaring her love."

"You think I'm gorgeous?" She batted her eyelashes at him.

"You know you are, but you can forget using your cute tricks on me. I don't chase women whose hearts are already given to someone else."

She smiled. "Flatterer. But seriously, Adam, your plan sucks. He'll just laugh at me."

Putting his hands on her shoulders, Adam leaned down to peer into her eyes. "He won't. Trust me."

"What if I shock him? It might ruin everything between us."

"What if everything between you remains the same forever?"

He could see that remark shot home.

"But what will I say?"

He smiled. "I may be going out on a limb here, Des, but I'd be surprised if there have been many opportunities where you've been at a loss for words."

"True." Her eyes followed Brian. "You'll think I'm being stupid, but I feel scared."

"I'm scared often," he assured her.

Des snorted. "Cressa told us what your job really is. You must have nerves of steel." She looked at him, saw his expression and said, "You're serious. Go on, then. Tell me what scares you."

"The idea of asking your sister to come to Texas with me for a few weeks."

"Really? Are you considering it?" Des's face lit up. "That's so cool. Oh, Adam, you definitely have to ask her. You guys are so right together. I'm sure she'll say yes. Is that all you're frightened about?"

He hesitated. He wasn't used to confidences, but he wanted to win Des's trust. "Just between you and me?"

"Of course."

"I am scared that if she comes, I won't ever want to let her go."

"Oh." Des eyed Cressa thoughtfully. "That is a

problem, especially with the job. She doesn't like to commit, you know."

"Yeah, tell me about it. Still, I think you and I both have to take the risk."

"Really?" Des drained her glass as she pondered his words. "Okay. I will if you will." He smiled at the resolve in her voice, the way she straightened her shoulders. "We'll risk our hearts together."

It was almost like having a kid sister of his own. "You betcha."

"Then I'm going to do it now, before I can wimp out." She handed him her glass and cricked her neck right and left, then wriggled her shoulders the way he'd seen actors do before a scene.

She took a step, faltered and turned back to him. He smiled encouragingly. "Go on. Good luck."

"Will you stay here and watch?" Des asked. "If it looks like it's going badly, you've got to come and rescue me."

He laughed. "How?"

"I don't know. Start a fire or something. I don't care how you do it. Please, Adam."

He couldn't resist her entreaty. "Sure. I'm right here. I've got your back. Go get him!"

He propped a shoulder against the wall, watching as Des went over to Brian, touched his hand and gestured to the deck outside. Bemused, Brian followed.

"What are you doing?" Cressa slipped an arm around Adam's waist. "Are you checking out my little sister?"

He wrapped his arm around her waist and pulled her close. "I'm here as moral support."

Cressa was intrigued. "What's she up to?"

The deck was lit only by the light from inside the living room. Des shimmered in the darkness, but Brian, dressed in a black suit, was only silhouetted. However, his face happened to fall in a shaft of light, making him look strangely defenseless.

"I hope you won't mind. Watch. I'm pretty sure she's going to get what she wants," Adam murmured.

Des was talking to Brian. He laughed. She took him by his arm, speaking more intently.

"Des usually does. What does she— Oh, you are kidding me." Cressa was incredulous. "She wants *Brian?*"

"That's right. She's been in love with him for years."

Cressa gazed at him. "Oh, we all knew about her puppy love when she was thirteen, but surely she's over it by now."

"She stopped being a puppy a while back and her feelings became something quite different."

Brian had stopped laughing and stepped back, as wary as if Des had a bomb strapped to her.

"Are you serious?" Cressa asked in disbelief. "Is this serious?"

"Yes, it really is. Do you mind?"

"No! I'd be thrilled. I would love someone to have Brian's heart, and he and Des have always had a really close relationship."

Des stepped up to Brian and stretched to kiss him on the lips. Brian reared back. As if calming a spooked horse, she put her hand on his cheek, helpfully guiding his face down to hers. Then she wrapped her arms around his neck. Brian's back was to them, but they saw her small thumbs-up, then the flick of her hand to shoo them away.

Adam laughed. "It looks like she can take it from here." He turned so Cressa was in the circle of his arms.

"But how did you know?" she asked. "I can't believe

it's been under our noses all this time and none of us saw it. Not even Juliet, and she prides herself on knowing everything."

"It's sometimes easier for an outsider to see these things."

Cressa laughed. "If you've just played Cupid for Des and Brian, you'll never qualify as an outsider in the Curtis family ever again. Ma will be delighted to make Brian an official member of the family."

Adam cupped Cressa's neck, stroking the fine skin behind her ear. "They're a long way from that. Brian's got a lot of reversing to do first, but hey, at least he's realizing he needs to change track."

Cressa shook her head. "For the son of an English teacher, that's one convoluted metaphor. But—" she glanced back toward the deck "—you did something good tonight, Texas."

Adam's thoughts, however, had shifted to more pressing concerns. Des had upheld her end of their deal. Now he had to pick the right time to follow through with his.

LATER, IN BED, Cressa snuggled into Adam's body, exhausted after glorious but don't-let-the-parents-hear giggly sex.

"All in all, a very good night for everyone. You survived my family well."

She heard the smile in his voice. "I didn't survive them. I love them. They're great people. A roomful of women with incredible noses."

She jabbed him in the stomach. Wow, he had amazing muscles. "No quips about the nose, got it?"

"I love the nose," he protested, running a finger down it. "It saves you all from being merely pretty."

She snorted. "And moves us into pretty awful."

He pressed his finger to her lips. "Stop fishing. You are all beautiful in your very different ways."

"Nah, Des is the only one who's really lovely."

"She's a stunner, but I've never been into blondes. Growing up as the dark kid in a blond family puts you off."

His other hand moved to stroke Cressa's hair, from the crown of her head down to the curve of her hip. She could feel the warm strength of his hand and nestled in even closer. If she could, she'd dissolve into his skin, she wanted him so much.

"I saw Katherine and Juliet interrogate you, but you seemed to win them around."

"Yeah, we had a good chat."

"What did you talk about?"

He shrugged. "Lots. How difficult Juliet finds having Mike work so hard. Whether they should start having kids. The biological clock versus career. Katherine, of course, is still pretty cut up over her ex."

"They're right." Cressa pressed her palm on his chest and shoved herself upright to peer at his face. The glow from the alarm clock gave her enough light to see his quizzical expression.

"Right about what?"

"The key to your charm."

"My charm?"

She just loved the way that word rolled warm and sweet and long from his lips. She loved even more his bewilderment. "You listen. You get people to talk about themselves and you actually pay attention."

"What's the big deal? People are interesting."

Was this love? Surely not. Juliet was wrong, but how else to define this overwhelming mushiness Cressa felt for Adam right at this moment? She leaned down and dropped a kiss on his nipple. She loved hearing his quick intake of air, too. "Most people like to talk about themselves. You honestly prefer talking about other people."

"But I know me, so that's boring." His tone was very reasonable.

She kissed his other nipple. "You have no idea how different that makes you. You get it from Alicia. When she talks to people, they have her complete, undivided attention. It's incredibly flattering and self-affirming."

"Your mom listens to you."

Cressa laughed. "Believe me, in a family of five girls and one actor, no one gets undivided attention. We constantly vie for it. That's why Katherine and Juliet play the perfect daughters and Des is such a drama queen. Portia escapes it all by slipping away under everyone's radar."

Adam shifted his head on the pillow to view Cressa more squarely. "And you?"

"What about me?"

"Don't be obtuse. Come on, confess."

"What?" Mystified, she propped her chin on his chest to look at him. He squinted down his nose. "You get it by indulging in unsuitable, short-term relationships, which culminated tonight in you bringing home your mother's worst nightmare."

"That's so wrong. It's not like that at all!"

"No?"

He clearly didn't believe her, but because they were only having a fling, she couldn't say she'd brought him home because she'd wanted to, because he was different.

Besides, Adam had clearly gotten bored with talking,

because his hand came up, wrapped itself in her hair to pull her head down into another of his deep, amazing kisses. Just as she was surrendering, she remembered what Juliet had said: "You are head-over-heels, girl."

I'm not, she thought. *I'm not at all.*

CHAPTER TWENTY-FOUR

FRESH FROM A SHOWER, Alicia wandered naked from the tiny bathroom in the sleep-out over to the bed where her clothes lay. The angle of the early morning sun was such that she glimpsed her faint reflection in the sliding door and she stopped short to see more closely.

She had not looked at herself naked and full-length in a mirror for some years. Shame at the flabbiness of a once-trim figure, shame at the aging of a once-young body, shame at all the self-abuse, had prevented her. Now Alicia examined her wavering self with a not-unfriendly eye. Her body was gaining tone again. Of course, it would never be the same as twenty years earlier, but it was certainly an improvement on this time last year. Her long walks and hours in the garden were paying off. As, no doubt, she thought wryly, were her nights of abstinence. Gravity was certainly having its way, but, she thought, hands on hips, not bad at all for fifty-one.

For a fleeting second she had a recollection of sex, hot bodies twined in the sheets.

With a shake of her head, she turned briskly to the bed and began pulling on her clothes—jeans that were now too loose, and a T-shirt, followed by a shapeless sweatshirt. Men her age were interested in women at least ten-, if not fifteen-, years younger. Besides, she'd learned long ago that she was a complete disaster when it came to relationships. If anything sent her straight back to the margaritas, it would be a close encounter of the male kind. She was so much better off without *that* to complicate her life.

She did miss sex, though. More so since she'd given up drinking. But now, she told herself, at least she had gardening and her blog. Not great, but a good start for a future she was reclaiming with every day she remained alcohol-free.

The air was cold as she stepped outside and into her waiting gum boots. The morning was gray and misty, the grass wet, the harbor waters a sheath of beaten silver below the gray clouds. Alicia glanced over to the house and saw through the French doors the far gleam of the kitchen light. Adam was up. He'd be gone in a few days, returning all too soon to Texas. These past few days since their revelations had been so good, had set them on a new path and it hurt to think that he had to leave just as they'd reestablished their relationship. Letting go was never easy for a mother.

She went into the garage for the spade and then walked over to the magnificent magnolia behind her sleep-out, planning to dig a flower bed around it. Who had planted this lovely tree? she wondered, as she blew on her fingers and rubbed her hands together to get the blood going. What generosity of spirit to plant a tree one might never see in its full glory.

"Whatcha up to?"

Alicia spun around. "Cressa! What are you doing up this early?"

Cressa grinned. "I know! It's obscene. But after Adam got up, I couldn't go back to sleep. I saw you from the window and thought I'd give you a hand."

"I'd be delighted."

She looked so vital, even as she yawned and stretched, her tight black sweatshirt riding up to show a flash of flat stomach. Cressa was filled with that energized well-being Alicia could vaguely remember from years ago. Sex. Lots of good sex. She hadn't tied her hair up and it fell like a cloak, oddly medieval in contrast to the combat trousers and boots.

"What's the plan?"

"I want a flower bed around the tree, so help with digging would be wonderful. The ground is horribly soggy and heavy."

"Right-o. I'll get another spade."

Cressa strode off to the garage. Though she'd just tumbled from bed, she was already filled with purpose. Such a strange mixture. She dressed like a warrior, was direct and decided in manner, yet underneath she was all at sea without compass or direction. She did a good job of bluffing, though. As someone who'd bluffed her way for years, Alicia could spot a fellow pro.

She was glad of the company, however. They dug together, spades biting into the grass to reveal the black clay below.

"How big do you want it?"

Alicia pursed her lips. "Probably out to about here. What do you think?"

Cressa brushed a strand of hair off her face with the back of her wrist and smiled. "That you're mad. They're going to bulldoze this whole place."

"I know." Alicia looked around at the garden, spangled by the night's rain. "That's why we should enjoy it until then. See those daffodils? They'll be gone in a few weeks, but for now they enrich our lives. As you get older, you know that everything passes eventually."

"Yeah?" Cressa dug her spade in and stamped hard

on it. With a grunt she lifted the load and flicked it sideways. "Well, I prefer things transitory."

"Why?" Alicia threw her spadeful onto the pile. Yes, she definitely was getting stronger.

Cressa shrugged, her eyes the same misty green as the hills across the harbor. "I guess I just thrive on change."

Change was the last thing Adam needed. Alicia's boy needed roots and the love of a steady woman. He'd drifted long enough, between short-term jobs and relationships. Surely he could see that.

Cressa stamped on her spade again, her hair billowing about her, and Alicia felt a shiver of apprehension. This casual young woman was going to break his heart. Yet for all her misgivings, Alicia couldn't rid herself of the feeling that with some truth and honesty, those two could make their way through to something very special. Time was running short, though.

"Why did you look for a sailing job right now, Cressa? Did you have the need for a way out?"

"Way out? What are you talking about? I got this job, Alicia, because you guys said I should follow my dreams." There was a sarcastic tinge to her tone.

The old Alicia would have apologized and accepted the answer. This new Alicia, with strong biceps, leaned on the spade and eyed the young woman. "Are you sure? Is the sailing job really following your dreams?"

Cressa threw another huge clod aside and stabbed her spade back into the earth. "Of course. What makes you think it mightn't be?"

Not a question, but a challenge. Alicia turned back to her own digging, keeping her voice light. "As a recovering alcoholic, I'm an expert on people's avoidance tactics."

She saw the quick sidelong glance. There was a pause, then Cressa asked, "So what were you running away from?"

Alicia pursed her lips. "At first I was escaping a bad marriage and impending bankruptcy." She smiled grimly. "That was in the good years. I drank to forget the past and to cope with the present. Later I drank to drown the realization that my life was the result of my poor decisions, which led to self-recrimination and, finally, self-hatred."

Cressa had stopped working and was looking at her with a mixture of awe and pity. "Wow."

Alicia gave a small smile. "Yes, wow."

Cressa rubbed her hands over the seat of her pants, twisted her hair into a heavy knot at her nape, then began digging again. "So were you, like, you know, a fall-down drunk?"

"No, I could do my job fine until last year. I never passed out in my food or danced drunk on the tables." She halted. "Alcohol just eroded me from the inside out."

"Homer Simpson once said—" and Cressa put on a deep Homer voice "'—ah, alcohol. The answer to, and cause of, all life's problems.'"

Alicia laughed. "That's so true. I learned all about the paradoxes of alcohol in rehab."

"Paradoxes?"

"Things like the fact women often drink to lose sexual inhibitions, but alcohol robs them of sexual desire. People drink to forget their worries, but alcohol becomes a worry in itself. You drink to be sociable, then lose friends because you drink…."

"So which camp did you fall into?"

Alicia struggled with one particularly irksome clod.

"I drank because I felt my life was going nowhere, and the booze robbed me of the drive to get somewhere else. I functioned just fine at that level." She added softly, "It just wasn't the level I wanted to be on."

"Didn't you like your job?"

"I loved it. But I stayed in the same place too long."

She straightened and put her hands at the small of her back, arching to release muscles. "So, that's my story. What about you?"

She envied the smooth, powerful energy of her companion, who could keep digging without flagging.

"I told you, I'm not escaping, I'm going *to* something, Alicia. I love traveling, meeting new people, trying out new things. Sailing will give me all that, with stunning locations thrown in, too."

"Sounds fun, but is it sustainable?"

"You betcha it's fun." Irritation was plain in Cressa's voice. "It's exactly what I want. As for sustainable, I have no idea about things long-term, but I'm sure as heck not going to land up locked in some job year after year, living in the same crappy home—" She stopped short. "Sorry, that sounded rude. I didn't mean it like that."

Alicia smiled, but the gloves were off. "I know you didn't, and I'm delighted you don't want to compromise as I did. However—" her tone became more pointed "—there are many roads other than the one I've followed and the wedding you fled. Your mother, for example, has done very well."

"Mum?" Cressa was surprised. "Hardly! Her life is exactly the sort I want to avoid. Same office, same house, same everything as far back as I can remember. Dad, now, has had the really interesting life, following his passion."

"Actually, your mother has achieved a lot. As principal, she faces new challenges every year, and every day is different. How can it not be with twelve hundred girls and nearly a hundred staff under her care? In addition, she's been a wonderful mother—look how close you all are."

"Only because she's bossy."

"Oh, Cressa! You sound just like a teenager. Your mom has to be bossy—a single mother with five daughters."

Cressa stared at Alicia. "She wasn't a single mum."

"Sorry." Alicia felt guilty. "That slipped out."

"I've got a wonderful father."

"I know."

"The best, in fact."

"I agree."

"But...?"

A moment of silence followed. Then Alicia asked, "Just how much was he around, Cressa, to do the day-to-day stuff?"

She hesitated. "It's the nature of his *job*. Mum's always pointed that out. Actors have to take work where they can. He'd be around more if he could."

"Of course he would." Alicia paused again, but some shared bond pushed her to defend Deirdre. "He wasn't, though, was he? Your mother is the glue that held you girls together. You should be grateful. After all, family is very important to you, isn't it."

Cressa stared. "My family is everything." She spoke slowly, as if weighing the veracity of the words for the first time.

"There you are," said Alicia, as she bent and pulled out a weed. "To plant a garden, to grow a family, needs constant care and stability." She was meddling, she knew, but for Adam's sake she decided to give getting through to Cressa one last try. "The life you describe is wonderful if you're doing it for the right reasons and not using it to run away. Pain has to be felt at some point, Cressa. It, too, is an integral part of life."

Cressa brushed her hair off her face, brushed Alicia's words away. "There's nothing I'm running away from now. Sure, I ran away from my wedding and Brian, but that was two years ago. Now I'm happy. Everything's fine, okay. As to pain—frankly, Alicia, I don't know what you're on about."

Once again, Cressa dodged acknowledging her baby, just picked up her spade and began digging.

Alicia followed suit, feeling she had failed. As long as Cressa remained locked in denial, it would erode her life as surely as alcohol had eroded Alicia's own.

CHAPTER TWENTY-FIVE

"THIS IS CRAZY," said Adam, "but kinda fun. I've never been to a sandbank party."

He was rowing with his own particular blend of elegance and economy of movement, the oars barely splashing in the waters stained yellow with the setting sun. The sky was clear and the moon hung low between two small mountains. His black hair was swept back off his face and Cressa wished she'd brought her camera as she tried to imprint his image on her mind. Hard to believe that in a few days this flesh-and-blood man before her would be reduced to a couple of photos and some memories. Good memories.

Filming for Cressa was over. The last action scenes with her character were completed. The location shoot was done, too. The community had invited the cast and crew to a farewell party on the sandbank. The locals had enjoyed the excitement of having actors in the midst, enjoyed the lift to the economy. Besides, any excuse for a party.

"You'll love it." She tried to sound enthusiastic. Usually she adored socializing, but, tonight, she wasn't in a party mood. "I can't believe everything is ending all at once. The filming, you going."

"And you off to sail the seven seas. Well, the Pacific at any rate."

"Yeah." She just didn't have any of her normal

anticipation for the next phase of her life. "I'll miss you."

There were three words she'd never uttered before.

Adam smiled but didn't say anything. He'd been preoccupied all day. Maybe his thoughts were already slipping forward a few days, forward seven thousand miles. It would be understandable if they were. What she couldn't understand was why it pained her to acknowledge this. He was only playing by her rules. Why did she resent him for that?

As they drew close to the sandbank, they could see people silhouetted against the dying light of the sun. A bonfire had been built and the generator hummed as the technicians set up the sound system. Motorboats, rowboats and kayaks were pulled up into a small bay tucked into the wide sweep of sand, and people were busy unloading ice chests, unfolding chairs and greeting old friends. Kids darted around, and farther down the beach a few teenagers were throwing a luminous Frisbee. The air was lively with chatter and laughter, but all sounds were still mellow and muted in the vast theater of the bay.

Their boat scraped sand. Adam shipped the oars and leaped into the water. Cressa moved to help him, but he said, "Don't worry, I've got it," so she sat back to enjoy watching him draw them ashore. There was something almost primeval in the act, plugging into the early days when a man always made land first. It felt ridiculously good, though she shot him a you-gotta-be-kidding-me look when he held out a hand to help her from the boat. He grinned as she jumped unaided onto the sand, and dropped a kiss on her head.

There was a shriek. "Cressa!"

Sam bounded forward and hugged her. "Bring your stuff and set up camp with us."

She led them to the circle of firelight, where Bridget was laying out cheeses and crackers on a wobbly table, while Jeremy and Hank sorted out the portable barbecue. Adam cracked a beer and went to join the guys, and Cressa took the plastic cup of wine Bridget held out to her.

"This is great!" said Sam, gesturing at the wide sky. "I'll miss this place. It gets under the skin, doesn't it?"

"Northland's special," said Cressa through a mouthful of cracker. "I've had some brilliant times in Aroha Bay."

"Especially recently." Sam nudged her, then looked over at Hank. "I've had a lot of fun, too."

"Yeah," said Bridget, smiling across at Jeremy. "Happy memories."

"Are you going to stay in touch?" asked Cressa.

"Of course!" said Sam.

Cressa smiled. "I wasn't talking about us, stupid. Of course we will. I was talking about them." She motioned with her chin to the men around the barbecue. The glow from the flames lit their faces, and Adam's skin looked almost gold. He stood with beer in one hand, barbecue fork in the other, turning sausages. All three men were chatting, but Steve and Jeremy were angled toward Adam. Strange, how Adam never pushed himself forward yet somehow became the center.

"Nah," said Sam. "Hank's going to Australia. Still, it's been fun while it lasted. Says he'll give me a call if he's back this way. Oh, look, garlic bread. I'll get the guys to start toasting this."

She stepped away and Cressa turned to Bridget. "What about Jeremy?"

"He's going to move down to Wellington to be with me," Bridget said. "He's fairly confident he'll get a job." Dropping her voice, she added, "He's talking marriage. I told him rubbish, that we've only known each other a few months and been going out a few weeks, but he says he's sure and is just waiting for me to make up my mind."

"Marriage?" Cressa was taken aback. "That's fast."

"Shh, keep your voice down. I don't want Sam to hear. She'll just make jokes—you know how she is."

"So what'll you do?" Cressa asked in lowered tones.

"I don't know. I keep thinking I'll say yes, but then I get scared. What if he's the wrong guy? Except, I imagine life without him and that terrifies me even more." Seeing Sam return, she spoke in a normal tone. "And you, about to sail away. How wonderful is that?"

"I know. Fate must have had my name written all over the job."

"When does Adam fly out?" Sam asked.

"Tuesday."

"So soon?" Sam glanced at Adam, her head to one side. "I'll say this for you, Cressa. You're a stronger woman than I am, being able to walk away from a glorious specimen of manhood like that. Come on, let's join the guys."

"You go. I'll just sort things out here." Cressa held back while Bridget and Sam went over to the men. She busied herself tidying the small table, but watched her two friends. Both were so alive in the moment, one with scant regard for imminent separation and the other on the verge of something both wonderful and terrifying.

Cressa ought to be excited, too. The *Maria Louisa* was the chance of the lifetime. But the joy of the evening was clouded with the forthcoming farewells. She so didn't want this clinging fear of saying goodbye.

"Cressa," Bridget called. "Bring the marshmallows. They should be dessert, but why delay wondrous joy, I always say."

And why let it go?

ADAM WAS ENJOYING the evening. Life was always fun with Cressa. They'd eaten burned sausages wrapped in bread and smothered in onions, tomato sauce and mustard. She'd said he couldn't leave New Zealand without experiencing the finest Kiwi cuisine. There'd also been steaks and salad, great wine, lots of talking, lots of laughter.

All the time, though, he was aware of the envelope in his inside jacket pocket. He'd acted on impulse, and a stupid one at that. Cressa had already chosen her path. Still, he owed it to Des. She'd taken the risk; he had to, too.

When the eating finished, the sound system was cranked way up and dancing began. He could see Cressa swaying to the music, ready to be drawn into the press of bodies, but he grabbed her hand. "Hey, let's go exploring."

He was kidding, of course. Nothing but a big sandbank stretched into the darkness.

"Sure."

As they headed away from the fire, their feet crunching on the shell-strewn beach, they suddenly saw shards of light shooting away under them. From the delighted yells of the teenagers, they'd just noticed, also.

"Phosphorescence!" Cressa exclaimed. "Man, we're lucky. It doesn't often happen in the bay."

It was like walking on a disco floor. Under the thin crust of shells, lightning jags raced away from each footstep. Adam tossed a big shell into the water, where it splintered the surface with brilliant sparks and sank, a fireball in the blackness.

"If it wasn't so cold, we could swim," said Cressa. "It looks fabulous being covered in green fire."

"Yeah?"

His tone must have given his thoughts away. She stopped short. "Oh, no way!"

"There are a couple of towels and a blanket in the boat."

"Tell me you're joking."

"If I hadn't seen you a month ago swimming at midnight, I'd think you were chicken."

It was too dark to see, but he felt the look she cast at him. "Chicken?"

He made a clucking sound. That got her. "You have the count of three to fetch the damn towels."

With a laugh he ran down to the boats. When he returned, she was hopping on one bare foot and swearing as she wrestled off her second sock. "We have to go to the island or our clothes will be soaked. The water comes up through the sand."

Phosphorescence lit their steps all the way to the tiny island at the far end. There they stripped, then put clothes, towels and blanket on the rocks to keep them dry. The moon was high in the sky now, pearl-white in the blackness; the stars stood out in sharp definition.

"This is bloody crazy," said Cressa as she tossed her jeans onto the rocks.

Adam would have agreed, but at that moment she

yanked off her T-shirt, then her bra. The moonlight on her breasts made him catch his breath. The cold, two seconds later, stole it completely as he threw off his clothes.

"The only way to do this is fast."

"Agreed," said Cressa, shivering.

"On the count of three. One—"

Both ridiculously competitive, they leaped together two counts early. When Adam surfaced, he could hardly hear Cressa's expletives; his mind was flash-frozen. His body, unfortunately, was not. Could one die of cold in Northland? Cressa's leap had been shallower because she'd tried to keep her braid, twisted into a knot on top of her head, dry. Now she floundered in the water, vigorously moving arms and legs, attempting to get warm. Liquid fire surrounded her and she looked exotic, a mythological maiden in fairy water.

"We gotta swim." The cold strangled his voice.

Their strokes were jerky as they began making their way around the island.

"It's really hard not to curl into a fetal position." Cressa's words came in gasps, as though turning to icicles in her throat.

Adam concurred. His whole body protested violently, but determined to push through, he concentrated on the beauty of the waters breaking bright around him, the sparkling bubbles that frothed on his limbs. As they got halfway around, the agony began to ease. His body was either becoming accustomed to the water or was completely numb. Cressa's breathing smoothed out from short gasps to something approaching normal, and by the time they were three-quarters around the island, they were able to exchange smug comments.

"This is fantastic," said Cressa, pulling up and

treading water as she turned slowly, gazing at the moon and stars.

"It is," said Adam, looking at the illuminated lines of her body. Unable to resist, he tugged her to him. She immediately wrapped her legs around his waist, and he cursed his numbness. Their lips were not so cold, however, and the warmth of Cressa's mouth was extraordinarily erotic in contrast with the freezing water. He kissed her deeply, the underlying pain of imminent parting added poignancy to the moment. The water was too cold for them to stay still long, though. With a sigh she broke off and leaned back, legs still wrapped around his waist, bathed in phosphorescence, with sparks of light caught on her cheeks. Adam groaned.

"What's wrong?" she asked.

"I have never desired a woman quite so much and have never been so completely handicapped."

She laughed and kissed him again. "I'm hot inside," she whispered against his lips.

He groaned anew, more theatrically this time. "I doubt I'll be able to find that out."

"Let's see," she said.

They swam back to shore and hobbled on numbed feet to their towels. As they rubbed off hard, they laughed, but still had to don all their clothes to stop their teeth chattering and quell the violent shivers that rocked their bodies. Then Adam spread out the blanket and they lay down, entwined, to continue the kiss. Cressa tasted of salt with a lingering touch of wine, and Adam thought how well that combination suited her personality. The ground was hard and lumpy, so he swung her onto him, and she sighed as she stretched her length against his, her hands buried in his hair as their kiss deepened. He wriggled his hands under her jacket, her sweater, her

T-shirt until they found the satin of her skin. His fingers had already learned her body and they roamed now to the points that he loved, to the places he knew would drive her wild. As she gave a little moan of pleasure and snuggled her hips closer to his, Adam discovered that his mind and body were back in communication.

"Glad to see you've recovered from the cold," Cressa murmured, and for the second time, they removed their clothes, this time slowly, layer after layer, savoring each stage, until they were flesh on flesh, Cressa's hair loose and warming them both. She was indeed as hot as she'd promised, and as they moved together, generating their own heat, Adam held on in sweet, delicious agony until Cressa let go that small wild cry she always gave just before climaxing then he let himself go and when they came together, it was as though the phosphorescence was splintering all around and inside them.

Both were breathing hard, and Adam held her tight against him. She clung to him.

"Really going to miss you, mate."

The hoarse catch in her voice made him ask, "Will you?"

"Of course."

"I've got a birthday present for you."

"Oh, Adam, what is it? A Stetson? I've always wanted one."

"No."

He reached over and pulled the envelope out of his jacket pocket. She took it with a quizzical expression.

"What's this? A gift voucher? Scared of buying the wrong thing?"

Very. But he had, all the same.

He watched her face as she drew the piece of paper out of the envelope. She had to squint as she tried to read in the dark. Then her face went blank. "Is this a plane ticket?"

"Yeah. An open return, leaving on my flight."

"Oh, Adam, this is way too much. A box of chocolates would have been just fine."

"You don't eat chocolates. You're too disciplined. Besides, I wanted to get you something memorable."

"This is memorable, all right. But I can't accept it. It's too much. It'll have cost you a bomb."

"You're worth it." He leaned forward and kissed her. "Besides, it's not as generous as you might think. It's also my present to me. You're my reward for all my hard study."

A smile flickered, but her eyes remained glued to the ticket. "Wow, I can't believe you're asking me to go to the States."

"Why not? Just for a few weeks, before flying back to catch your boat." He tried to sound casual, tried not to show that he scarcely dared breathe. "It'll be fun."

Various emotions crossed her face. Doubt, excitement, happiness—the beginning of fear. She started to shake her head, so he added quickly, "Only for a holiday. Come hang out for a few weeks. You'll love Texas."

She pushed herself up, shivered and began pulling on clothes. Without her warmth, he shivered, too, and followed suit. That kept them busy while she made up her mind.

This was crazy. What had he been thinking? She was all set to say goodbye. He was crazy to have gotten involved, knowing she'd break his heart at some stage.

"What about your MCAT?" she asked.

"I can study during the day and you can go sightseeing."

"I guess."

She still sounded dubious. Clearly, the idea had been a dumb one. They put on socks and shoes and rose together. *Finish it now,* he told himself. *Give her an out and yourself a break. Neither of us needs this.*

"Look," he began, "just forget—"

At the same time she said, "Okay, for a month."

She didn't fling her arms around his neck the way he'd hoped, but she hadn't refused, as he'd feared. Execution temporarily stayed. He pulled her back into his arms. "A month? That would be great."

Anything could happen in a month.

CHAPTER TWENTY-SIX

THE UNITED STATES WAS VAST. Cressa found it hard to conceive how huge as she peered out the window of the airplane to see land stretching to the horizon. "Is that the Grand Canyon?" she breathed.

"Sure is," said Adam, craning to look over her shoulder. "It's real good to see America again."

The airports were vast and teeming with people. The Texas countryside was vast and flat.

"My stuff's in storage," said Adam. "I gave up my apartment when I went to New Zealand. A friend is lending me his home in Galveston while he's away in Europe for a couple of months. He left a car at the airport for us. We'll get my bike tomorrow."

They found the big SUV and drove down to Galveston. Everything was both the same and different. There were freeways, but they were broad and concrete and looked more like giant, never-ending driveways than roads. Everyone drove on the wrong side. Traffic lights were strung across the roads on wires. Despite being light-headed with fatigue, Cressa couldn't bear to close her eyes. When they drove across a massive spanned bridge to Galveston, the sense of unreality expanded.

"I can't believe I'm driving through a pop song."

The house blew her away. Built high on stilts, it was right on the beach, with the Gulf of Mexico spread before it. Inside, the place was large and gracious—fat

sofas, enveloping armchairs, big beds heaped with pil-
lows, several gleaming bathrooms and a huge kitchen
with every appliance she could think of, plus a few she'd
never imagined.

She tried texting her sisters, but her cell phone didn't
work in the States. "Cheap piece of crap!" She tossed it
on the table in disgust.

"You can use mine," said Adam, yawning, "but not
now. C'mon, Cressa, bed."

"It's only five o'clock," she objected, but at that
moment she, too, yawned widely, almost dislocating her
jaw. Adam didn't argue. He simply grabbed her hand and
dragged her into the main bedroom, which overlooked
the sea. The sight of the bed proved irresistible, and
within minutes both had stripped and tumbled between
the sheets to fall instantly asleep.

When Cressa awoke, the room was in darkness and
she was disoriented. The regular slush of the waves
was reassuring, however, as she slowly realized she
was indeed in America. Beside her, the bed was empty.
Squinting at a clock on the nightstand, she saw it was
4:30 a.m. On the back of the door she spied a long dress-
ing gown, and she slipped it on before going in search
of Adam.

When she stepped outside, she was immediately
struck by how hot and humid the night was. It felt deli-
ciously languid. Adam was on a swing out on the deck.
He'd showered and shaved, and was wearing clean jeans
and a black T-shirt. In the moonlight he looked like
a French philosopher, all moody elegance with deep,
shadowed eyes.

His face lit up when he saw her. "Hey. Glad to see
you're alive. You were so sound asleep when I left you
I wondered if you'd ever wake up again."

He scooted over to make space for her, and she leaned into him, enjoying the athletic strength of his body.

"You look beautiful." His hand slipped beneath the satin robe.

"It's so lovely here." She gestured to the tranquil scene. The sea was black, and the faint moonlight picked out the whitewash breaking rhythmically along the beach. No hills interrupted the horizon and the sky arced high.

Adam smiled down at her. "Isn't it."

She'd never seen him so relaxed. The heat and the serenity of the night had somehow dissipated his usual coiled energy. Or perhaps he was just content to be home again. In New Zealand he'd always seemed exotic, but here, on this deck swing, he suddenly belonged.

"I can't wait to show you all the sights. Galveston's beautiful, and I'll take you into Houston for some shopping. Then there's the Alamo, of course. Seeing as you're fond of pop songs, I can take you up to Pasadena."

She laughed, arching under his stroking hand. "I want to see everything, but you also have to study. I'm not here to distract you."

"Not sure if I can resist." He kissed the top of her head.

"Seriously, I'll be out of the house from early morning to evening. No way will I interfere with your work. It's too important."

His arm tightened around her. "Yeah, it is. Thanks."

She smiled. He was finally learning to say that something mattered, to say he cared.

HE TOOK THE FIRST DAY OFF, however. They unpacked, and he was delighted to find a letter from Cole waiting for him.

"I told him about the MCAT and said I'd be staying here," Adam said as he ripped open the envelope. "He's banned me from visiting until the exam is over." A grin spread over his face as he unfolded the paper. "Actually, it's for you, Cressa. Look. I sent him a couple of pictures of you."

He passed her a cartoon sketch of a kiwi and a coyote snuggled together. The sketch made her chuckle, because the kiwi had her eyes, her nose fusing into the bird's characteristically long beak, while the coyote had Adam's features. There was a note at the bottom:

Hi, Cressa. Adam told me all about you. I'm really looking forward to meeting you, but I hope you understand if I say I'd rather we wait until I'm released. Cole.

She glanced up. "I thought he wasn't getting out till the end of the year."

"He isn't."

"I'm only here for a month."

"I know." Adam bent over and picked up the cartoon, his hair falling forward to screen his face. "He's really clever at drawing, isn't he?"

"Yeah, I'll frame it when I get home."

LATER THAT MORNING Adam drove her into Galveston. She was enchanted by the long piers, the lovely houses and old storefronts. They ambled down the sunny streets of the main shopping area.

"Man, I'm going to have to buy some different clothes," she said. "Jeans are way too hot."

She dragged Adam into several surfing shops to get

an idea of the prices. In one store window she saw an advertisement for a temporary assistant.

"That's me!" she said.

"Cressa, it's supposed to be your holiday!"

"Nah, I enjoy working. It's the best way of getting to know a new place. Besides, it'll keep me out your hair. Come on."

Mike and Tim, who owned the shop, were at first dubious. They were both in their early sixties, faces ravaged by too much sun, too much surf and probably too much pot. Despite their renegade looks, their long hair and surfer clothing, they were disconcertingly bureaucratic.

"Have you got a green card?"

However, when they inquired about her accent and chatted a bit about the surfing scene in New Zealand, they were less worried. Then she let slip that Jake was her cousin.

"Jake Finlayson? *The* Jake Finlayson? No way, man!"

The job was hers, beginning the following day. She was almost skipping as she left the shop. "It'll be such fun!"

Adam laughed and spun her around to kiss her. "I love that you are so wholehearted. So crazy."

She kissed him back. "What's crazy? I want to experience everything I can in this month. It's a way to get to understand you better. Which starts right now. I want to see where you grew up."

He pulled back. "Definitely not. It's not pretty. There are much better things to see, instead."

"I don't care. It's important. Besides—" she drew a key out of her pocket "—I told Alicia we'd check up on the place."

DEFEATED, Adam drove her to the trailer park. She had never seen one before.

"It's nicer than I expected," she said as they drove slowly up and down the rows of mobile homes.

"The trailers vary a lot. Some are horrendous. Others have been done up well."

They certainly were a mixed bunch, ranging from ones painted in jaunty colors like Gypsy caravans, with tiny, well-tended gardens and hanging baskets, to the frankly deplorable, with peeling paint and rusted air-conditioning units.

"This is it." They stopped in front of a blue trailer. The paintwork was faded, the grass overgrown. It was not so much run-down as unloved. The inside was the same. The unit was small but well-appointed, the furnishings shabby now, but of good quality. The air was stifling and stale, from the place having been shut up so long and Adam opened some windows. Walking through the deserted home felt strange, almost as if someone had died there.

The back bedrooms were tiny. The boys' room still had the bunks they'd grown up in, and a few faded posters.

"Mom left them up because she said they reminded her of us."

Sass's room had been converted into a study. It was filled with books and had a desk under the window, which looked down the trailer-lined road. Cressa imagined Alicia sitting there, marking and preparing lessons at night and over weekends. The room was peaceful enough, but the whole trailer felt desolate, no doubt the result of it being locked up for months. Sass had come in to clean and tidy up, but Alicia had preferred not to return to live in it. She'd wanted to make sure her addiction was truly conquered before she risked sliding back into old habits in familiar places.

Cressa wandered back to the small living room. Hard to imagine having three children here—Sass, driven to succeed; Cole, the golden boy; and Adam. No wonder he'd taken off on his bike, gone wild. This place was far too tiny for a young teenager bursting with energy. No wonder he'd learned to fold in on himself, to hold in his thoughts and feelings. There was no space for privacy. Either people showed what they thought and felt, or they learned to hide it. How different from her own home. Although there had been many sisters, each had had her own room.

What a fighter Alicia was. Cressa smiled as she trailed her finger along a bookshelf, one of many tucked into any available space. Books had been her lifeline, she'd said, after her children had gone.

Cressa looked up to see Adam watching her. "Well, what do you think?"

"I think your mum is amazing—she just battles on, whatever the odds, doesn't she."

Cressa loved the way Adam's dark features lit up with his smile. "Yeah, she's really something." He grew serious. "I should have been around for her more, though. Leaving her on her own was wrong."

Cressa slipped her arm through his. "Kids have to leave home. We all have our own roads."

He looked down at her, face inscrutable. "How do we know when roads are meant to merge or diverge?"

Suddenly, she wasn't sure if they were still talking about Alicia. "I don't know. I guess when it feels right."

Adam didn't say anything for a second, then he

moved toward the kitchen. "Do you want a drink? We may find some herbal tea or something."

But she wasn't going to allow him to pull away from her like that, and she leaped onto his back.

"Hey, whoa," he said, staggering under her unexpected assault. "Whattaya doing?"

She wrapped arms and legs tightly around him. "Not letting you slip away, Texas. Don't think you can use those avoidance tactics on me."

He laughed but crossed his arms over his chest to hold her arms. "What avoidance tactics?"

"You think I can't tell when you turn impenetrable? Your drawbridge goes up, and just now you were about to bring down the portcullis, too. However—" she bit his ear "—I'm up to your tricks and I've stormed your defenses."

"Oh, yeah?" he said, and backed her into one of the flimsy walls.

"Oof. Yeah. What are you going to do about it?"

"This!" He carried her piggyback through the doorway into his mother's bedroom and with a twist flung her onto the bed. He began tearing off her sandals.

"Adam, we can't!" said Cressa, scandalized. "This is your mother's room."

She loved the ruthless look on his lean face.

"Yes, we can. You gonna stop me?"

He was unzipping her jeans.

"It's just so wrong," she argued as she raised her hips so he could strip the jeans off.

"What she doesn't know won't hurt her." He tossed them aside.

"It's just—" she objected, her voice muffled as her T-shirt was hauled up over her face "—one of those taboo things."

He shoved her back so she was prone on the bed, his face alive with mischief and laughter. "But you love being bad. Enjoy it."

So she did, and far from it feeling wrong, making love here in the home where he'd grown up ended up feeling incredibly right. It was as though she was being woven into the fabric of his childhood, while at the same time they brought new warmth, new love into this flimsy family home.

CHAPTER TWENTY-SEVEN

OVER THE NEXT TWO WEEKS Cressa was surprised to find herself falling in love with America. She hadn't expected to be charmed by everyone, awed by the sheer size of everything, from the milk bottles to the cavernous washing machines to the margaritas served in what looked like fishbowls.

She didn't miss her family as much as she'd thought she would. She talked to her sisters on Skype regularly, and now she had different adventures and experiences to share with them. Her Facebook pages were lively with comments about the photos she'd posted of new sights, from beach mansions on stilts to ornate graveyards and the beautiful wooden counter of the milk bar.

There were other surprises, too. She had never expected to return to accounting, but one look at the shop's books had so appalled her that she'd taken the paperwork in hand. She hadn't expected the satisfaction of getting systems going, and was shocked to discover that beneath her freewheeling persona lurked her mother's military precision. Tim's and Mike's delight made her feel good. Surprisingly good.

But most of all, she hadn't expected to relish the day-to-day domesticity of living with Adam. She loved seeing his boots by the back door, his razor in the bathroom. She didn't even mind picking up his socks, though she could tell that would get old pretty soon. She loved kissing him goodbye in the morning as though they were straight out of a 1950s movie. When she came home, Adam would rise from his desk to wrap her in a huge bear hug that lifted her off her feet. Sometimes he carried her straight off to the bedroom or took her then and there, against the wall or on the floor.

"I can't get enough of you," he explained. "Gotta make the most of every opportunity."

She wasn't complaining. Not at all.

Cressa knew how hard he had to struggle to hold his restless energy in check, knew it demanded every scrap of his fierce determination to focus on his studies rather than obey the demands of a body that craved action. When his incarceration became too much for him, they'd jump on his bike and drive into the night along the endless highways, beneath huge Texas skies.

Other nights they'd make simple meals and veg out in front of the television before going to bed for incredible sex or slow gentle making out or even just sleep, which in some ways was almost more intimate than sex—a comfortable sharing on a whole new level she'd never experienced.

There were other changes, too. Because of the languorous heat, Cressa bought a couple of skirts and some gauzy tops. Alicia's blouse was perfect. Having a new image was fun, like discovering a different side to her personality. One night she found silver-and-turquoise earrings and a bracelet tucked under her pillow.

"Oh, Adam!" She flung her arms around his neck. "How did you know I've been lusting after Mexican jewellery?"

He kissed her nose. "Seeing you being brave enough to be feminine these days is great."

She stepped back a pace. "What do you mean?"

He gestured to the skirt and top, her loose flowing hair. Touched one of the hoops in her ears. "Don't get me wrong. I love your tough girl image, too, but it's like you trust things enough to be more vulnerable."

She snorted. "Yeah, right. Any more of that sort of talk and you'll be the vulnerable one, mate."

But deep down she knew what he meant. She could feel the heat of Texas melting her from the inside out, the warm Gulf winds eroding her edges. Sometimes when she loitered along hot streets, idled on the long piers, she felt she was floating inside a magical bubble where nothing was real except Adam. Here he was the center of her universe, the core of her being.

She hadn't expected any of this.

Most of all, she hadn't expected to keep forgetting about her upcoming job and to start imagining a different future. She thought what fun it would be to travel up through the States to Seattle. She'd always wanted to check out those houses on the water, having watched *Sleepless in Seattle*. It might be fun to cut across to Wisconsin because of *That Seventies Show*. She wanted to do Pasadena, San Francisco, El Condor Pasa and all the other songs. Maybe she could come back over during Adam's holidays and they could have adventures together. A long-distance, no-strings relationship could work. It would have all the fun and none of the boring bits of a normal relationship.

Cressa's thoughts were fully engaged in considering such exciting possibilities one bright Saturday morning, two weeks after her arrival. She was stacking the dishwasher when Adam burst into the kitchen, his face alight with excitement.

"Cressa, you'll never guess!"

"What?" She was hard put to think of anything that could have chased all the shadows from his face.

"She's answered me. She's finally contacted me."

"Who?" But even as she asked, Cressa felt a chilly hand steal around her heart.

"Stella! Isn't that incredible?" Laughing in disbelief, he snatched Cressa up in a hug and began spinning her around and around. She tried to laugh, too, but she was rigid in his arms. He was too happy to notice. "She's still here in Texas! In Dallas. And she wants to meet me. I just can't believe it."

"Adam, set me down and tell me about it." Cressa made an effort to sound pleased for him. He placed her back on her feet, but too excited to stay still, he began pacing.

"It was on my Facebook page this morning. She says she's checked out all the photos and things, and now she wants to meet me."

There was wonder in his face. Joy lent it a new beauty. "I've sent her my number and said she can call. Or for her to send me her number and I'll phone her." He held up a hand and stared at it. "Can you believe it? I'm shaking."

"I'm not surprised." Cressa struggled to sound happy. "It's fantastic news. Just out of nowhere."

A lightning bolt, destroying her fantasies in one strike.

Adam suddenly appeared anxious. "What if she doesn't like me? What if she thinks I'm nothing?"

This made Cressa smile. "Adam, she will think you are the most amazing person ever."

"But her stepdad is some rich prick. I won't be able to compare with him."

Adam looked so vulnerable that she stroked his arm.

"You'll be different, that's all. She'll still think you are wonderful."

His smile was blinding. "I just can't wait to meet her. We'll go as soon as we can."

We? Cressa was registering that word when his cell phone rang. Adam snatched it up.

"Adam here... Stella, oh, my God, I just can't believe this."

Cressa didn't wait to hear more. A father should have privacy for his first conversation with his daughter. As she slipped out of the kitchen, her last sight was of him clutching the phone to his ear as though it were lifeline and he was finally being drawn back home.

Cressa walked down onto the beach, where she drifted aimlessly, her arms wrapped around herself. She couldn't go too far or Adam might not find her. This didn't have to change things. She could still fly over, go on trips with him. They could still have the fun times she'd imagined. He could see Stella when Cressa was in New Zealand. No problem.

She shook her head to rid her eyes of tears, and dug her fingernails hard into her back as she squeezed her arms around herself. This was ridiculous. She was making a fuss over nothing. So Adam was happy to get his daughter back. Cressa was pleased for him. Really pleased. She pictured his face blazing with joy and disbelief, and felt herself being swept away by factors moving too swiftly and out of her control. She was reminded of the same helplessness that had engulfed her on her wedding day.

She heard footfalls on the sand and turned just as Adam caught up to her. He flung his arms around her and lifted her off her feet as he planted a smacking kiss on her lips.

"Now! We're leaving right now! Can you believe it? We should get there in about four and a half hours. Stella sounded so cute but so grown-up. She's nine, after all. Amazingly self-possessed. A bit cautious and polite—so damn polite." He laughed. "That'll be Crystal! The kid will have been brought up knowing exactly how to behave. That's good. C'mon. We'd better get going."

Adam grabbed her arm, but Cressa resisted and he stopped, puzzled. "What's up?"

She shrugged, uncertain herself. "Look, maybe you'd better go without me. Get to know the kid on your own."

All emotion disappeared from his face. "Yeah? Why?"

"It's your relationship. You don't need other people there."

"Other people? You."

She tried to explain. "What I mean is this is your thing. Yours and Stella's. And Crystal's, too, I guess. I don't really have a place there."

"You mean you don't want a place there."

"Oh, Adam! You make it sound like I'm reneging on some sort of understanding we have. That's unfair. I'm leaving in a few weeks."

He shoved his hands into his back pockets and looked at her. She felt she had to justify herself. "C'mon, you know I only came for a short time. And it's been great—it really has. I had been thinking maybe I could come back during your holidays and we could hang out, go look for adventures, that sort of thing. There's lots I want to do in the States. But this family thing..." She shrugged, holding out her hands. "That's your trip, not mine." She realized she was babbling, but couldn't stop herself. "I'm not the family sort. I've made that clear from the start. Heck, I don't even believe in marriage, and I certainly don't buy into the whole happily-ever-after."

He was silent, deathly silent. He was unnervingly still, too. The shadows had returned to his face. When he spoke, his voice was raw. "You're really going to do this, aren't you? I can't believe it. You're going to throw away everything that we have together." He shook his head. "For me these past weeks have been incredible— the best in my life. I'd so hoped you were feeling the same. I've been praying that when the time came, you wouldn't leave. As for your not buying into the happily-ever-after—what, do you think people who marry are in some way conning themselves? People don't marry out of certainty, Cressa. They marry in hope. Hell, marriage is the biggest gamble in life. As a risk taker, I'd have thought you'd appreciate that."

She shrugged again. It was meant to be a helpless, I-don't-know gesture, but it must have come across as I-don't-give-a-damn, because Adam's face tightened.

"From the moment we met, you've been a torment, Cressa, you and your notions of being wild and free. No strings, no commitments. Just fun."

His words cut deep. "I thought you were happy," she cried resentfully. "I thought you liked being with me."

"Despite your stupid notions, Cressa, not because of them. I love being with you because I love *you*, damn it. I love you so much I've even toyed with the idea of not doing my MCAT so we can lead the sort of life you hanker after."

She was appalled. "That's crazy. I'd never ask that of you. I know what the exam means to you." She stopped short, searching for the right words. "Adam, it *is* you."

The words sounded stupid when she said them, but he nodded.

"Yes, it is," he said. "You're right. We are what our dreams are. There you are, thinking about meeting up a few months a year for sex and a good time, and here I am, wanting it all. *It all.*" He gave the last words slow, hard emphasis. "I want a wife, Cressa, not just a part-time lover or a long-distance girlfriend. I want a family. Yeah, I want to do the trips that you mentioned, but I want Stella riding pillion. No, I want more than that. I want an SUV packed with kids and camping stuff. I want a family, a home and a career—the whole damn picket fence."

High above them a seagull wheeled, uttering its harsh cry. Cressa didn't know what to say, how to answer. The wide-open spaces of the Galveston coast suddenly seemed too much. She felt swallowed up. She was filled with a need for the green hills of home, for the safety of Aroha Bay. For a world where the scale was reasonable and the people predictable. The men were manageable. Only Adam, she thought bitterly, could make a pro-posal sound like a challenge. The one challenge she couldn't take on. But before she could begin to frame an answer, he stepped close and clamped her arms with fierce fingers.

"Don't say it," he said. "Don't you dare." His face was very near hers, his breath warm on her cheeks. Cressa couldn't help herself. Even though her words were push-ing him away, her body instinctively leaned closer, as if drawn to him. But Adam held her at bay. His voice continued low, but granite hard with resolve. "You know what, Cressa? I'm going to save us both from repeating patterns. To save you from being the one who quits yet again and me from being the one left. I've had one wife walk out on me, so I'll be damned if I'm going to set myself up to be a groom left waiting at the altar. This time *I'm* going to walk away."

She made an incoherent sound, but he shook his head.

"No, I'm leaving right now. My daughter's waiting for me and I've got my life's path. I don't know whether I can make it work, but I'm not taking any detours for some woman—however much I may love her—who doesn't know who she is or what she wants."

Don't leave, Cressa screamed inside. *Don't you dare bloody leave me!*

His fingers tightened and hurt her arms, but no way in hell would she admit to the pain. He pulled her to him, and unresisting, she let him kiss her goodbye. If he'd kissed her harder, she would have opened her mouth, let him in, but his lips just rested on hers and she kept hers stubbornly shut.

"Goodbye, Cressa." He breathed rather than said the words.

Then he was gone.

She waited, the only person on the long expanse of beach. The waves pulsed; the seagull shredded the air with its wrenching cries. She heard his motorbike roar to life and drive off. She waited until the sound dissolved into the air around her. She waited for what seemed like hours. But he never came back.

CHAPTER TWENTY-EIGHT

THE RIDE TO DALLAS was long. Adam barely noticed the road for the first hour. He had just made the biggest mistake of his life. He'd seen the conflicting emotions in Cressa's face. He could have—should have—talked her around. Been patient. Taken her offer of visits. They might have turned into something permanent. She'd be thinking he was just another Brian. But they weren't the same. How had Des put it?

"They're too similar and too different at the same time."

"Oh, right. Whereas Cressa and I...?"

"Are completely different and exactly the same."

How would Cressa ever get that if Adam didn't make it clear to her?

Every instinct urged him to turn the bike around. He'd been unable to stop himself from glancing out the bedroom window when picking up his keys and wallet. She'd just been standing there on the beach, hugging herself. All alone in America. Hell, she was all alone in her life; she just didn't realize it. Filling it with sisters didn't change the fact that deep down, she refused to let anyone near. How could he abandon her when he loved her more than anyone else in the world?

It was because he loved her with every fiber of his being that he kept on driving. He had to. It had nearly killed him when Crystal had left. He wouldn't survive Cressa deserting him. He wasn't Brian.

On the open road, Adam let the bike have its head and ripped up the miles. *Think of Stella*, he told himself. *Don't look back. Look forward. There's nothing else for you.*

THE HOUSE IN DALLAS did nothing to allay his fears. As he found his way to one of the wealthiest areas in the city, he could feel his old anxieties of worthlessness reemerge. When he drew up in front of the property, he checked the number several times. The gates were huge, the driveway long and lined with stately trees. Taking a deep breath, he pressed the bell and spoke into the intercom. The gates swung open.

What the hell did Crystal's husband do? Adam pulled up in front of the house itself and stared at it as he stripped off gloves and helmet. It was several stories high and seemed to have an unnecessarily large number of windows. Was the place really all for one family?

He walked up the wide flight of stairs to the massive front door, squared his shoulders, drew in a deep breath and rang the bell. He was relieved when Crystal opened the door, not some maid or butler.

"Adam." Her voice had the right pitch of welcome, but her eyes were hostile. "Come in."

"Hey, Crystal." He didn't know the etiquette for greeting a runaway wife. Kiss her on the cheek? Shake her hand? He settled for a compliment. "You're looking great."

She always had been lovely, tall and willowy. Now she was dressed in an elegant skirt and blouse that enhanced her excellent figure. Her hair, once brown, was streaked with blond and bobbed. He thought of Cressa's small body, muscular and curvy, thought of her mass of long hair, and his stomach clenched.

"Thank you." She turned to lead the way into a large, sunny room with expensive-looking sofas and tables and lavish curtains. A tall man in a white shirt and well-pressed jeans was rising from a chair, and he held out his hand. "Adam. It's good to meet you. I'm Wayne."

If Adam had thought greeting a long-lost wife awkward, he found confronting the unknown rival who had stolen her away even trickier. "Wayne," he said, adopting Crystal's minimalism as they shook hands.

"Have a seat," said his ex-wife. "I'll get Stella. She's out back."

The men sat down opposite each other. Wayne relaxed and crossed his legs. Adam perched on a chair and fumbled his helmet from his lap onto the floor beside him.

"This is awkward," said Wayne. "I don't know what to say."

"I suppose you could start by apologizing for running off with my wife and kid." Adam had rehearsed speeches a thousand different ways over the years, though most ended with him smashing his fist into the bastard's face.

"I do," said Wayne. "Although, in the interests of historical accuracy, I would like to point out that she ran to me. I was, however, more than happy to receive her." Then he abandoned his tycoon-at-home demeanor, uncrossing his legs and leaning forward. "Adam, I have felt very bad over the years. If I found out Crystal was having an affair, it would destroy me. I didn't realize at the time—or didn't want to face—how horrible it would have been for you."

"I didn't know—didn't even guess." Adam looked at

Wayne and decided he must be twenty years older. "Till she was gone."

Wayne flinched, his eyes steady but watchful. "She said she didn't tell you anything in the note. I thought that was wrong." Adam remained silent. "We met in the park. I used to go jogging. She'd be at the swings with Stella."

Adam knew the park he meant, with its paths that wound through the trees down to the swings. There were always people running, always mothers with their kids. "It was a long time ago," he said. "I'm over it. I'm only here to meet my daughter."

Wayne nodded. "That's good. I'm very glad you're here. I've never been comfortable about... But it was Crystal's decision to make, not mine. You know how she is."

Adam suddenly remembered Crystal's sulks when she didn't get what she wanted. Her ruthlessness in fighting for what she saw as her rights. Remembered how nice she was once she'd got her way and how he'd be unable to enjoy it, feeling played. Whatever Cressa's faults, she was always direct and honest. Adam didn't envy Wayne one bit and could feel some of his hostility toward the man soften. "Oh, yeah, I remember, and believe me, I do understand."

Wayne smiled but didn't say anything. Clearly, he was loyal and loved Crystal. Stella was in a stable family, then.

The door opened. Adam rose and turned, heart in mouth. Crystal stood with her arm draped over a little girl's shoulder. She was a thin child, all nose and sharp cheekbones. She had blue eyes like her mother and straight black hair. He tried to see the plump baby in her features and acknowledged with a pang that the toddler was gone forever. He really had lost her. Yet here in front of him was the flesh-and-blood daughter old enough to look for him, old enough to want him.

"Hey, Stella."

"Hey." She sounded shy, but she was checking him out.

Wayne broke the awkward silence. "Adam, it's been a long drive. How about an iced tea? Crystal and I'll get you something to drink."

"That would be great," He couldn't take his eyes off his daughter's face.

Crystal's arm tightened. "You go, Wayne. I'll stay."

Stella shook off her mother's restraint and came to sit down in the chair Wayne had just vacated.

"I enjoyed reading your Facebook comments to me."

Adam sat down, also, legs suddenly weak. "That's good. I wanted—" He broke off, uncomfortable under his wife's cold stare as she, too, took a seat.

I know when your drawbridge is going up.

"I wanted you to know I was always thinking about you."

Stella smiled. She had a lower tooth missing. That was so cute. He ached to touch her, but was afraid of spooking her. Not that she appeared to spook easily.

"What were you doing out back?"

"Climbing trees."

"Yeah? High ones?"

"The tallest there is," she said with dignity.

"Stella's also a reader," said Crystal. "Just like me."

"What else do you like to do?"

Stella wrinkled her nose in thought. "Riding, skating, baseball, running and swimming. And drawing pictures."

That's my kid, he thought exultantly.

"What sort of skating?"

"Inline and skateboard," she said.

Definitely mine!

"Stella's very good at her schoolwork, too," said Crystal.

He glanced at his ex-wife, irritated by her interruptions, but suddenly noticed fear in her eyes. Surely she wasn't afraid he was somehow going to take Stella away, steal her love. Then he remembered Crystal's expression when she'd told him her parents weren't coming to their wedding. She'd been devastated and from then on had hated it when he had to go away.

"That's good," he said with a flicker of a smile to Crystal. "School's important. I wish I'd been better at school."

"Mommy says you were a rebel and a dropout."

Crystal appeared uncomfortable but defiant. There was the sound of clinking, and they all turned as Wayne reappeared with a tray of glasses and a big jug, already frosting. She shot him a look of relief and he nodded reassuringly. Adam, catching this exchange, felt regret. She'd have never felt reassured living with the hopeless kid that he'd been. Why hadn't he seen her vulnerability under her poise? *She was always a damaged little thing. You couldn't hope to provide her with the security she needed.*

Wayne chatted easily as he poured drinks for everyone. He asked about New Zealand and Adam told them about the wedding.

"Stella said there're photos on Facebook of Sass's wedding to some *surfer.*"

Crystal's emphasis made Adam grin. "He's not just

some surfer. He was one of the world's best big-wave surfers."

"Even so, it's a strange choice for Sass. She could have had any man she wanted."

"She *got* the man she wanted." Adam had to struggle to keep the edge from his voice. Crystal's snobbery had always riled him, mostly because they both thought she'd married beneath her.

Wayne broke in smoothly. "You have a brother, too, don't you?"

"Yeah."

"Cole," said Crystal, smiling. Cole always had that effect on women. "He was the coolest boy in the school. What happened to him? Did he become a sports star?"

"Not exactly."

"So what's he doing?" she asked, making an effort at conversation.

"He's in prison."

Again it was up to Wayne to break the silence. "And what are you doing these days?"

Adam very nearly dodged the question. However, he was through feeling ashamed of who he was, what he stood for.

"I'm studying for the MCAT exam. I hope to go to medical school."

Crystal's eyes widened. "You? A doctor?"

Her surprise was to be expected. If it hadn't been for his accident, he'd have probably turned into a quite different sort of man. The sort she hadn't wanted to spend the rest of her life with.

"That's admirable," said Wayne, and he looked as though he meant it. Stella, unimpressed, pointed to his helmet.

"Did you come on your motorcycle?"

"Sure did."

"Will you take me for a ride?"

"No!" said Crystal. "Motorcycles are dangerous."

All those days and nights she'd have spent worrying that he would kill himself had left their mark.

"Please," begged Stella, ignoring her mother and fixing imploring eyes on Adam.

"Stella," Crystal warned.

Adam didn't know what to say. He couldn't bear to say no to his daughter. Yet he didn't dare antagonize her mother.

"Now, Crystal," said Wayne, "why not let Adam give her a short ride? Just around the block." Adam watched Crystal waver. "You've always said that Stella inherited her extraordinary sense of balance from her father."

She'd probably said "her no-good father," but what the heck, a compliment was a compliment, and Adam felt a bit more hopeful.

"Trust me, there's no way I'd ever do anything to endanger Stella. We'll go around the block at twenty miles an hour if that's what you want. She'll wear my helmet."

Stella eyed him scornfully. "I don't want to go *slow.*"

"There, you see?" said Crystal to Wayne, flinging a hand toward her daughter. "I told you—just being in the same room as Adam brings out her wild side."

Adam glanced at his daughter and raised an eyebrow. "Wild side, huh?"

She puffed out her chest. "Yes."

Their eyes caught and they grinned at each other.

Adam saw Crystal send her husband a look of pained entreaty, but Wayne just laughed. "Honey, you're beat.

Accept it." He halted any further dispute by standing. "Stella, go get a jacket, sweetheart."

Adam braced for an argument—they used to argue so much—but Crystal amazed him by sitting back. She still gnawed her lip, but Wayne, it seemed, really did have a way of coping with her. Much as Adam didn't want to, he couldn't help warming to the guy.

Outside, Adam hunkered down to adjust the helmet's strap around his daughter's chin. *His daughter's chin.* Being with her felt surreal. He had to stop himself from leaning in and creeping her out by inhaling her little-girl scent. He was still dying to hug her, stroke her hair, tickle her as he used to when she was tiny, but it was all still too soon for such displays of affection.

"You just hang on and lean with me, okay?"

"'Kay," she said. "Promise me we won't go slow."

He glanced up the steps to where Crystal stood watching the proceedings, Wayne's arm around her shoulders.

"We won't be long."

"Take as long as you like," said Wayne. "Go as fast as you feel is right."

He and Adam nodded to each other.

Adam mounted the bike and helped Stella scramble up behind him. She was as agile as a monkey. Her little arms came around his waist and he had to fight the impulse to hold them. He peered over his shoulder. "You okay?" She nodded, eyes shining through the visor. "Here we go, then."

He took off slowly down the driveway. Ridiculously, his mouth was as dry as it always was before some big stunt. What if he screwed this up? What if he crashed? What if he said the wrong thing? What if Stella decided he was a no-good, deadbeat jerk?

They reached the gates. He couldn't help himself. He patted one of those tiny hands that clung to his jacket. Her arms tightened around him.

"What are you waiting for?" his daughter demanded. "Let's go. And when we get around the corner, go fast, okay?"

He laughed. The years suddenly stretched ahead of him, all those teenage adventures that would make him shake with worry as much as his escapades had terrified Alicia. Karma. Retribution. Man, he just couldn't wait!

CHAPTER TWENTY-NINE

THE HOUSE WAS VERY STILL when Cressa went back inside. Although she'd been in Texas only a few weeks, her belongings had spread amazingly. Tracking them down and shoving them into her large bag took a while.

When everything was packed, she looked around. Adam would come home to an empty house. Again. The thought of repeating patterns was strong, so she sat down and wrote a note saying that she would stay in Alicia's trailer until her departure date. She wished him well in his exam and his future relationship with his daughter. She thanked him for the time together and said it would always be special. Her words sounded lame, but she didn't know how else to say things and she wanted to finish on a sort of positive note. Then she slipped out and put the key under the third flowerpot by the back door.

Alicia's trailer was like an oven. Cressa threw open the windows and turned on the air-conditioning, knowing one action sabotaged the other. She put away the groceries she'd bought, then paced through the trailer, deciding which room to be in. At first she planned to sleep in the boys' room, but it felt like Adam's turf. When she went into Alicia's room, she was immediately assailed by happy memories of lovemaking. That's all Adam would be—happy memories. Funny, when one of her flings usually finished, she felt fleeting regret and a huge dollop of liberty. Now she just felt used up.

She lay down on the bed and curled into a fetal position. What should she do? Get an earlier flight home? No. Even though she yearned for her family right at this minute, going home early smacked of failure. Besides, she'd told Tim and Mike she'd run the shop while they had a long-weekend break.

She stared up at the ceiling, listened to the hum of the air-con unit. She was all alone. It was the strangest feeling. She knew only Adam and her workmates. She and Adam hadn't yet linked up with his friends. He'd said he didn't want any distraction until the MCAT was over. Then he'd kissed her on the nose and pointed out that because she was over only for a month, he wanted her all to himself. She'd laughed and punched him for being such a girl.

Cressa covered her eyes with her arm as though she could blot the scene from her mind. She'd have to keep busy or memories would overwhelm her. But she could do this. After all, she'd never needed a bloke in the past to enjoy herself. She'd have a ball, make the most of her remaining time in Texas.

Starting tomorrow, she thought, reaching for the TV remote. Starting tomorrow.

OVER THE NEXT TWO WEEKS, Cressa gained seven pounds. She made it to work every day on time and, she thought, in good spirits. She therefore resented the sidelong looks she received from her two bosses.

"Cut it out," she said. "You guys keep eyeing me funny."

"That's because you're acting funny."

"Whattaya mean? I'm fine."

The men exchanged glances. "You are too fine," said Tim. "You're too bright, too cheerful. You laugh too long at really bad jokes."

"Are you objecting to a happy employee?"

"Are you happy?" Mike appeared skeptical.

She rolled her eyes. "'Course I am!"

"How's Adam?"

She shrugged and opened her eyes wide. "Fine." Under the scrutiny of her bosses she added, "Okay, so we've split up, but very amicably. His daughter's come back into his life, and what with his exam and everything, we figured it was better to end things sooner rather than later."

She hated the sympathy that washed over both men's faces. "I'm really sorry to hear that, Cressa," said Tim.

"There's nothing to be sorry about. Like I told you, I'm fine."

It drove her crazy that from then on, ignoring her protestations, both dudes treated her with clumsy gentleness and—maybe she was imagining it—reproachfulness.

Her sisters' responses held no ambiguity. They were reproachful bordering on accusatory.

"You broke up with the guy right before his exam?" Juliet was shocked.

"I didn't break up with him. He broke up with me." Cressa was getting very tired of explaining this, and strode into the kitchen to make a milkshake. She wondered why she was running up Alicia's phone bill just to be yelled at.

Katherine didn't get it, either. "I can't believe you walked out on him on the best day of his life. I really hope you didn't spoil his reunion with his daughter."

Des took it hardest. "Oh, poor Adam! That's the

cruelest, dumbest thing you've ever done, Cressa. As bad as leaving Brian at the altar, except Adam won't have another sister to help mend his broken heart." An idea struck her. "Hey, what about Portia?"

"They are entirely unsuited," Cressa snapped with as much venom as a woman with a mouthful of chocolate can muster.

Des gave a gurgle of laugher. "Snippy, snippy!"

Cressa cut the connection.

Only to Portia did she confide the whole horrid exchange on the beach—his declaration of love, his sort-of proposal. "I mean, it's clear Adam doesn't get me at all if he thinks I want to buy into all that family stuff. He's mad."

But Portia, usually her mainstay, was troubled. "I thought you and Adam were a good match."

"Yeah, it was fun, but you know me, I like to be footloose and fancy-free." Cressa scooped another spoonful of that wonderful cookie dough ice cream she'd just discovered.

"Poor Adam. After all he's been through."

I've been through a lot, too, she wanted to cry. Only, of course, she couldn't say anything.

Worst of all was her mother's response. She'd been so sure that at least her mum would be happy that she and Adam were no longer together.

"Oh, Cressa," said Deirdre with an impatient sigh. "When will you ever grow up?"

"What are you talking about? I thought you hated Adam."

"I *never* hated Adam! Though I was miffed about my suit," she conceded.

"Well, you certainly didn't want us to get together. You were against it from the start. You pegged him as a deadbeat. Now that he wants to be a doctor, you've changed your tune!"

There was silence on the other end of the line. Then her mother said in a low voice, "It's true I didn't like it when I thought Adam didn't have a steady job, because I know from experience how much an unreliable income and constant absences can strain a relationship. I want all my girls to have dependable men—someone like Brian. Now, of course, it turns out that Adam has a phenomenal ability to stick to his chosen path. But the main problem was always Adam's nationality."

Cressa choked on her margarita. "You don't like Americans?"

This made Deirdre laugh. "Of course I do. It was just *this* American. He frightened me."

"Adam? He'd never hurt a fly!"

"No, but he had the power to carry my precious daughter away to live in another country. Then you went and got your sailing job, and I realized I was going to lose you one way or another."

Cressa tried to make sense of all this. "I thought you didn't like Adam because he was all wrong for me."

Her mother sighed again. She sounded sad and regretful. "I didn't like Adam because I could see you were besotted and I was being selfish. Now I think he's the perfect man for you."

After that conversation, Cressa finished a whole jug of margaritas. These days she was getting darn good at making them.

She couldn't tell which was worse: going to bed alone or waking up alone. Or having no one to come home to at the end of the day. No one to laugh with. When her feet were sore from standing all day, she couldn't have one of Adam's amazing foot massages that turned her to mush and at the same time made her horny as hell. She missed having a razor in the bathroom, socks strewn across the floor. She was dying to know how his studies were going. Some days the impulse to phone was so strong she needed a whole tub of ice cream *and* some margaritas to fight it.

Evenings were long. She tried to read but couldn't settle. She simply couldn't be bothered with any form of exercise. Instead, she filled the hours with television and food. She'd fall asleep with the blue light of the screen spilling across her bed, and when she woke up, as she did several times each night, the disembodied voices of unknown characters in unrelated scenes comforted her.

The days crawled by, until she had only two left in the States. Saying goodbye to Mike and Tim would be really hard, but she was relieved. Now she could go home and forget Texas and Adam and the whole sorry mess.

She cleaned the trailer from top to bottom. She scrubbed floors and sinks with a ferocious intensity and rubbed the windows until they were a millimeter thinner. She vacuumed and washed and even ironed. Her efforts were strangely therapeutic. Her mum would've had a heart attack if she'd seen just how domesticated Cressa could be. But through all this furious activity one ugly little truth burned.

She was jealous of Stella.

Despite her cheerfulness, her cleaning, her eating and her drinking, she couldn't get the kid out of her mind. Only when Cressa was sitting on the steps of the trailer her last evening, drinking a coffee, with everything cleaned, packed and ready to go, did she finally face it.

Not that she was jealous of Stella for stealing Adam's attention from her. She was jealous because she would never have the chance to find *her* son. He was buried. Dead and buried. Brian visited his grave, but she never had. After all, she hadn't wanted him. He'd nearly catapulted her into a life she hadn't wanted.

Slowly, Cressa drew her wallet out of her bag and unzipped it. From the hidden compartment she pulled the photograph, folded in half. The crease did not go through the face that lay in frozen serenity. A face that could have—should have—whooped with laughter, crumpled with concentration, blazed with anger. Cressa touched the photo with her index finger. Poor baby. Poor Felix. Brian had come up with the name. She liked it. Her son, Felix. He'd been so entwined in her conflicting feelings about Brian, the wedding, the future, that she hadn't been able to think of him in his own right. Hadn't dared.

Crystal was a huge mistake, but Stella wasn't. She was the best thing that ever happened to me.

Cressa would never have the chance to utter a sentence like that.

Felix would have been two now. Talking. Leaving toys everywhere. Killing her with his antics. She'd been robbed of her baby and she was furious with the whole world. Part of her had died that day and she'd never had the courage to confront the pain. *If you don't make yourself vulnerable, you can't ever be hurt.* So much easier to move on as if nothing had happened.

Except she seemed to have run out of road. Here in Texas, land of the long straight road. She tried to laugh at the irony, but somehow the laugh turned into a sob. Bowing her head on her knees, Cressa surrendered to the grief she had kept at bay for far too long, and wept.

CHAPTER THIRTY

ADAM THREW HIMSELF into his studies. Nothing to hold him back now, to distract his attention. All good. Great, in fact. At last he had the space he'd been needing these past few months. He was up at 4:00 a.m. and worked through to early evening, breaking at midday for a punishing run down the beach. At two-hour intervals he did push-ups, sit-ups, chin presses. Yet none of it helped to consume his burning, restless energy. Only the daily exchanges with Stella gave some relief. Sometimes he and Stella chatted on the phone; sometimes they exchanged just a text or two. He was careful not to rush things. He'd rushed Cressa, and his efforts had blown up in his face. He and Stella had a lifetime ahead.

The intensity of his concentration kept emotion in check. He couldn't afford to wallow. He'd done that when Crystal had left. Well, not this time. But there wasn't a corner of his house that didn't carry the memory of Cressa. He even delayed changing the sheets as long as possible, because at night he could still catch breath of her scent.

Part of him was always listening in case her feet came up the steps. Maybe she'd breeze back as though nothing had happened. She did that sort of thing. But she never came. The days passed until it was the afternoon of her flight home.

The phone rang. Heart racing, he pounced on it.

"Adam?"

He sagged against the wall. "Mom!" He tried for upbeat. "How're things?"

He'd phoned her, of course, straight after visiting Stella. She'd been so excited to hear about her granddaughter that he hadn't told her about Cressa. What was the point? So the visit ended earlier than it should have. Big deal. But now, from his mother's tone, he could tell something was up.

"Oh, Adam, Deirdre called me today to tell me you and Cressa split up."

"Split up? We were never really together. It was only ever a short-term thing."

"Deirdre blames Cressa."

"Why? I thought she didn't like our relationship."

"She's very upset. Explained to me that she was against the relationship because she was so sure you were going to carry her daughter off to another country to live. I understand, you know. I feel a bit the same about Sass. But Deirdre says that worse than her losing Cressa is Cressa losing you. She hadn't seen her so happy in years."

Adam was dumbfounded. "What about Brian?"

Alicia laughed. "Deirdre now feels he and Des are far better suited, and she's delighted she doesn't have to lose him as a son-in-law. But she's very concerned about losing you."

"Women," said Adam, shaking his head. "You know, Mom, I'll never understand them."

"Never mind that now. What are you going to do about Cressa?"

"There's nothing I can do. Her flight takes off in a couple hours. She's leaving me, just as she was always going to."

"Deirdre says *you* broke up with *her*." Alicia sounded remarkably disapproving.

"Only because I all but went down on my knees and proposed and she rejected me."

"So you *did* break up!" Alicia was incredulous. "Adam Walker, I've never known you to be a quitter."

He was incensed. "*Quitter?* Mom, what's wrong with the reception? Why can't you hear me? Cressa doesn't love me—okay?"

"No, Adam, not okay. You find your daughter and are over the moon about it, and you fling a proposal at Cressa out of the blue. How do you think she was feeling?"

"What are you talking about?"

"Her baby, Adam. Her son."

He was silent.

"Adam?"

"I didn't think."

"No."

"So you figure…?"

"Yes. Yes, I do."

"Mom, I gotta go. Her flight leaves real soon."

He barely heard her wishes of good luck as he flicked the phone shut, grabbed his jacket and keys. He glanced at his watch. Man, this was going to be tight. But with more hope, more giddy excitement and more fear than he'd ever felt, he dashed out of the house.

He rode his bike like a maniac, dodging between cars and cursing her broken phone, taking the smallest of gaps that would have had even Cressa drawing in a breath. He parked the bike and ran to the terminal in record time. The airport was really crowded and that didn't help, but he found her check-in counter almost immediately. He went up and down the long queue. She wasn't there. He tried asking the check-in clerks if she'd already gone through, but they told him they weren't allowed to give out information. He tried bribing the security official at the door but got laughed at. He tried paging her, but she either didn't hear or knew it would be him, and refused to respond.

He waited till the very last person had boarded her flight. He waited until they began checking in the next flight. He waited until the plane had taken off. He thought that maybe, like in the movies, she would order the plane to turn around and would come running back to find him there, waiting. The crowds milled around him. People hugged one another in the ecstasy of reunion or in the sorrow of parting. He was jostled by those who had somewhere to go, someone to meet. The din of announcements barely pierced his consciousness.

He'd blown it. He had failed. In his sorry life of failure and misadventure, this was the worst of all. Mom was right. He should have convinced Cressa. He should have fought for her. Should have done everything. Cressa always said he retreated when others got too close. She'd been so good at not allowing him to do that.

He had no choice. Straight after his MCAT, he would have to go to New Zealand and get her back.

CHAPTER THIRTY-ONE

CRESSA HAD SPENT a long afternoon waiting in the silent Galveston house, wondering where on earth Adam could be. She smiled with relief, but she was shaking, too, when she heard the fumbling of keys, the surprised expletive when Adam discovered the door unlocked. What if it was too late? What if he'd learned to hate her? She'd learned to hate herself.

His quick footsteps sounded through the kitchen. She got up, running her hands down her jeans. This past half hour, she'd rehearsed over and over what to say. Adam burst into the room and stood absolutely still, his face white.

"You!" he said. "What the hell?"

All her carefully worded speeches fled from her mind. Which didn't matter, because in three strides he had closed the distance between them and snatched her into an embrace that threatened to crack her ribs. His ruthless kisses robbed her lungs of breath and her knees of strength. She sagged into his arms and surrendered in head-spinning joy.

When they finally came up for air, Adam smoothed her hair from her face, as if seeing her face better reassured him that she was real.

"I've spent the whole damn afternoon at the airport." The wonderment in his eyes belied the accusation in his voice.

"You have?" She felt weak with relief. Images of Adam hooking up with past girlfriends had filled her mind since the moment she'd returned to his house, only to find him AWOL. "I've been here waiting for you. Damn. If I'd known you were going to do the whole airport scene, I'd have gone there, instead. I feel so cheated! That would've been such a turn-on."

"Seeing you is a turn-on." He sat down, pulling her into his lap. "I can't believe it. I thought you'd gone."

She leaned against his chest. It felt so good. "I was wrong," she said simply. "I got it wrong. I nearly walked out on the only thing that gives my life meaning—us."

He wrapped his arms tightly around her. "It was my fault. I wasn't honest. I should have told you from the start all I wanted was a lifetime with you."

"Damn straight! You changed the rules on me." Then she snuggled in closer, trying to infuse herself with his strength. "But I'm not complaining."

He laughed. "So what the hell is all this, Cressa? Not that I'm complaining, either, but don't you have a boat to catch?"

She shrugged. "I walked away from the perfect man. Now I've walked away from the perfect job. I phoned them yesterday. They were very understanding and have their choice of several hopefuls who've been hanging out on the dock every day. But tell me about Stella."

"Sure you want to know?" He sounded suddenly solicitous.

"Of course I want to know. Got a photo?"

They had to untangle themselves so he could pull his phone out and show her two shots—one of Stella dwarfed by his helmet and perched on his bike. The other a close-up of her grinning cheekily.

"She's gorgeous. Just look at the nose on her. Poor kid. Man, is she ever about to join the right family. My sisters will gobble her up. She's one of us already." Cressa clicked back to the one on the bike. "Action girl, too, I see."

"I have it on her mother's authority," said Adam, "that she's wild just like me."

Cressa laughed. "I love her more and more."

Adam took the phone back and gazed down at his daughter's image. Reading his face was easy now. Paternal love and pride were written all over it. And still that sense of wonder that Stella had really entered his life again. Then he glanced up at Cressa. "Are you okay with this? Why the change of heart?"

She smiled self-consciously. "You want the truth? I had no choice. If I stayed away any longer, I'd have to book into a diet farm."

He laughed. "I thought you felt a little different. Cuddly," he added hastily. "It suits you."

"Yeah?" She trailed her hands down his chest. "Well, feels like you're in even better shape than when I left you."

"No sex. All that energy has to go somewhere."

"Mmm. Now, here's a whole new dilemma. Do I withhold sexual favors to keep my man with the body of a warrior?"

"Sex burns up a lot of calories," he countered.

"Then have you ever got your work cut out for you, starting right after your exam."

"Don't you worry," he assured her, threading one hand into her hair and drawing her to him for another mind-numbing kiss. "I can manage both very well."

They didn't even make it to the bedroom. The carpet was perfect. Everything was just perfect.

AFTERWARD THEY LAY together under the light blanket Adam had fetched. "Why did you come back— really?"

"The question should be why did I run out. On the beach I suddenly felt I was facing the same situation I'd faced two years earlier—a ready-made family, expectations, a train ride into the future with the tracks already laid down."

"Yeah, I figured that out, but by then it was too late." Adam sounded rueful.

"It's probably just as well. I needed to work things out for myself. It took some time, but when I finally sat down and analyzed the situation, I found that it was opposite in every single way."

"Yeah? How so?"

She chuckled. "For a start, Adam, you are anything but perfect and our future is anything but clear. We're going to be making it up as we go along, and who knows how it will turn out. I like that—the big unknown. The only thing I know for sure is that I love you. When I walked away from Brian, I was certain it was the right thing to do. When I left you, I couldn't rid myself of the feeling that I'd just made the most terrible mistake of my life."

"It was my fault for pushing you into a corner," Adam said. "I dropped Stella on you without giving a thought about your baby."

"Felix. His name was Felix."

She could feel Adam smile into her hair. His voice was gentle. "That's a nice name."

"Yeah, Brian chose it. I've spoken to Brian. We spent a couple hours on the phone, talking and crying. My poor baby. I was so conflicted about him from the start. I thought I ought to marry because of him. Now I realize

I had the choice all the time to be a solo mum. I just got caught up and confused. When he died, I felt it was all my fault, that I hadn't wanted him enough, loved him enough. I couldn't face thinking about it, so I pushed it all away." She gave a watery laugh. "Alicia's been great, too. We've talked lots about denial. It really helps to know how badly your mum screwed up and still came out right on the other end."

Adam's arm tightened. "So we can talk about Felix now? Are you okay about that?"

"I really am. Brian and I both accept what happened. Brian coped so much better with Felix's nonlife than I did, and not being able to help me drove him crazy. It was the final part of the road we had to do together."

"Brian's one of the best."

"I know. He and Des are doing well together. Finally I phoned Mum. I did a lot of talking and crying with her, too. I'd driven her wild with anxiety, as well. She said she'd phone your mum. They've become the best of friends."

"That's great. Mom needs good friends in New Zealand."

"Enough of me. How are the studies going?"

He shrugged. "I think I've got it under control."

She knew all about his control. "That's fine, then." Her head was resting on his chest, where it belonged.

He sounded almost shy as he continued. "Once the exam is over, I thought I might contact Adahy. I found him on the internet. He's still traveling, doing minor performances. Shouldn't be too hard to track him down."

Surprise and delight propelled her upright to look at him. "Oh, Adam! That's fantastic. What made you decide to do that?"

"Finding Stella. All these years I've wanted so much

to be a part of her life. Who knows, maybe Adahy might be pleased to find he's got a son and a granddaughter. Maybe I've got a whole other family out there that Stella also belongs to."

Cressa cupped his jaw and smiled. "Stella's going to be rich in families. We'll make sure of that." She turned his face slightly so she could look straight at him. "Was there another reason?"

His sinfully thick lashes began to sink to shutter his eyes, but she tightened her grip. "Don't you try that evasive trick on me! Go on, say it."

"Yeah," he said reluctantly. "I admit I'm a bit curious about him, too."

She laughed and gave his chin a teasing tug. "There, that wasn't so hard, was it? Give me ten years and I'll have you chatting about your feelings as easily as a girl."

His hand shot up to capture her wrist and he flipped her onto her back, where he proceeded to kiss her thoroughly. She realized that after such a difficult confession, he needed to reestablish his alpha male dominance, so she let him. Okay, also because she enjoyed it.

When they finally came up for air, he still had her wrists pinned to the carpet. "And what happens after ten years?"

His eyes drilled into hers. She writhed, but his weight held her down. She widened her eyes in mock bewilderment. "What do you mean?"

"You know what I mean. Go on, say it."

"Oh, very well," she conceded. "After ten years, there'll be another ten years." He released her wrists to begin tickling her and she shrieked in laughter. "And another ten, then another and another, forever. Stop! Oh, stop!"

Adam stopped, a satisfied grin on his face. "That's better." He lay back down, gathering her to him. Now he was serious.

"You know Cressa, this is going to be a long road. The MCAT is just the beginning. If I do get into medical school, we'll be poor for a very long time. I won't even have a home for you—let alone a vineyard and a yacht."

"I didn't want them then. I don't want them now. I just want to be with you. However, when I spoke to Alicia, she suggested we might like her trailer home. She's planning to stay in New Zealand for the time being."

Adam made a face. "It's not the most romantic start to a relationship."

"It's been a good place for me. It'll be a great place for us, you'll see. As for money to live on—" she smiled "—I'm going to be an accountant and support you."

"No!" He sat up so suddenly that her head bumped the floor. "Cressa, this won't work if it begins with compromises and sacrifices."

She pulled herself up so she was sitting next to him, leaning against the sofa. "It's not a sacrifice. I've learned a few things since coming to the States, and one of them is that I like making businesses run. I get huge satisfaction balancing Mike and Tim's accounts. Go figure, huh! I still don't want to do big company stuff, so I'm going to stay my own boss and work with small businesses. After all, that's what I liked best in all my different jobs—improving the systems, making them run better."

He laughed, putting an arm around her and holding her safe against him. "What about the need for adventures, new experiences?"

"That's where you come in. I realized that your SUV

full of camping equipment and kids—starting with Stella, of course—would include ropes for rappelling, flashlights for caving, snorkels and fins."

"The SUV can also tow a boat, and on the racks we'll have skis—in the far distant future."

The image pleased her. "Yeah. I also know that your backyard will have trampolines and a big climbing frame."

"Stella already climbs like a monkey."

"Excellent. The other kids will, too."

"Others? Are you sure?"

"I think so. Not for a few years, though."

"No rush. We have all the years in the world. For the first time since we met, we're not up against the clock." He was suddenly serious. "So is this it, Cressa? We're talking love here—commitment, wedding, kids—the whole package. Are you truly up for it?"

She turned so she could look right into that dark, beautiful face. "Yup," she said. "I truly am. Family's always been the core of my existence. I know that now. Besides, if I want to stay in the States with you, we'll have to marry. The rest—kids, family home, careers—will come in good time." She leaned up and kissed him. "I've discovered my fantasies have changed, and all of them now contain you, so yes, I want it all. With you, I want it all. With one proviso…"

"You've already got my heart and soul and my undying love. What else is there?"

"I want the damn picket fence, too."

Adam gave a shout of laughter and gathered her into another bone-crushing embrace. "You shall have the home, the career, the kids and yes, even the damn picket fence. But I have a proviso, as well."

"And what's that, my fine Cherokee?"

"I can satisfy my wicked desire for you whenever and wherever I want."

"Ha!" she said. "That applies for both of us."

"Agreed!"

"Wow, that was easy."

"That's because I'm easy. And so, my fair Valkyrie," he said, looking dangerous and adorable as only Adam could, "I'm choosing right here, right now."

With a growl he pounced on her, and she shrieked with laughter and put up a bit of a fight—as a Valkyrie should, just to let the warrior know he wasn't going to get everything his own way. She was soon defeated, however, by their mutual laughter, desire and love— yes, love! Unbelievable to think he'd once doubted its existence. And as she surrendered, Cressa discovered the fantasies hadn't completely disappeared, after all; in fact, the dream was just beginning. And that, she thought, was more than enough for any Valkyrie.

* * * * *

Harlequin
Super Romance

COMING NEXT MONTH

Available July 12, 2011

You can find more information on upcoming
Harlequin® titles, free excerpts and more at
www.HarlequinInsideRomance.com.

REQUEST YOUR FREE BOOKS!
2 FREE NOVELS PLUS 2 FREE GIFTS!

♦ Harlequin®
Super Romance®

Exciting, emotional, unexpected!

USA TODAY *bestselling author B.J. Daniels takes you on a trip to Whitehorse, Montana, and the Chisholm Cattle Company.*

RUSTLED

Available July 2011 from Harlequin Intrigue.

As the dust settled, Dawson got his first good look at the rustler. A pair of big Montana sky-blue eyes glared up at him from a face framed by blond curls.

A woman rustler?

"You have to let me go," she hollered as the roar of the stampeding cattle died off in the distance.

"So you can finish stealing my cattle? I don't think so." Dawson jerked the woman to her feet.

She reached for the gun strapped to her hip hidden under her long barn jacket.

He grabbed the weapon before she could, his eyes narrowing as he assessed her. "How many others are there?" he demanded, grabbing a fistful of her jacket. "I think you'd better start talking before I tear into you."

She tried to fight him off, but he was on to her tricks and pinned her to the ground. He was suddenly aware of the soft curves beneath the jean jacket she wore under her coat.

"You have to listen to me." She ground out the words from between her gritted teeth. "You have to let me go. If you don't they will come back for me and they will kill you. There are too many of them for you to fight off alone. You won't stand a chance and I don't want your blood on my hands."

"I'm touched by your concern for me. Especially after you just tried to pull a gun on me."

"I wasn't going to shoot you."

Dawson hauled her to her feet and walked her the rest of the way to his horse. Reaching into his saddlebag, he pulled out a length of rope.

"You can't tie me up."

He pulled her hands behind her back and began to tie her wrists together.

"If you let me go, I can keep them from coming back," she said. "You have my word." She let out an unladylike curse. "I'm just trying to save your sorry neck."

"And I'm just going after my cattle."

"Don't you mean your boss's cattle?"

"Those cattle are mine."

"*You're* a Chisholm?"

"Dawson Chisholm. And you are…?"

"Everyone calls me Jinx."

He chuckled. "I can see why."

Bronco busting, falling in love…it's all in a day's work.
Look for the rest of their story in

RUSTLED

Available July 2011 from Harlequin Intrigue
wherever books are sold.